A SCI FI ALIEN FATED MATES ROMANCE

SKY ROBERT

Broken Books
Kent, WA 98030

First published in the United States of America by Broken Books LLC, 2023
Copyright © 2023 S.M. McCoy writing as Sky Robert
Editing by S.M. McCoy/Sky Robert
Version Second Edition: ISBN: 978-1-7322475-2-9
Cover Design: Taurus Colosseum Cover Design

We all feel alien,

But to someone we are the universe.

To all the alien lovers out there, who are into limbs with a mind of their own, body parts that vibrate, pulse, and throb while some primal instinct bonds you to another organism in blissful romance. You knew what you were getting into when you picked up this book, and if you didn't then you should really read the descriptions of the books you read first. Enjoy your alien smut. No shame.

Praise for the Trillume Universe

"Excellent book, good intro into this series. Well-paced, excellent descriptions and world building, realistic and fascinating characters. Very good balance between internal dialogues and action, also very hot sex scenes. Reminds me of Viola Grace and Loki Renard, two of my favorite authors. Waiting with bated breath for next books!" **5-star Review of Her Alien Exchange - Terri**

"Loved it!
Running from a bad relationship, Violet jumps into a situation that could be termed jumping from the frying pan to the fire. Luckily she meets Roe-el who is everything Violet wants in a man. Roe-el's people look at humans as mere pets, not a species they would mate with. Then he meets Violet and all his misconceptions are put to the test. These two are absolutely perfect for each other." **5-star Review of Her Alien Exchange - Jeanéva**

"Oh my goodness, I wasn't sure what to expect because this is my first time reading anything from Sky Robert. I was very pleasantly surprised by how vivid the characters are and by the detail of the world building. I'm so intrigued to see what is going to happen in the rest of the series." **5-star Review of Jewel of the Alien Bandit - Jenna**

"It's got fated mates, forbidden romance, action, political intrigue. The love story between Trent and Mabel is beautiful. Fighting for what you believe in and a coming of age story since Mabel doesn't know who her family is. I highly recommend this book if you read the first." **5-star Review of Her Alien Prince - Melissa**

"I have to say the more I read this, the more I love the story. One thing you do that I enjoy is you don't make the female heroine stupid. I see this often in other stories and I usually can't finish them due to frustration at the blatant silliness of the characters. Tis is not how you write your characters (thankfully). In fact each of the characters here act according to the personality you showed us throughout the story. Well done. I wish I could write as well as you do. Your imagination and storytelling is wonderful." **5-star review of Her Alien Prince – Tori**

TABLE OF CONTENTS

Chapter One
Luan

Loric, my mother's adviser, and my pain-in-ass watcher, was a pushover for the most part, so I didn't think I'd have any problems convincing him or my mother to delay another cycle of the mating ceremony once again. There were more important things to worry about, like how the planet Krelis was trying to devalue our jewels so they could scam us out of more food imports.

Sure, we could survive off of eating some of the more edible jewels, but they were hardly what I would call delicious, and as more and more of our population bred with outside species, the more and more varied nutrition our offspring required to survive.

It just wasn't sustainable, and our already complicated mating rituals only increased the stress on our slow population growth.

"Are you thinking about the krelins again?" Loric asked, lifting a brow and shaking his head.

His blue skin was finely chiseled, which most of my friends have told me is delicious. If only he were part of the mating games more often they would have devoured him. I can admit he is quite attractive, even his sapphire jewels down his arms are impressive.

Almder, our leader, and my mother, would not have chosen him as an adviser if he were not skilled, and powerful in both mind and body. The more jewels displayed on an estreld's arms the more powerful they were. It is the way the land has blessed our species to absorb more of the moon's rays.

Papers were spread out on the desk of Loric's office while he worked on his next diplomatic game plan to assist Almder.

In frustration I slammed the book in my hands closed before replying, "Of course I am, not only is food tastier from the krelins, but they know our offspring are becoming dependent on their supply for nutrition and they are trying to rob us!"

I stood, storming across the room, and rushed out the open door to head directly to the library for another book. There had to be something that could help me figure out a way to reverse the pressure from the planet Krelis, and regain control of our trade market.

Something perhaps in the journals of the almder's before my mother. One of them had to have dealt with unreasonable trade mongers before.

Loric casually strode alongside me, his longer legs able to help him catch up to me without effort.

"Do you not trust our Almder?"

There he went again, trying to make me feel ashamed, or guilty for even trying to help. Of course, I trusted my mother, but she had enough on her plate already with making sure our population didn't go extinct after a few more generations. It's only because of the last five cycles of Estreldez opening up the mating ceremony to offworlders that we were seeing any uptick in offspring.

"There's only so much one estreld can do," I insisted, "and my mother doesn't have to do it alone."

He had to know I'm right about this. He's seen how hard I work to learn what I can to fill my mother's role of Almder one day.

"She doesn't," he objected, obviously offended by my statement. He was her adviser, and he did help her, but what did that have to do with whether or not I should help?

"You know what I mean." I wasn't going to tip toe around Loric of all beings, I've known him since we were both offspring ourselves. He was like a brother to me, but like a brother...

3

he got on my nerves. He followed me through the halls and unfortunately we were stopped by one of my mother's other advisers, Mabel.

"Luan, Almder has summoned you," she informed.

I pursed my lips, not wanting to be distracted from my task, considering every shipment was another chance for Krelis to withhold for more payment. It wasn't Mabel's fault that my mother was impatient.

Nor was it her fault that the mating ceremony was coming up soon.

Ten male mates were chosen every planetary rotation of the moons around Estreldez to lead the mating ceremony. Some are from Estreldez, and others are chosen from far away planets to port in, under diplomatic award, to increase the odds of fertility. Many of Estreldez's females participate in the mating games after they feel the pull of their shoulder glands pulse, letting them know that they are likely to be ready to release their eggs. I've never once felt such a pull, and I'm several cycles past the age of mating, as my Almder would say.

The Almder is the leader of our clan on Estreldez, and my mother, I conceded internally with a groan. I couldn't stop her plans for me indefinitely. I'd avoided the Moon Mating Ceremony for many cycles, and she's graciously allowed me to watch instead. But, my mother was becoming more testy of late about my participation and I'm pretty sure it had to do with Loric.

He's always lurking around like a glorbin flighter, those creatures are always flitting about when they see something shiny. Our whole planet was shiny, our specialized trade was our abundance of jewels, which the glorbin flighters gladly eat for breakfast. The jewels are fun to toss at them, especially if they are fast enough to catch them. And I'm equally entertained by teasing Loric about my interest in the ceremony when he's been talking about it so much recently. He's been acting more unusual and dropping many hints over the last moon cycle, trying to convince me that joining the mating ceremony may be something that I would enjoy.

Loric watched me with that smug expression on his face, almost like he was saying I told you so. How would he know if my mother was calling to tell me to stop researching and join our mating ceremony this cycle? I glared at him, before taking Mabel's arm and being led to the assembly cove.

The room opened up into an open air courtyard carved from our favorite stone of black tarnpul, the strongest of our mineral deposits, and the most reflective of the moon's rays. Shaped in a cone, lifting up from the ground on all sides to create a dish that helps focus the moon's light for us to absorb. This was where only the chosen came to have a better chance at successful mating during the ceremony. I cringed at the thought. I've had to sit with my mother during these displays to show my support and I never understood why I had to watch front and center, when the whole thing was recorded for the whole planet. I could easily watch from my room if I wanted. There was no need to be so close you could see the seams of a male's shaft open to fill their mate. I shook my head to rid myself of the thought.

"Where have you been hiding?" My Almder stood from her seat wearing her traditional robes draped over her pale white skin, her jeweled arms and chest on full display.

"If I were hiding then I wouldn't be here," I grumbled.

She was always so dramatic when she found I'd been avoiding her advisers. Loric was different, he's always following me when he's not meeting with my mother to tattle on me.

My mother sighed, waving off the advisers that were gathered in the assembly. All except Loric left. "This is not the time for word play, My Jewel. You are well aware that we have another Moon Ceremony coming up, and it's time you join the others in a show of support, and to hopefully one day provide our clan with another heir."

I gulped heavily, this was not the conversation I wanted to get into. Every Moon Ceremony was always the same, she'd ask if I felt any 'tingles' in my shoulders to signal my readiness, and then I'd say, 'no', and then she'd smile, pat me on the head and say, 'One day, my daughter.' And that was that. There was no serious conversation about joining, or that I should join.

One day couldn't be today, couldn't be now.

And she was the only person that could make me.

Not just as my mother, but as the leader of the Estreldez. The leader of our clan.

My Almder.

"I do not feel any—"

She cut me off. "Not all feel the urge until they meet a compatible mate, and even then participation increases the odds of that happening. How do you think it looks to our clan that you have been of age for many cycles and have not shown your support but to watch?"

"You watch," I countered accusingly.

Narrowing her eyes at me she continued, "I'm much too old to participate any longer. I was blessed to have secured a female as an heir, and it is my burden that I was not able to provide you with siblings." The irritation faded from her, replaced with a sadness that made my stomach clench. I did not want to remind her of the loss she had endured with my siblings.

For every one of them she lost, she had plucked a jewel from her back and displayed them on the crown she wore. Off-worlders would think my mother was displaying her wealth, but it was her greatest loss that she clung to in mourning. No other Almder had ever worn anything more than a simple crown of tarnpul, which for us was displaying our power. The jewels, they are remembrances of her children. That was why I am her favorite jewel, the one that survived.

The one she was now sentencing to join the Moon Ceremony.

I shook my head, unbelieving that she would force this upon me.

"I'm not ready..." I choked out.

"Jewel of Estreldez, it is not if we are ready to serve but that we are able. I do not wish to burden you with this task, but our clan needs hope. And seeing you participate will give them that. Will you deny them that small kindness?"

Pressing my lips together I glanced over to see Loric staring at me, and even his blue eyes were watching me with a sense of hopefulness. Was that what our planet has come to? The mating games were all voluntary, my mother never demanded anyone participate. But she was asking it of me?

There was no denying her request.

I was participating in the next cycle's Moon Ceremony, and I could only pray that my eggs remained fully attached at all times. It would be embarrassing to have them release, and my wings sprout for all to see. That's what happened when a female Estreldez was fertile, and there would be no backing out of the games if that happened. My mother wouldn't hear of it, I would have to choose one of the mates provided, and if they weren't from our planet...

I would never see the mates again.

Never see my mate again, if I had one.

Sometimes, I wondered if the reason I never wanted to participate was because as long as I only watched, I couldn't be hurt. As long as I never knew if my mate was out there... I wouldn't have to give them up.

Chapter Two

Vareo

I rubbed my face in disbelief, re-reading the transmission once again. I'd heard of rich psychopaths before, but this was too good to be true. Being a system pirate wasn't always easy work, most of the bounties were extremely illegal to the Lunar Administration, but they were spread pretty thin these days, and the pay was better than the regular bounty fare. Whoever this rich fucker was, they were offering enough credit to make me tattoo their face on my left asscheek if that's what they wanted.

"What's the job?" Carmen asked from behind me, slinking her arm around my neck. Her tongue licked at my ear, and I grinned thinking about all the other things that tongue could be capable of. We'd never gone that far, but that never stopped her from teasing. She was the one that got me into this career path to begin with, and I knew she'd sooner shoot my nuts off than let me touch her.

That was fine by me, but the long cycles alone had my mind addled with urges that were tough to ignore, and that's exactly why Carmen did it. I ignored her, and pinched her cheeks to focus her on the screen.

She would have tried to kick my ass, but she was just as stunned as I was at the price tag on this black market lister.

"That has to be a glitch," she finally said.

"You could leave me the fuck alone with that kind of credit." The offer was enticing, the only problem was whether it was legit or not.

"With that kind of credit, you'll have paid off your debt, and have credit left over to buy your own small planet." I swiveled in my chair to see the glitter of profit in her eyes. She could finally get off my heap of metal, and tell her bosses, the necia of Necias Delta Fal, 'I'm a free agent.'

Necia were a fiery bunch of alien outlaws, where their main trade of their planet was basically being mercenaries for hire. How I got involved with them wasn't exactly my choice, but I blew my chance at escaping when I was a boy.

"If it's real," I added, trying to bring reason back into both of our credit hungry egos.

"Even if it isn't real, you still have to show proof to Jax that you're going to pay up, or she'll gut you."

"I thought that was your job?" I gave her a wry smile, and she gave me a wink in return before her extra finger bones sliced from her flesh, and dug into my throat. I shook my head, feeling her grip loosen, unable to follow through with her threats just yet. I wondered, however momentarily, that I could have thought of Carmen as more than a thug. She was pretty by any standards, dark hair hung short at her shoulders, hazel eyes that changed color depending on what she wore, and a tight jumpsuit that revealed all her curves. But necia were a rough breed, and it would be easy for her to morph her bones from her skeleton into weapons like a creepy pin cushion. I would have shivered at the thought, but any movement would have given me an extra close shave.

"Don't test me. I've been kind to you, haven't I, Vareo?"

My Adam's apple bobbed, feeling the pressure of the sharp bone. But, this wasn't the first time she threatened me, and she needed me for the credits. I was worth more alive, and I've long since found her threats towards me to be more bark than bite. Easing the weapon of her extra finger bones away from my skin with my own fleshy finger, I smiled.

"Kind as a krelin's horn up my—" It was the kindest endearment I could ever muster for her.

"Don't be crass." She shoved my face with the palm of her hand back towards the screen that was flickering due to the repairs that my ship badly needed. Those credits were tempting. "Go screw a few Estreldez females and bring back their prized jewel. Even if the job's a scam we can milk them for what they're worth, or sell the jewel on the black market, and take whatever the buyer has for trying to fuck us."

"Aren't you the picture of propriety," I mocked her eagerness to send me out to pimp myself to an alien planet so I could steal their treasure. That was a first, but it was the only way we'd gain access to the planet Estreldez. They weren't open for tourism, and kept strict closed borders. In fact, it was only recently that they even allowed offworlders to join their mating ceremony. Though, really even that was a very select few.

Which had me doubting whether we could even get the job.

"How are we supposed to get an invite?" I wondered out loud.

"Maybe that's why the credits are so large. Figure it out."

Carmen sauntered off to go comm Jax about the job. She wasn't going to let me turn this down. Somehow, I had to find a way onto the invite list. As much as having my go with a bunch of alien women might have been appealing, the idea of having children that I'd never see again was not. My dad was never around as a kid... I swore I'd never have children if I couldn't be around for them.

I'd have to steal the jewel and get off planet before the mating could ever be consummated. Get my credits, and I never have to see Carmen, Jax, or any other necia outlaws again. Glaring at the screen, and all of those zeros at the end of the credits meant certain freedom, but I highly doubted the necia would give up easily even after they got their credits. They probably never expected anyone to make enough credits to pay off their debts when the costs kept on rolling in to cover the operation's overhead. Plus, I wasn't dumb. They weren't known to play fair, and just like they'd screw over the client if they didn't hand over the agreed upon sum it was just as likely they'd do the same to me.

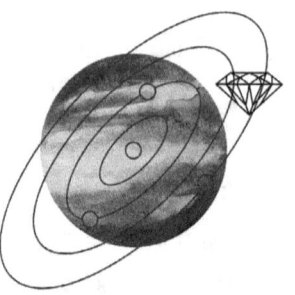

Chapter Three
Luan

There was no reason to be nervous. The likelihood of my eggs releasing was low, and even less so that any of the potential mates this season would be compatible. Nothing to worry about, I assured myself. I would join the Moon Ceremony, show my support for the future of Estreldez, and be back to protecting our planet from the krelins in a blip of existence.

I shouldn't have been happy about how dismal our mating chances were, but before my mother, all the Almders before her were able to summon successful matings with the moon's blessing. The moon god has forsaken us for many generations, and if the krelins knew how deep that rift was, we'd be in no position to bargain for our food at all. They would invade, and all of Estreldez would be even more screwed than we already were.

"Does the ceremony trouble you so much?" The crease between my brows worried Loric, and he was always an optimist about the state of our species. Convinced that when we were both old enough that we would find the answers we were searching for, he would say it was the way of the moons, and there were lessons to be learned. Loric was much too wise for his cycles, but I didn't doubt his conviction because he wasn't like the rest of the planet thinking prayers would solve things. He actually did things, met with diplomats, conferred with our scientists, and put in the work when he wasn't tasked with following me around.

I groaned. "Does my mother actually believe that my participation is a better use of my time than trying to figure out a solution?"

"How are you supposed to solve a problem if you don't have all the facts?"

Glaring at him, I suppressed the urge to smack him for insinuating I haven't been pouring myself into the research of both diplomatic solutions for the krelins, and our population decreases. Our older generations are more than half of our population, and past their mating cycles. If we didn't find a solution soon, even with our long lives, our species would be extinguished at this rate.

He held up his hands in a cease fire before I could yell at him. But even that gesture was false when his next words were, "Maybe participating in the ceremony will give you new insights into the very problem that you seek to solve?"

"Has it done you any favors?" I snarked back. Now it was his turn to narrow his blue eyes at me. It wasn't my intention to pit us against ourselves, we both had the same goals. He's joined the ceremony many times, but none of his matings have taken hold. That was the same for most of the Estreldez males, which is why most of the selected mates for the ceremony have been selected from offworld systems.

"None of them were mine, you know how our biology works."

"I know," I huffed out exasperated. It wasn't his fault. His seed was sterile until a compatible mate was found, just as it takes a certain amount of chemistry for our eggs to drop from their sacks.

Loric sighed, and sat down next to me in the library. He wrapped his arm around my shoulders and pulled me into his chest. Nose nuzzling into my white blond hair, he whispered, "Are you afraid that under the mating moon you'll find a compatible mate, or that you won't?"

His words were daggers into my heart, hitting so deep into my buried fears. Which one was I more afraid of? He was right, so painfully right.

If my eggs dropped then I wasn't broken, but I'd have mated with a potential stranger that would leave our planet after the ceremony. I shook my head, that sounded awful. How did the other females do it? I mean, I understood that a mating ritual wasn't binding to offworlders or even to us without a true bond the same way it would for our males, but they all leave.

Every one of them leaves.

They come for the fun of having sex, and we allow them to mate with us to help our population growth. It was an understandable transaction. They knew we used their genetics for procreation, but Estreldez was viewed as an exclusive sex harem instead of a planet in desperate need of scientists to help our declining spawnrates.

I adjusted to look up into Loric's blue sad eyes as he watched me struggle with this realization. A part of me wondered then, how it would be if I found Loric to be my mate. I gave him a small smile knowing he wouldn't leave me. But Loric had been responsible for many female's eggs dropping, and he has yet to be fertile with any of them. I didn't think I could handle that kind of rejection from someone I cared so much about. If we mated, and had no spawn... he would try with another. That was our way.

"I'm afraid I will find a mate, and he'll reject me," I admitted out loud. Whether it was Loric or an offworlder, it was better not to have a mate at all. I'd still have Loric, and I'd never have to know if I was broken or not.

"It would be his loss," he murmured into my hair, squeezing me to him, holding back all of my worries. Would Loric be mine? He was kind, smart, and a powerful estreld. Anyone seeking a mate would be ecstatic to claim him, and many have tried.

I pushed away from his embrace, and gathered my wits about me. Shoving all those insecurities away I told him something I've never said to anyone before, "What if I don't wish to have offspring? What if I want to travel the systems to find new resources and technology to help our planet from out there?" The ceiling was decorated in a mosaic of jewels made to look like the star system above our planet. they twinkled in the light filtering through them from the outside.

Loric gazed up at the library's ceiling with me and then shook his head. It wasn't something he dreamed about, I knew he'd always want to stay on Estreldez. And I knew he wanted a family, children to call his own.

"Luan..." I knew that tone of his. He was about to bring me back down from the stars my dreams expanded to. He traced one of the colorless jewels embedded on the top of my hand. It was a gesture that was usually comforting, but not this time. This time it felt like he was pressuring me.

I pulled my hand from his grasp. "There are plenty of willing estrelds to repopulate our lands. What we need are answers, new solutions, and they could be out there." My arm jerked to the ceiling, and I stormed off once more to find my mother.

Loric did not follow this time, staying seated staring up at the constellations of our star system.

When I arrived at the assembly garden, Mabel was rushing out so distracted that she nearly toppled me over. I steadied her by the shoulders and thought I saw tears in her green eyes before black hair covered her face as she exited.

"Mabel?"

My mother beckoned me in preventing me from following after to see what was wrong. "Mabel has been informed by the M.R. that she is no longer eligible for the ceremony. More and more of our clan have been found to be infertile before their time. We need a win, My Jewel, something to boost the hopes of Estreldez."

Biting my lip, I knew exactly where she was leading with this conversation. She needed me to be that beacon of hope. She needed me to successfully mate during the moon ceremony. There was so much pressure building on my shoulders, that if I didn't feel it before I certainly felt it now.

The sadness in her eyes, the exhaustion, it was all there for me to read in her features.

"Mom–"

She lifted a weary hand. "I ask a lot of you," she cut me off, already knowing I would object once more to joining. "When you are Almder you will be faced with tough decisions, and that urge you feel now to protect our clan, and find a solution worthy of journals you pour over in our library will grow to be unbearable when you must act even when you are uncertain. Because our clan needs the best solution right now, until there is a better one in the future.

"My Jewel, I know one day we will have a better solution, and you may well be the one to find it, but for now, for this ceremony you are needed to show your support. Even if you find yourself unable to mate, you will be seen as resilient and dedicated to doing everything within your control to save our future. Everything I can not." My mother took off her crown and stroked the jewels across the band of tarnpul. Her white hair had grayed, even her skin was silvery with age, yet she still retained a strong healthy glow about her like the largest moon orbiting Estreldez. And like the largest moon, she seemed the farthest away from me, even now. Those silvery eyes distant in her grief for her lost children, and the many lost generations of our clan.

My heart swelled for her, for our clan, and guiltily for myself for what I must do. She knew exactly what to say to convince me to join the moon ceremony, but I would make sure she agreed to do things my way next.

"I'm only one estreld, and we need to send someone out into the systems searching for new technologies, new food sources, and new alliances—" I pleaded, cut off before I could continue.

"And you want to be that someone," she finished for me. "My jewel, you will get what you want, but it must be someone else who does it. Plan your team, and I will approve their mission.

Whatever they need will be theirs, but you are the future of Estreldez."

What she was really saying was that I would be the queen one day, and must stay on Estreldez for our clan. I bristled at the idea that this was it for me, managing from the assembly garden for the rest of my days, sequestered to the palace. My dreams of exploring myself all done through others, merely waiting for a miracle to come.

Did she not understand what I wished for our clan? My fists clenched at my sides, as my Almder, no longer my mother in my eyes, replaced her crown atop her head. The action was not lost on me, this was no longer a negotiation.

"As you divine, Almder." I punctuated her title, and turned on my heels to leave. Mabel wasn't the only one to leave the assembly room in tears today. My eyes burned with frustration, and exactly what my mother wanted from me... and determination to change her mind, even if it meant going against her wishes.

I would go to our moon ceremony, and I would leave with one of those mates, even if I had to stow away on their ship to do so.

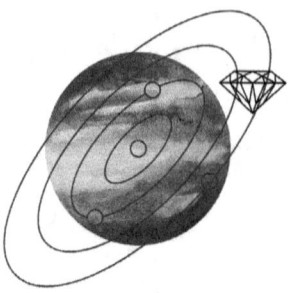

Chapter Four
Vareo

G etting an invite to the Estreldez Mating Games was more difficult than I anticipated. Sure, the price tag on the job was more than worth the effort, but they were requiring a full physical examination, credentials, references, and a detailed history like I was cataloging my life's existence for their judgment. Obviously, the only thing I could give them that was accurate was my physical exam, as they required that to be done by their own scientists on one of their orbiting moons. The largest moon called Lupa.

Carmen wanted to forge my background as some prince of a distant star system traveling the planets searching for a mate, but who would believe that kind of bullshit? The best lies were based on molecules of truth.

And I was no prince material.

I was an outlaw, working for the necia scum of the DVQ Trillume system on Necias Delta Fal that invaded my planet and considered the fact that they saved my life a debt that can be paid off with a sum of credits that would normally be unattainable. This life was all I knew.

"Vareo from planet Sholonus. Says here you're a bounty hunter?"

I grunted my confirmation as they scanned my body with their medical wand that looked more like an anal probe. If they tried to stick that anywhere on my body I would throttle the light pink male with matching hair. I knew the estreld were a colorful lot, but I assumed they'd be a bit more built.

Considering the whole planet was so well guarded, and every source I tapped for this mission said they were powerful, I wasn't expecting beings so scrawny. The pink male rolled up his lab coat revealing a few small gems decorating his forearms that had a slight glow to them. He caught me staring and smiled at me.

"It's common for offworlders to stare. Often I must explain that these are not the same as the jewels on our planet, they are organic and help estrelds to connect with the moon's radiation."

All I could think of is what would happen to him if I removed them from his flesh, and how many credits I'd get for them? Though, I considered if they were organic like he said they probably didn't keep the same as a normal rock would. That's probably why they had to explain to outsiders anything at all, I wasn't the first one to think of harvesting something so shiny for profit. I kept my face neutral, not wanting to scare the small male.

Instead I gave him a smile in return, and nodded. Compliments were the best strategy to avoid most awkward situations. "I'm sure they come in handy to impress your females."

My research showed that this planet valued their mating above most things, and all the male's coloring were part of stimulating the females of this planet to drop their eggs so that they can find out if they are compatible for breeding. How their scientists haven't found a way to detect compatibility without having to actually copulate was beyond me. And what exactly it meant to 'drop' their eggs was also an unnerving concept. I had no intention of breeding with any of them, but mating was the only diplomatic waiver to entering their orbit.

The male blushed, and turned a darker shade of pink at my comment, apparently he was scrawny and shy about the very reason I was even here.

"Yes, well," he cleared his throat then stared at his read out of my scan. "Your physiology seems to be compatible, and in peak condition." He handed me a cup. "Please deposit your specimen for analysis."

I stared at the plastic receptacle, then back at the pink scientist.

He stammered, more than a little intimidated by me, "Do you need assistance?"

I scoffed, of course I didn't need any damned assistance to shoot my seed into a dish. I just assumed their little medical scanner could do all of that analysis without a sample. I wasn't dumb, even the necia had a device you stuck your junk into and it took a sample with a tiny nanobot. No mess, no fuss.

Holding up the cup, I searched the room and found it lacking for any privacy. Were these estrelds voyeurists?

The scientist cleared his throat to get my attention. What the fuck was he expecting from me?

He sighed, uncomfortable that he had to explain something, but it was obvious that it wasn't the first time he had to do so. "The sample cannot be tampered with. I'm required to remain here to ensure its integrity. Even the nanobots have been known to be hacked, and we've had to resort to baser methods." He wrinkled his nose, seeming to be as displeased about the development as I was, but it wasn't shame that I felt.

Just I didn't find the guy to be all that attractive, and staring at his pink face didn't elicit the kind of mood needed to provide him with what he was asking for. Then the screen in front of him flickered, and he swiped it to accept the comm.

I stilled at the image of a woman with flawless pale skin, platinum blond waves of hair, and the eyes that glowed like the moon's radiation. My cock pulsed, growing at the mere sight of her. A moon goddess, wearing nothing but a slip of fabric revealing rows of diamonds decorating her skin. She was beauty, and then she spoke.

"Xol, I need you to give me a list of the diplomats arriving, and ships they will arrive in."

"We haven't narrowed down the candidates for the ceremony yet. There seems to have been a miscalculation of invites, and–"

"It doesn't matter, if they've passed their exams, and came with their own transport then it only increases the odds of a successful ceremony. Let me know when you have the list ready."

She was feisty, and the way she demanded what she needed had my cock hard. I liked it when a woman knew what she wanted and took charge. Before the examiner could reply her transmission ended, and I unzipped my pants before I lost the after mirage of her face in my mind. Giving the pink guy a wink I closed my eyes to let my surroundings disappear so all I saw was her.

It wasn't difficult to finish after months of blue balls on a ship with a psychopath. The mere thought of Carmen had my stomach recoiling, and I grimaced, readjusting myself and shoving the cup at the estreld without its cap. That was his problem now. It was lucky that I finished before thinking about the way Carmen would zap me with a jolt of electricity after teasing me with a rub of her breasts on my shoulder, causing a trained reaction to flinch when she touched me.

"Be careful what you wish for," I teased the guy. My balls were still uncomfortable, and despite relieving myself into a cup I still felt backed up. Nothing was quite the same as the real deal, and what I wanted was that bossy bejeweled estreld wrapping herself around my shaft, and telling me exactly how she liked to be finished off. My erection was slowly coming back, and I adjusted in my seat to accommodate it.

The scientist lifted an eyebrow and I smiled. "Don't tell me you need another sample?"

He gulped down his extra saliva, and shook his head unable to speak. He couldn't handle a spitfire like her, even if he wanted to.

"Your sample is viable. You've signed a waiver allowing us to utilize your specimens for research purposes. A guide will be assigned to you to assist with your involvement in the ceremony should you have any further questions."

"Just one. Is that woman participating in the ceremony?"

He stammered, "It will be her first year to attend in an official capacity."

That's all I needed to know to have a renewed interest in attending the Estreldez Mating Games. Who said I couldn't have a little fun while on the job?

Chapter Five

Luan

There were always at least a few offworlders that have tried to enter the moon ceremony for the 'fun' of it, without an invite from Almder. Estreldez has, over recent years since opening to diplomats, been given quite the reputation I've found of being an exclusive, highly-sought-after invite for a pleasurable time. I rolled my eyes. This wasn't a brothel, this was our very existence on the line and they treated us like a commodity.

I flipped through the images of the mating candidates, and stopped abruptly on one in particular with hard brown eyes so dark they reminded me of tarnpul deposits before they were polished. This one was definitely not invited by my mother. He appeared to be a warrior, chiseled jaw line, battle formed into a mask of determination and a lifelong built distance between himself and anything that would harm him, emotions included.

"He's handsome," Mabel commented over my shoulder. "In a dangerous kind of way."

I scanned his file. He was a bounty hunter, that made sense, and he was in peak physical condition. But, what didn't make sense was where he said he was from. Sholonus was destroyed before I was spawned. I've read about many failed civilizations to better prevent our own from suffering the same fate, and he didn't look anything like the natural inhabitants of Sholonus. Was my data incomplete, or was he hiding something?

"He's one of the pleasure seekers," I informed Mabel. Definitely not a true diplomat seeking to further bond our trade or alliances with assisting our repopulation efforts. Not that I really cared about his motives. I'd seen his kind over the years, and he'd leave as soon as he'd had his fun, and he'd be much too distracted to notice an extra passenger on his ship.

I grinned wickedly, he was perfect to get me offworld. Once I was settled, I'd inform my mother where I was, and have her send my selected team to me, or I'd threaten to never return to my duties as future Almder of Estreldez.

"He has strange scars on his skin, they are black as his eyes and hair."

I nodded. A tingling in my gut made me stand, and pace the garden. Why was I getting nervous? He's seen battle, would I not be safe when he discovered me on his ship? He wouldn't want to cause an incident, he would take me where I requested, right? I was second guessing my plans at using him for my escape.

"Mabel." She watched me wear a line into the dirt at my feet. I pressed my lips together doubting my own resolve. "You've been part of the M.R. team and an adviser to Almder for a few years now..."

She bit her lip, still raw about her new status as infertile from her previous report to my mother.

"Yes."

I regretted reminding her of something that upset her, but she'd understand more than anyone else what I was trying to do. Most of all, I trusted her.

"I need your help to search for new technology and treaties that could help us save our clan."

"Of course, anything I can do to help." She was eager to distract herself, and it was the reason she joined the M.R., Moon Mating Research, team to begin with. I knew I could count on her.

"As you know there is only so far diplomacy can reach from inside the palace. That's why we send delegates out as representatives, and the voice of the Almder across the current system." She already knew all this, but when you asked for someone to go against the current Almder's wishes, things needed to be prefaced and the reasons clearly positive. "And though my mother has many more years of leadership, she has agreed to form a team to go outside of our current system to seek out new solutions, and alliances with my direct involvement. My support will be well received by any planet or species to increase our chances of forming those bonds, being the future Almder of Estreldez. It is why I must personally acquire those relationships myself being an integral part of the team that explores the systems until it is my time to take over my mother's duties."

Rushing that last part was probably the reason why she furrowed her brow with a mix of confusion and disbelief. I had basically inferred I had my mother's approval for joining the team, when really I only had her approval to form the team, which in my opinion was the same thing. I was forming the team, and I decided I should be the diplomat of the mission to seek offworld assistance to our cause.

"Luan... you are forgetting you would be putting our whole planet's future in jeopardy by leaving the safety of Estreldez. You are the future Almder, the Jewel of Estreldez, and easily a target by those that wish to control our resources, or worse enslave us."

Frowning, this was not how I envisioned this conversation going. She was supposed to support me, and be on my side of things. My relation to my mother was always kept quiet outside the planet during the moon ceremony. No one should even know who I am until I've made it to the first planet for treaty and trade discussions. People talked, I thought suspiciously. Any one of the previous mates or diplomats could have said something, but no one should know my name outside this planet. They were all under oath.

"We are not cowards." I bristled at the implications of why we should be sequestering ourselves to our home planet.

"No, all of our warriors have proven themselves against the krelins before our treaty. We are not cowards. You think this will show our strength to have you part of the mission." She understood, and I breathed a sigh of relief. "I won't tell your mom what you are up to, but that's the best I can do."

My shoulders sagged. She wouldn't help, but she wouldn't deter me either. That was something.

I nodded sadly.

"That will have to be enough, then."

"The games will begin soon." Mabel stood. She was here to make sure I attended, though sometimes I forgot that Mabel and Loric were at their core my mother's advisers, and therefore hung out with me because they were tasked to do so. My heart grew heavy, not willing to accept neither of them were my friends after all the years I'd known them.

"Mabel. We are friends." I needed her reassurances, that this wasn't one sided, even if she lied to me, I needed to hear the words.

Her green eyes softened, and she pulled me into a hug. "We are." With a heavy sigh she continued, "I will see what I can do to help you, but right now we must see if any of the mates can make your shoulders tingle."

I blew off a laugh, holding her tightly. "I've seen the games before, and I have my doubts."

She pulled me back, her hands giving me a gentle squeeze on my biceps. "It is different when they display their talents to you personally."

"I don't understand." I watched her skeptically. Had she felt her eggs drop before? She spoke as if she knew that I would feel the tingle myself, that she had felt that very same thing when someone had displayed themselves in games before.

Mabel glanced away shyly, embarrassed. "As a scientist of behavioral analysis, I've interviewed many that have successfully mated. Some knew as soon as they saw them, and others needed to be in close proximity. You've been far from attentive during the previous ceremonies, participating may change things for you."

Grumbling, I followed Mabel away from the gardens and towards the viewing decks along with every other eligible female clamoring for the chance to mate during the peak of the moon's radiation.

I had no intention of mating with anyone. I had more important things to do, like plan how I was going to sneak away onto the bounty hunter's ship. What was his name again?

Did it matter?

Of course it did, my mother always said using someone's name has always endeared a person towards you. Showed interest and respect. I stared at the picture on my view screen again. The image lifted from my wrist jewel, my stomach twisted. Nerves again.

You're going to help me, Vareo, I know you will, I thought.

Even if he didn't know it yet.

Chapter Six

Vareo

No one said anything about playing games before the ceremony, and I still haven't located the jewel of Estreldez. My guide was just as bright as my examiner but green coloring, and male as well. He was in better shape than the others I've seen going about their business. He wore a strange uniform that made him look like meat tied into sausage skin, loose beige clothing tied and cinched at his junctions. Though his torso was draped open displaying his toned muscle, I could see his ribcage. Either he needed to eat more or all the estreld males were skeletal like that under their lab coats.

"What kind of games?" I asked, suspiciously considering what tests I had to do on their moon before arriving on the mainland.

"Every mate must do their part to encourage as many females to participate in the ceremony as possible. If you do not catch the attention of a mate then you will be escorted back to your ship and be unable to participate in the ceremony."

We were passing by a large black stone courtyard and my eye caught on a large diamond at the center.

"What's that used for?"

"That's where the ceremony will be held, you will not be returning to this assembly garden until you're chosen. The jewel at the center helps focus the radiation of the moon's rays being gathered by the tarnpul," he explained lazily. I smiled as the diamond in the floor disappeared from sight. There it was. The Jewel of Estreldez. Ripe for the taking while everyone was distracted fucking each other, I'll grab the fist-sized diamond right under their gyrating bodies.

"So, what is it that gets an estreld excited?" I teased him, but it was a valid question. Even this green male turned a deeper shade of embarrassment at the topic. Their whole ceremony was about mating. They were sensitive for being the ones soliciting me to procreate their species.

"Displays of power, intelligence, and skill," the green estreld replied evenly. I scanned him over once more assessing what he'd have to offer in those departments and he continued, "We start with gaining their attention." And with that, we entered a room within the palace set up like a stadium, if it could even be called a room. The stands were filled with estrelds, all female and I was the last of the males to arrive. Seeing as the whole floor level was packed with potential mates and their handlers. There was even a krelin in the lot of them. He was easy to spot, even in a crowd, as everyone was giving him a decent girth of space, like a bubble no one dared enter.

And I found I was indeed wrong about the estreld males being all scrawny, or ill-fed. My eye caught on a particular blue one that was nearly as large as I was. Nearly, I joked internally with a grin thinking about how I could still take him down if it came down to a fight. But, I wasn't here to cause trouble, at least not until I was long gone from this system and the best strategy was always keep your strongest threat to your goals closer than your end game.

"Who's he?" I pointed to the big blue estreld with his tied sausage pants, and no shirt to display his muscles, along with his rather large organic jewels the scientist was telling me about. He seemed to have many more jewels on his arms than the examiner, or the handler that stayed glued to my side. I'd have to figure out a way of ditching my handler at some point.

"Aw." I hadn't even asked the handler what his own name was, and he didn't seem to mind when he saw who I was re-ferring to. "He's the Amlder's favorite adviser, and the Pride of

Estreldez, Loric. Many females join just for a chance to mate with him, but he only chooses one each ceremony."

"Only one?" The handler made a point to say 'only' and it made me think that it wasn't normal, especially with the way the planet was described as the best kept exclusive pleasure destination. Selling forged invites for a chance to be evaluated and make it into the games was a common black market scam, and only a few of the dealers were shady enough to trust their forgeries to be up to the challenge of making it to the examination. Lucky for me, even before the too-good-to-be-true job posting the necia had already dipped into the market craze of creating forged invites, and they were damned good at it.

"Yes, every mate is allowed to procreate as often as their anatomy will allow them to during the ceremony. Diversity is encouraged, though copulating multiple times with one female has shown to bear positive results as well."

That's what I thought he meant.

"Why only one then?" I motioned my chin over to the blue guy named Loric.

"He is an honorable estreld, and if his efforts spawn in another female he would wish to stay with her. It's rare for an estreld male to be compatible with multiple mates, but he is aware that he risks a small chance to spawn with someone he isn't fully compatible with, and he does his duty while still mitigating his chance of meeting both his true mate, and the mother of his spawn in the same evening. Though our clan would praise him for both, he does not want to make a true mate sad."

So the blue warrior was a softy after all. I didn't realize their true mates would be sad if their male had an offspring with another female. I thought they were all very open about that kind of stuff considering their mating games, but apparently some of them were more traditional.

"So, we're just supposed to mingle with the competition?" I changed the subject, scanning the crowd of females staring at us like a herd of blorgenpines gathered to be slaughtered for flavor packs. Those flavor packs were a godsend with the gruel you have to endure on long space travel.

"Normally there are only ten mates chosen for the ritual, but as you can see many mates have been accepted this cycle. The Almder will arrive soon to start the games, and Salph will introduce the mates to the participants."

"Right..."

I took the opportunity to make my way closer to Loric, the stoic blue estreld in the back, and folded my arms over my chest, grunting while scanning the females. Appearing dissatisfied with my search was a sure bet for any protective softy to start up a conversation to be defensive on their behalf. I didn't need him thinking I was a complete asshole, but I could easily adjust the chat in my favor once he initiated contact. Trust is never built between marks when they think you're talking to them because you want something, but when they are the one that talks to you, well then, their guard is down because they think they are the one in control.

I kept my back to the male, further cementing that I have no intention of approaching him. Tapping my foot to increase the anxiety levels of most who were paying attention only psychologically sped up the desire for my mark to take action sooner than later. Preferably before my act was interrupted by the leader of the planet, and the whole mating games. I needed to solidify my ally in this show and gorble parade.

"Bunch of gorbles," I mumbled just loud enough for my friend to hear, but it was my handler that finally gave in.

"Gorbles are a strange breed. They may appear to be worthless beasts, but it's really a matter of what you consider valuable. What they lack in practical use, they make up for in emotional support, and have been shown to be quite protective of beings that bond with them. Fascinating creatures."

What was his name anyway? I now regret not asking so that I can properly mock him in my thoughts before utilizing his rant to my advantage.

"Is there a reason why all of the mates are topless, and puffing out their chests like gorbles waiting for a snack?" It was better to make fun of my competition than it was to make fun of their females. I didn't have anything bad to say about their women here, not if I could catch the eye of that one I saw on the vidcom earlier. "I thought you said we were trying to impress the females," I added for good measure, and my handler smiled now at ease that I had no disrespect for their species but for most of the mates they've brought in offworld, though my comment did apply to their own estreld mates too.

Loric came up from behind and inserted himself into the conversation, right on cue, "You should take the opportunity to remove your own shirt as well, it is customary for potential mates to bare themselves to show their health and for an estreld, show how many loh they've manifested."

"Is that what you call the organic rocks on your skin?" I wondered, and it was off topic for developing our frienemy bond, but I could learn a few things on the way. "If that's the case then you have most of us beat, including myself."

His expression was still guarded but he played along. I still thought I could take him on, loh markings or not. "I'm not trying to beat any of them," he said smoothly putting a hitch in the male bonding, but also making him out to be the kind of guy I probably would have kept around if my life wasn't a shit show. That will only make betraying him a little more difficult, but only a little. "There's only one I'm interested in, and hers is the only opinion that matters."

"All of Estreldez is praying for your successful mating, Loric," my handler remarked, making my job easier by the second as he led the topics along, making everything appear more organic and less orchestrated. "Even your admirers have such high hopes that Luan will respond to your efforts."

Now, we were getting somewhere.

"Luan? Is she the one you are interested in?" I pressed lightly. Being a wingman to his mating success would go a long way to letting me fly under the radar while I went about stealing their jewel and getting the hell out of this star system. As far away from the necia as possible.

Loric's expression hardened, giving my handler an admonishing glance before responding. Maybe he didn't want to reveal his pick to anyone, but it seemed to me his pick wasn't so much a secret to anyone on this planet.

"Ignore the crowd, and focus on pleasing the one that catches your essence." So he was going for a redirect by offering me advice. I could work with that.

"Sage words." I grinned at him and gave a clap on his back in camaraderie. Who knew if the gesture was universal or not, but he seemed to loosen up a bit after the contact. And then I saw her.

Loric was right about one thing, her essence was hard to ignore. All of the commotion of the females in the crowd, and the potential mates milling about stilled in my vision as I took her in. The vidcom didn't do her justice, she looked like a god's damned ice princess that could crush my organs with a stare. The determined set of her jaw, and the hardened gleam in those silver eyes had me wondering what it took to have her melt against the heat of my own determination, to hear her pant my name as I traced my fingers down that glowing flesh of hers. My blood pumped in anticipation, feeling my need for her swelling my now constrictive pants. I now understood why the estreld choose those bunched up loose fabrics cinched in with leather, it was probably a lot more comfortable to let yourself have a bit of space to grow. I grinned to myself and turned to my new friend.

"So, when you find who to focus on what do you do to get their attention?" I asked Loric.

I had no intentions of mating with any of them for the job, so I never took the time to learn their mating customs, but I'd make an exception for her.

"A display of power, and then find a way of making contact with them. Research has found that touch can trigger their mating hormones. Then it's up to them to choose you for the games, and ultimately for the ceremony."

"Got it." I figured ripping off my shirt was too obvious, and there were plenty of pectorals on display already that I'd have to find another way of getting her attention.

Her eyes, so much like the moon, searched the sea of males, and stopped when they met my dark eyes, clouded with my desire to hear her strong voice shake when she tells me how she wants to be pleased. My chest expanded faster and faster as adrenaline made every other thought besides her drop away.

What kind of magic did she hold over me? I didn't care.

A low growl of possessiveness came over me as I thought, mine.

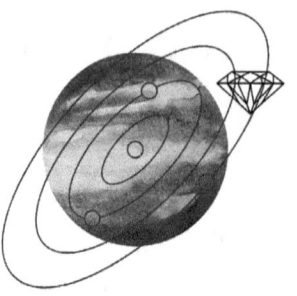

Chapter Seven
Luan

Almder came out with a soft yellow glow about her, dressed in traditional light robes that complimented her loh jewels and the beauty of her silvered hair. For a moment I completely forgot about how she was forcing me to spend the rest of my life, even before I became the next Almder stuck on this planet. There was so much more good I could do for our clan offworld, and she just couldn't see that yet.

It was strange not being the one up there introducing the history of the moon ceremony to the offworlders this cycle, talking of time honored traditions and granting a blessing for a successful mating. The radiation from the moon's rays absorbed into my mother's loh burst out in a warm breeze across the room. My own loh buzzed with the contact, that was the power of a true Almder, the ability to not merely strengthen yourself, but to give strength to others. With my mother doing the blessing this year, it's sure to be more successful than the cycles she's asked me to take over.

Salph took over when my mother made her way to her viewing pod, our viewing pod where I would have been playing a game of who may choose who in the ceremony later.

I could already see a few estreld's rolling their shoulders back from the tension building in their bodies. Their eggs will drop soon at that rate. Flauna in front of me made a small whimper and a few more loh popped from between her shoulder blades, she would participate in this cycle's ceremony for sure.

She turned around excited that her eggs dropped without even touching one of the mates. Her blue eyes alight with joy she noticed Mabel and me were there and giggled.

"He may not be lit with the moon's radiation, but there's just something about him. I need to know his name." Flauna took my hands in hers and practically begged for me to tell her about whoever caught her eye before the dance of eld. I could understand her nerves, even I requested the list before the games, though for different reasons.

"Which one?" Clicking on the list, Vareo's image popped up first as the last file I was on, and Flauna's eyes lit up before I could swipe to the next male.

"Him! How did you know? What is his name? Look at all of his scars, he must be very powerful."

"Or very reckless," I grumbled back to her, feeling an odd desire to dissuade her from her choice.

Mabel said his name, offering it to Flauna. "Vareo, a bounty hunter passing through the star system. He seems like a fine mate, even if his motives may be credit-inspired rather than diplomatic."

"Doesn't matter what got him here, all that matters is that he's here now," Flauna cooed. "He's looking this way." She blushed turning her blue skin a bit purple in the cheeks. Her loh between her shoulders was pulsing, and they grew a bit in size. This should have made me happy to see mating signs, but I found myself scowling instead. I turned my glare onto Vareo, and a different kind of heat twisted my stomach, my anger dissipating. Maintaining my glare was becoming difficult, but that grin of his was so smug I was resolved to keep him at a distance until I've stolen his ship for a ride to the nearest star system. Since he was just passing through anyway, I might be able to make the whole trip with him none the wiser that I had stolen aboard. I could just slip out at his next stop. Bounty hunters usually made a pit stop at the outlaw planet Necias Delta Fal, and I could find a new transport there easily enough with a few jewels, and a guarantee for more once I was delivered to my destination.

"That's unusual," Mabel muttered, her attention distracted in a different direction from the large bounty hunter. She nudged me towards another male with yellow eyes, and golden blonde hair. He blinked and I noticed he was also staring at us, double lids clearing his vision. I gulped back my distaste for what he reminded me of, a krelin, but he seemed different from the delegates sent from Krelis before.

"He's the ambassador from Krelis," Mabel had already swiped my still open screen to his file.

"But he's... participating," I finished her thought for both of us. That was highly unusual for any of the Krelis delegates to subject themselves to an exam and do more than be an observer of the ceremony. Almder always gave Krelis an invite so that they weren't offended when we relied on them for the trade of their hewve lard, and other nutritional supplies. Not once have they participated.

Did he actually think anyone would mate with him? I practically scoffed at the idea. They were a brutal hive-like species, and any offspring from them could be considered a security risk.

He was probably planning how to invade our planet and steal our resources right now, making my mission to find other trade agreements that much more important. They were already strong arming us during trades for more than agreed upon at time of delivery, one step away from being considered an outlaw themselves.

I folded my arms instinctively protecting myself from even his stare, but didn't turn away from him. I was not afraid, at least I wouldn't let him know I was.

"Any estreld who has already seen a potential mate, please give them an offering of tarnpul inviting them to the dance in celebration of another cycle of the moons," Salph instructed, and Flauna bounced from her seat. As did many other estreld who felt the pull of their mating loh. My stomach twisted in knots knowing who she was giving her tarnpul offering to. We all accessorized ourselves with various tarnpul for the ceremony. I had several tarnpul rings, and even a headdress beaded with bleached tarnpul to match my hair. I twisted the ring on my thumb nervously, and it was Mabel who touched the bangle on my wrist to get my attention as Flauna approached Vareo.

Trying to ignore them I bit my lip and gave Mabel all my attention. Then I noticed her pained expression.

"What is it?"

She cleared her throat. Unable to say it herself she pointed to my screen, that I still had yet to close. There was a message from my mother reading:

You'll offer the ambassador of Krelis some tarnpul, My Jewel.

How could she call me her jewel and ask me to do such a thing at the same time? I fumed.

"One piece of tarnpul doesn't mean you'll mate with him," Mabel tried to reassure me that this was merely a show of respect, and not of interest. We could only hope he wouldn't take it that way.

Heavy footed, I made my way down the rows of seating to reach the males, in particular the one called Trent, from the planet Krelis. My whole body tensed up the closer I got. A heat surged up my spine, and my breathing was becoming irregular. Was I sick?

Mouth dry, I watched as Trent was making his way through the crowd to eliminate the distance sooner. No, no, no, I repeated in my mind. Too quick, I needed time to think of what to say. He was one of the few males that still had his shirt on, thank the moons. His leather armor had intricate designs across it that I hadn't noticed until he was standing before me, his nostrils flaring, sniffing the air. From behind him wind gushed making other males make space for him, and wings emerged from his back. Leathery, and some part iridescent with a gorgeous yellow shimmer to them.

I gasped, unable to stop myself from being breathless at the display. He was uncharacteristically handsome for a krelin, and I had no idea that they had wings...

The burning sensation crawling up my spine intensified, and the humm of the crowd murmuring amongst themselves was distracting.

Trent reached out his hand, and stupidly I accepted it with my own.

"Luan." He knew my name... and the way he said it was deep and husky. His yellow eyes slanted with his double lids once more, reptilian or insect like, but I didn't hate it.

I should dislike it, but I found myself unable to look away.

Recovering myself I spoke, "Will you accept my offering?" I unclasped the bangle of tarnpul from my bicep and it fell down to my wrist. With a gentle hand he slid the jewelry from my hand on to his without releasing his grip. His thumb caressed my skin, and my back was practically on fire.

Then I heard another's deep voice in the distance, as if he were right next to me, "Focus, power, touch." I grinned to myself, amused that he was repeating the words like a mantra.

Chapter Eight

Vareo

L oric already had a swarm of females around him, giving me the chance to slip away and work my way towards the silver beauty, but she hadn't even budged from her seat. Still glaring in the viewing decks, and then a spritely girl with blue hair, and a soft blue tint of flesh flung her arms around me. If she actually weighed something I might have lost my balance, but when I guided her back to her toes, and firmly back on the ground, she patted a stone that hung around my neck now. This was their tarnpul offering the what's her face was talking about.

"Do you accept my offering?" she asked after she'd already had the damned thing wrapped around my neck. It wasn't an offering at all, it was a hostile takeover. A low growl was surfacing in my throat, and I tried to suppress it. The handler had told me I couldn't go to the dance without an offering, and I wasn't about to dismiss a free pass, just in case it was my only opportunity. I quickly found she wasn't my only opportunity at all, as a few other estreld females approached, and one after the other was draping tarnpul jewels across me. I had bracelets on my wrist, even a damned ring on my pinky, I felt like I was at the outlaw gambling parade on Necias Delta Fal. All these bits of tarnpul alone would pay for the next few months of maintenance on the ship, maybe even get my screen fixed so it didn't glitch anymore. As long as Carmen didn't get a hold of them, this trip wouldn't be worthless even if the job was a scam.

A glow caught my attention, and I stilled watching the gauzy fabric of the estreld I had set my sights on billow behind her. Those silver eyes were hard set, determined, and heading down here towards me. I waited, and tensed as the krelin male parted the space of mates for him to meet her trajectory.

And Loric said this wasn't a competition of gorbles. His insectoid eyes were already targeted on her, and I could smell his glands warding off other males from approaching.

"Pardon me, ladies," I gave a small tilt of my head, and worked my way through the now tightening crowd, as everyone had stopped to stare at the two of them.

She was glowing like the moons, and she was stunning. A fierceness to her face, and that's what I wanted to see in her as she stared down her foes. She couldn't possibly want to mate with a krelin, I assured myself.

I had to reach them before he started a traditional krelin mating ritual, some males were known to spray their mates with their scent so no other male will touch their prey. Not that it's harmful, but my nose has always been sensitive to that odor, and it's been known to trigger hormones in females that's a pretty powerful drug-like state making them more susceptible to their 'charms'.

He wasn't going to spoil this ceremony for me by taking the one female that made having to go through that examination seem worth it. I'd already imagined burying myself inside her slick folds, and hearing my name on her lips.

Wind blew through my hair, and I cursed. He was one of those krelins... one with wings. He was a warrior within his hive.

Fuck.

He'd be more difficult to get rid of than I thought. Once they set their sights on a mate, they usually saw red when faced with other suitors. Most of the time they'd sooner kill the competition, even if they were part of their own hive. Dangerous creatures.

I didn't know what was coming over me, but I couldn't let it go. It would have been better to ignore her and focus on the job, but I couldn't walk away.

Focus on the objective. The girl.

Give her a powerful display. What was more powerful than saving her from the clutches of a krelin?

They needed touch to trigger their loh or something like that.

The krelin was already holding her hand, and stroking her fingers. I growled at the sight. Clenching my fists, I prepared to throw him off of her if he even thought of spraying her with his mating glands.

There were better ways of getting what I wanted that didn't involve violence, I reminded myself and chanted, "Focus, power, touch." Stick to the plan, Vareo, you just need to prevent his mating spray, and convince her that he's not a worthy mate.

And you are? I thought grimly. No, of course not, but I was better for a one night stand than a krelin was. My gut felt like acid was tearing its way through the fourth black depths of Trillus Magus. Did I want more than one night? I shook the thought from my head.

Focus.

Power.

Touch.

Her head turned from the krelin's wing display, which I tried to convince myself weren't that impressive, to catch me mid stride. My heart hammered in my ribcage under her scrutiny, then the whole crowd went silent as she glowed brighter, and putting the earlier light show of the leader of the estrelds to shame.

She was the moon herself, trapped in the body of an angel. And when I thought she couldn't be any more impressive, she sprouted jewels from her back that layered and layered like unsheathing an arsenal of daggers made of diamonds, spread out from her shoulders like her own set of wings. Deathly wings, that looked like they could stab the krelin if he got out of line, I smiled at that image in my mind. She'd be a force to be reckoned with, and I wanted her even more.

She had no idea how she tore through my control, making me want to pull her into my arms even with all of Estreldez watching. They seemed to be the voyeur kind of species that wouldn't be too concerned about it, but there were things I wanted to do to her that I'd prefer to keep to myself.

My cock pulsed, already preparing itself despite the current circumstances that I was choosing to ignore. Like the krelin that was still holding her hand, and expanding his wings in an act of dominance. I wrinkled my nose as the waft of his warding glands intensified, it was a good thing the females couldn't smell it themselves... they'd be repulsed instantly.

She spoke finally, interrupting the heavy air between the three of us, "I'll see you at the dance, then." Her tone was dismissive, and I grinned feeling relieved that she wasn't affected by the krelin's advances. She slipped her hand from his grasp, and turned abruptly from both of us.

Stunned, it took me a moment to realize she was also dismissing my own attempt to get her attention. She was leaving. I didn't even get the chance to greet her, or ask her name.

Someone bumped into me from behind, and I watched as Loric passed by to pursue her himself. I glared after him and, coming to my senses, I followed after. As he got closer to her his blue loh morphed before my eyes, extending out like spikes from his arms.

He was a walking weapon, even the loh on his back grew up and out curving like odd wings of his own. Did all the estreld have these?

They weren't the same as the diamond wings of the beauty escaping, but dangerous all the same.

It was odd that the kerlin didn't make any attempts to spray or claim her when she left. I took a moment to glance over my shoulder, and like he was waiting for me he lifted an arm to show off a bracelet bejeweled with tarnpul. He gave me a victorious smile, and turned his back to me. The bastard, was that one of her offerings?

My insides boiled at his bold claim that I was distracted long enough for more females to surround me. One of them clung to my arm, and cooed.

"He's chosen her, I'm so jealous."

I grumbled. "He's just an insect."

She giggled. "No, not him. Loric. He's chosen Luan to be his mate this cycle."

"Yes, I already knew that." He'd told me as much when we spoke, and then I looked up to see who he was standing in front of. My silver beauty.

Luan.

Of course we'd be going after the same mate. Mate, that word felt strange to say, but right when I referred to her. So what if this ridiculous ceremony was meant to help the estrelds repopulate their species; while I was here... she was mine. What she did when I was gone, was her business, but even that thought irritated me.

Her bedding with that krelin, or even my frenemy Loric was out of the question.

Loric was glowing an obnoxious blue, and he seemed to pulse in her presence, making me grind my teeth watching him. Her cheeks were blushing a sweet pink, and it was for a man that wasn't me.

She removed a ring from her thumb, and placed it on his finger as she bit down on her lower lip.

They may have won the round, but the games weren't over yet, and I had plenty of tarnpul to join the dance.

"Aren't they perfect?" The girl was still clinging to my arm.

Then the host chimed in, "It looks like this cycle's moon ceremony is shaping up to be one for the history books. May the moon bless us all. For every offering you will have the opportunity for one on one time before the dance, so hand out those tarnpuls quickly!"

"Oh, excuse me." The girl on my arm released me, but left behind a necklace she tied around my wrist. "See you soon." Her curvy hips swayed through the crowd, and I didn't have much time to introduce myself.

"So this is Luan," I interrupted Loric's moment. I was a shitty wingman, not that I wanted to cock block him specifically, just from her. "You are more fierce than the rays of a Trillus sun. May the moons give many blessings upon your mating." I took her hand into my own and bent down to kiss her fingers, carefully slipping off one of her rings as I withdrew. When I lifted my gaze there was that fire in her silver eyes once more.

"I have not agreed to mate with anyone yet," she objected, and I smiled back at her, pleased to hear that.

"My apologies for assuming." I gave Loric an apologetic shrug that he struck out despite being given one of her offerings. While their attention was on my shoulders I pocketed the ring that would guarantee me a one on one meeting with Luan.

Loric explained, "It is customary to wait until after the rest of the games to make any commitments." He too leaned in, though instead of kissing her hand he pulled her in to brush against her cheek and my blood heated. For someone that wasn't trying to compete he did a good job of stepping up a notch from my hand peck.

I could still feel her skin on my lips, and I ached to press my mouth to other parts of her willing flesh. And this Loric was in my way. My chest rumbled involuntarily, a warning sign to those that knew what I was, but I doubted anyone knew much about Sholonus, since my planet was destroyed. I cleared my throat hoping no one noticed.

"When you're ready," Loric whispered to Luan. If he hadn't been after the same mate then I would have clapped him on the back, and rooted for the suave move, but all he did was bring out the carnal protective instincts of my shol side.

"I'll be in the library for the meetings phase of the games." She was gazing at me when she invited Loric for his one on one, and I couldn't help but feel included. Giving her a bow of my head, I would certainly see her soon after I picked my handler's brain for more details on the rest of the games.

See you soon, Luan.

Even her name meant the light of the moons, but I wanted her to shine for me alone.

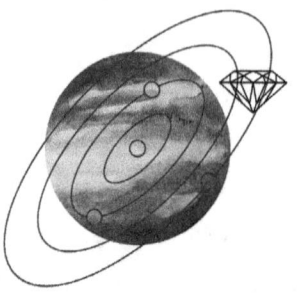

Chapter Nine

Luan

Not until after it happened did I understand what I had just announced to the whole of Estreldez. I buried my face in my hands, embarrassed that I'd dropped my eggs, and displayed my mating loh to every male like I was yelling at the top of my lungs, "Fuck me."

"It wasn't that bad..." Mabel tried to console me. Of course she didn't understand. To her this was a success for her to research later when she interviewed everyone after the ceremony. Hell, she was probably holding herself back from interviewing me now while it was still fresh.

I shouldn't be irritated at her for it. That was her job, and it benefited the clan.

"How is this possible?"

Not even some of the matings that had successful offspring showed their mating loh to people during the first phase of the games. I flushed thinking about what all of Estreldez thought of my display.

Mabel answered that for me too, "You've given the clan a lot of hope for the future. It may not seem like it now, but a strong response like what you've shown is a positive sign for mating, and in every instance of the mating loh appearing there has been a new spawn."

That terrified me even more.

"I'm not ready to have offspring yet," I blanched, "this cycle was supposed to be a 'show' of support, not anything more. And to have it happen for... a krelin no less." I shivered. That's who was holding my hand at the time, and if he was supposed to be my true mate what did that mean for the future of Estreldez?

But when I saw the dark coal eyes of the bounty hunter I stilled. He looked as if he would devour me, and heat pulsed through my loh. Was that what happened when the mating loh were out? Every glance and touch turned my insides to mush, and was destroying my inhibitions into granting all- access-passes for any who showed interest?

I groaned, fully disappointed in my lack of control. Rubbing the spot on my hand where Vareo's lips burned my skin like an imprint I squeezed my thighs together feeling my loh react once more. The room brightened, and Mabel blushed realizing my not so private thoughts are practically exposed with every glowing jewel on my skin.

Even Loric's mating loh responded to mine, and my heart was racing so fast. Every touch was sensitive, and his cheek brushing up against mine was so different from all the other times we spent together. I wanted to slap myself to prevent myself from hoping Loric was actually choosing me to mate with. I've seen his mating loh for other females during previous ceremonies, for estreld males that could merely mean that he was feeling protective of me after seeing who I chose to show my own loh to... Trent.

How could my mating loh choose Trent, a krelin?

"He's quite handsome." Mabel shrugged, noncommittally. "His file says he's a warrior, and one of the leaders that help protect our system from outlaws."

"He's practically an outlaw himself with how the krelin have been extorting us for our minerals and rock deposits."

She lifted a brow, a small smile lifting the corner of her mouth. "And the bounty hunter isn't?"

"What does Vareo have to do with this?"

I even called him by name, and Mabel's smile grew. "Don't think I didn't see how you responded to him. Maybe you're just into strong outlaw types, even Loric has been known to ignore orders and implement strategies without the Almder's approval."

"Really?" I didn't know that about Loric, he always seemed a bit ridgid in his desire to follow rules. Maybe that was only around me.

My neck heated thinking about how I had bent the mating games traditions by allowing Vareo to get away with stealing one of my rings. It wasn't officially offered to him, but I hoped that I'd see him later and he wasn't just trying to earn a few extra credits by selling off the tarnpul later.

He had plenty of tarnpul from other potential mates, I frowned thinking about how many offerings he received. He had no flashy coloring, he didn't show off his physical health by removing his top coverings, and he had no loh to glow in the moon's radiation. Why were so many females interested in him?

Mabel eased her hand from my grip, shaking out her fingers at my tightening hold.

"Luan?" I must have had the appearance of a visp ready to pluck her loh from her skin to feed myself. Viscous, was the word. The idea that someone else would mate with him made me ready to claw at them.

"Why do I feel so possessive?"

"It's common for the mating loh to want potential mates to choose them over others. The feeling passes after you've copulated with them. Biologically we seek mating to replicate ourselves, and once seed is inside us we feel more free to choose.

Many have found they've enjoyed the ceremony much more after the first mating of the evening, and go to find other compatible mates while the moon is still at its brightest."

I felt relieved that it was normal, and sighed. I just needed to mate with one of them and then I'll feel more like myself again. Images of Vareo's strong arms wrapped around me made me squirm in my seat. My core heated, and a strange wetness leaked from my insides. Mating season was disgusting, I grimaced.

This will all be solved once I ravage him, and I can focus on more important things. A horrified thought crossed my mind, would I have to mate with all three of them?

As if reading my palling face Mabel added, "You don't have to mate with any of them. The mating loh is a powerful feeling, but just like you had the strength to walk away from them earlier, you can walk away from them again, even at the peak of the ceremony. You are a strong estreld. It is by your choice, and grace alone that one of them may mate with you. And whomever you choose, whenever you decide will be a lucky mate."

"Thank you, I needed that." I pulled her in for a hug. I still planned on mating with Vareo before the ceremony ever took place. I needed a clear head to avoid Trent, and mating with Loric was much too likely to create spawn I wasn't ready for, and he would wish to imprint on me with the way his loh was responding to mine. I could always mate with him another time, when I was ready. But Trent... if he was the reason my mating loh came out, then he was the most dangerous of all. He could be my true mate... and mating with him would bind me to a species that was trying to strong arm Estreldez into being part of their hive and expanding their control. I couldn't do that to our clan.

"Do you need me to stay and supervise your ceremonial greetings?"

I could handle myself.

"No, I know you have others to interview. I'll be fine."

"What did you feel when your mating loh came out?" Mabel asked real quick before retreating.

"My nerves were on fire, and my shoulders burned. The thought repeated in my head, mine."

She nodded, and left me with my thoughts.

I had to get rid of that echo. Please don't let the first mate I see be Trent. I had to mate with Vareo before I was alone with the one that turned my insides into goo. Mabel may have thought I had all the control in the world, but we didn't have enough research on whether that was the case with mates that triggered our imprinting. I knew that's what was happening to me, even if Mabel wouldn't say it.

"Am I the first to arrive?" his deep voice asked from the doorway, my breath caught.

I stared at Vareo's broad shoulders, and his odd coverings that hid the scars I knew were under them.

"Do you have an offering?" I smirked at him, knowing full well he had my mother's ring. Why had I let him take that one?

It was a risk that he wouldn't show to return it. But here he was. Now, in front of me.

He was so unusually handsome. His ears were pointed, I hadn't noticed that with his black hair over them before. He wasn't wearing any of the tarnpul offerings from the other females. I smiled at that.

He strode over to me, lifted my hand and replaced my ring upon my finger. My skin tingled where he touched me, and then without another word, he walked over to the stack of books I had been pouring through the last few days and sat down to pick up the first one. I paled realizing which book had been placed there last.

"It's not an easy book to get a hold of. Most of Sholonus's history is lost." He flipped through the pages, finding the marker I placed in one of the sections floating out. He grinned from pointy ear to pointy ear. "We aren't so different, though I suspect you knew that since I passed all of your exams before arriving."

I lifted my chin not willing to be mocked by him for wondering if he really was from Sholonus or not. Knowing his anatomy would definitely help me figure out if he was lying on his file or not. Forgeries were becoming more common. Instead of shying away from what I'd done, I'll embarrass him with the facts I'd learned.

"Is it true that even when you are not mating your mating organs are always outside of your body?"

He lifted an amused brow. "Does that intrigue you? Or are you more excited about the 'folds of skin that harden to rock' bit?" He quoted the book's reference and I blushed, remembering the next part was about how it expanded and filled to make contact with as many nerves as possible before hardening.

His legs were spread wide as he sat back relaxed with the book, and I could make out the large shape of his external organ under his tight coverings. My loh brightened with anticipation. Luckily my mating loh weren't out, but I felt my back burning with the need to free him from his odd clothing to see for myself what he's been hiding.

He picked up another book, and then another, reading the titles, scanning the contents. His interest in what I've been reading made my stomach flutter. Did he really care what I was interested in?

"I'm pretty sure the necias stole some technology from another system that might help your scientist with your food replication shortage. Maybe even research on why your males aren't getting the job done."

"And you know this for a fact?" I clipped sharply. How could he know what the necias outlaw planet has or doesn't have?

What planet did they steal from that might help my clan? He was going to tell me everything, and then he was going to take me to that planet.

I stalked over to him, and the closer I got the more my shoulders burned to release. His mating organ was strained against his pants and my loh pulsed with need. I may have been upset that the necias was holding back vital information for my clan, but my anger wasn't towards Vareo. He took an interest in my clan's problems and shared leads on a solution, for that I felt even more eager to see just what the textbook got correct about his species.

His voice was husky, those tarnpul-colored eyes were hooded with matching desire. "It's only speculation, but for you I'd risk a bounty on my own head to confirm it as fact."

Before I could back away he stood, pulling me to him. Those lips pressed into mine, softer than I would have anticipated. Like he was waiting for me to reciprocate, and letting him know that I wanted what he was offering. And I did, I wanted all of him, more than just a kiss. With a flick of my tongue, I opened my mouth to him, and my body molded to his embrace that was tighter now. My whole body tingled with heat, and my core throbbed until I couldn't concentrate enough to keep my mating loh under control. My loh vibrated and expanded behind me. Fuck it, I thought wrapping my arms around his neck and threading my fingers through his dark strands to pull him in, deepening our kiss.

His mouth moved in rhythm to mine like it was always meant to be this way. He was always meant to taste this intoxicating. My tongue traced over his teeth that just like in the book on his species I'd read were elongating, as shols were known to be carnivores, and I wanted him to devour me.

His hand wrapped around my waist brushing against my mating loh, making me shudder with all sorts of sensations I'd never felt before.

My legs clenched, feeling my glands wet my core for entry, a trickle of fluid leaked down my thigh, but this time I rubbed myself up against his strained pants feeling the thick hardness of him as the fabric wicked up my juices. Then I heard him groan, a low rumble vibrated in his chest.

I squeaked against his intensified kisses as I felt his organ pulse against me. Breaking away from his mouth, I arched back. His strong arms held me firm against him, supporting me as I moved, feeling the bundle of nerves at my entrance ache and throb with the contact.

Panting, I wanted more. Wanted to feel everything he had to offer. That hard cock of his freed from his tight fabric, and filled the emptiness that longed for him inside me. Vareo's cock pulsed again, and I buried my face into his chest to stifle a moan into his shirt. Why was he still wearing clothing?

He guided my rubbery legs over to the cushioned bench and one of his hands trailed a fire down my skin until he cupped my entrance while he nibbled at my ear.

"Say my name," he whispered.

I was speechless, unable to even say that. Then one finger stroked the nub of nerves, then tapped at my entrance. Circling my slick pussy he teased a finger in and out. Then two fingers stroked and pulsed making my mouth dry, and my breathing quickened, wanting more.

"Say my name," he repeated. "I want to know you enjoy what you're feeling."

Oh, and I did.

I didn't want him to stop.

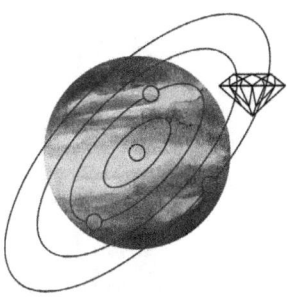

Chapter Ten

Vareo

M y whole body quaked with the need to drive my cock into her eager pussy. Every instinct in me screamed to claim her before anyone else could. Her juices soaked through my pants, and I was hard enough to rip the fabric between us with one calculated thrust. Her soft moans into my chest made me hold her firm against me, not even able to focus on anything but how she felt against my skin.

My fingers probed and explored my mate with precision. I needed her to crumble in my arms, and for mine to be the only name that ever escaped those lips of hers.

Her diamond wings were blocking us from view of anyone that might interrupt us, but I couldn't take her here. Not like this.

What was wrong with me?

She was willing, and open for me, and I held myself back like a fool.

You want her to want you.

It was a stupid thought, since none of the estreld ever kept any of their mates, but I knew as soon as I kissed her and my canines extended that if I mated with her... I wouldn't be able to let her go. My Sholonus instincts would take over, and I'd kidnap her from her own planet to make sure she'd never leave my side.

My chest vibrated with the need to claim her. Even my cock pulsed as I pressed her thigh against me while I cupped her ass in one hand, and teased her entrance with my other. I rubbed my thumb against her clit as I slid in and out of her, wishing it wasn't my finger deep inside, but my shaft.

Her whole body glowed and shivered, as she clung to my shirt and wrapped her arm around my neck to pull me closer. Luan's soft moans drove me mad with need.

"Say my name," I begged her.

Luan lifted her firm ass in the air, adjusting herself towards my cock, and she whimpered as I pulsed against her bundle of nerves. Holding her to me I kept my cock rubbing against her as I sunk my fingers into her eager haven, matching my rhythm. Her wings folded over us, and they were warm against my back. I didn't worry about whether they would cut me or not, it would be worth it.

"Vareo," she finally rasped, and my heart swelled with emotion at hearing my name on those perfect lips of hers.

As I felt her shudder her release, I bit my tongue to prevent myself from completing my own. I couldn't afford to let myself feel anymore than I already did, for her sake.

The life of an indentured outlaw wasn't what she deserved. And while I still had some control over myself, I wouldn't steal her away from her home planet.

Fuck, what was I doing getting distracted with mating someone I couldn't have. I needed to focus on what I came here for. Stealing the jewel of Estreldez.

Holding her to me as she panted, I could smell her juices in the air and I tried to memorize her fragrance for later, the scent of her need for me and no one else.

I growled possessively as I sniffed the top of her blond hair, she smelled of wild flowers from my home planet. Cost a sum of credits to find the seeds for them, and an incubator to supply them with the correct nitrogen levels. All I had to do was come to Estreldez and the true flower was here all along.

"I like the way your body pulses like mine," she admitted while stroking my chest. I regretted not ripping the shirt away when I had the chance, now I wanted nothing more than to feel her fingers against my skin. My cock still ached to complete what we started.

Luan trailed down my shirt, toying with the top closure of my pants, and my blood pumped faster at her advances. I groaned with an intake of air as her palm rubbed my shaft and her fingers cupped my balls.

She giggled. The sound brought warmth to my chest. I needed to hear more of that sweet laughter, but I couldn't let her continue. Grabbing her hand to still her as she clutched my cock she peered up at me with a raised eyebrow. Her silver eyes glowed with mischief.

"If you continue I won't let you go."

That seemed to clear her head, and replaced those lusty orbs with fear. She adjusted her silky dress, repositioning the slit of her skirt back to her smooth thigh. Not that covering up would do anything to bar me access to that pretty pink center, it was the terrified expression on her face that stilled my hard need, and dulled my throbbing cock.

I had expected that kind of reaction, but it didn't lessen the sting. Of course she didn't want to be mated with me if it meant leaving her planet.

Estreldez wanted offspring, not someone taking one of their viable females. I'd be on their bounty list for more than stealing a diamond, but one of their prized breeders too. I'd never make it out of the star system with my shit piece of an excuse for a ship. That wasn't part of the job. She wasn't part of the plan.

She's yours.

I gave her one of my reassuring smiles, as if I were merely joking. No need to scare her.

She turned her eyes up to the ceiling, only now did I notice the jeweled constellation design above us. This whole planet had a wealth of stones that they could decorate every room with murals like that.

"Do you really think the necia know of a planet with the technology that could help my clan?" She gnawed on her lower lip, worried about discussing this with me.

It wasn't common knowledge, but what did I care if the necia were pressured into sharing the tech that could help the estreld scientists with their mating system, or even their food shortage.

"Even if they don't have it, they know who does," I was sure of that much.

That fire returned to her eyes, and before I could ask what she was planning a male cleared their throat to get our attention. My arms were still wrapped around her, and her wings of diamond daggers were now unfolded and spread out ready to strike.

I should have sensed them enter the room. Having them sneak up on me like that only confirmed my suspicions that I couldn't afford to spend more time with the intoxicating estreld female.

I had to grab the jewel and leave.

"You know the rules, Loric, one-on-one time is not to be interrupted." She was already standing and pressing forward towards the male who now gave me the death stare. So much for frenemies, it was straight enemies with how he caught me touching her, though he didn't know the half of it. My cock twitched, remembering the feel of her clenching around my fingers. I shoved my hand in my pocket hoping he didn't have the same scent receptors that I did.

"You're being summoned for one of those one-on-ones in the garden." Loric didn't appear pleased with telling her about this. "Almder has made it perfectly clear that she wishes for you to stay with him for as long as possible to be polite, and you can return for the dance."

Her tiny fists bunched up revealing what she thought about this arrangement.

"Are you forfeiting your own time?" She asked through gritted teeth.

"No, in exchange for delaying our own time, Almder has granted us early leave from the dance to the royal grotto."

Luan waved her hand dismissively. "It's unlike her to meddle with the ceremony like this."

"Things are strained with Krelis, and you've expressed an interest to her many times that you wish to build more diplomatic relations. This is your chance to prove to her that you can do what you've been pushing for. Talk with the krelin and figure out what the hive wants. Find a better agreement between our planets."

I suppressed scoffing at the very idea of reasoning with a krelin. His display earlier told us exactly what his intentions were with Luan. If she wasn't careful with this meeting she'd be bargained to be his mate, and when you mate with the hive you become connected with them. He'd take her back to Krelis, and she'd be stashed away with the rest of the females on that planet. Brainwashed, the lot of them. The idea of Luan becoming one of them had me inching closer to her protectively.

Would she be better off if I stole her away for myself? No, at least with the hive she'd be safe. The life of an outlaw wasn't meant for her, though she'd give a bounty hunter a run for their credits with those impressive wings of hers.

She seemed to be considering what Loric had to say, and nodded. "I'll speak with him." She was firm in her decision, and she emphasized that it would only be speaking, which settled relief to my tense muscles. It shouldn't matter to me that she might be with another male since I wasn't claiming her myself, but it did bother me.

And before I could protest, she was sweeping out the door, and Loric stood between us preventing my instincts to follow.

Loric watched me with those sharp blue eyes of his before he spoke, "There are different releases of our mating loh that you may not be aware of. There is sexual attraction, and then there is fated mates. She's found her mate this cycle, and if it isn't you then you must step aside."

"You care about her," I surmised.

"I love her," he corrected.

"Does that make you her fated mate?" My jaw tightened even asking. I meant for the question to come out as a challenge, but there was worry at his answer that I hoped wasn't noticeable.

"A female estreld chooses her fated mate. It's a feeling that builds within the mate the more contact they have with her mating loh."

That explained why I was feeling such possessiveness. I smiled understanding that my feelings were not my own, they were hers pooling out of her mating loh. That means as long as I avoided her while her mating loh were out, I could leave here without going insane for not stealing her away with me.

"Like an infection," I clarified to myself. Once I left this planet I would be fine. It was such an intense feeling I almost mistook her for my Shol mate, that was something completely different than whatever toxic radiation her loh put off.

He squeezed my shoulder, as if giving me reassurance, despite potentially being in the way of him mating with Luan.

"It is a gift to be bonded with Luan in not merely her bed, but her very soul. After our one-on-one in the grotto I will know whether she has chosen me or not."

A flair of jealousy heated through me, and I took a step forward prepared to launch at him before reason stopped me. This was all part of the virus I told myself, I just needed to get off planet with the jewel to be back to normal. My fists flexed, and though I prevented myself from attacking him for even thinking about doing things with Luan in the grotto, I couldn't ease the tension in my muscles.

I wanted to say he could have her, but the words would not leave my tongue.

"Whether you are compatible with her or not will not sway me from pursuing her as a mate. She is the first to have stirred my own mating loh. I've been waiting for her to join the ceremony for many cycles. You understand, don't you, outlaw?"

My mouth dried as he seemed to pinpoint my secrets with a glance alone. He didn't call me bounty hunter. I nodded, but kept my face neutral.

Without meaning to, my competitive side surfaced. "If you were certain you were her true mate, then you wouldn't have any need to assert yourself. You don't want me to be chosen."

Loric smiled at me, his manner schooled from years of training, he was a diplomat if ever I saw one. Calculating his next move. "I'm sure you have thought of what you would offer Luan if she were to choose you. Perhaps a plan to stay on Estreldez to raise your offspring together, and use your connections to create new treaties for the continued prosperity of the clan."

The bastard hit low with his words. Offspring, being land bound to this planet, and knowingly mocking the fact that my outlaw history would bring more problems than it would solve. All humor fell from my features, and I knew I had met my match in manipulation tactics. He saw right through me, and might have already known I was messing with him from the beginning. He was not someone to eat up my bullshit without a fight. And his blows were direct hits.

I had no intention of breeding an offspring that would be left behind like my own old man did to me. And I certainly didn't have any desire to be stuck on this planet. And as reluctant as I was to admit I felt something for the blasted female, I didn't want to bring her more trouble.

"I'll be taking my leave after the dance, and before the ceremony."

I brushed past him, and he grabbed my shoulder, making me stiffen. He gave me a gentle squeeze, and he eyed me with relief.

"Thank you for your understanding."

I gritted my teeth, and glared at him. "This was an agreement of circumstances, nothing more."

He withdrew his hand, amusement not gone from his blue eyes. "Of course. I'll be sure to let the shuttle know you'll be departing shortly."

He was nothing if not persistent in his efforts to remove me from his planet. I admired that about him, if things were different we would have got along well together. He'd be a great outlaw if he decided to leave his planet. Wits, and power. I still remembered the way his loh expanded into lethal weapons all up his arms and down his back. He'd be handy to have on a mission. Technically he was assisting me even on this one, giving me the excuse to leave early with no extra suspicion about why I was doing so. That meant I didn't have to wait to steal the jewel. The sooner the better.

Though my insides struggled against that concept, the virus coursed through me making me feel ill at the prospect of leaving Luan. Damned mating toxins.

"I'm not the one you should be protecting her from." I wasn't sure why I wanted to help the guy after his dominance display, but I did. "If you let that krelin spray her with his own mating glands, he will steal her from your planet and she'd be part of the hive's harem. Treaty or not, krelins will take what they've marked as theirs. First your jewels, then your females, and eventually your planet."

I wasn't saying it to threaten him or his clan, but they were being naive if they thought they could simply make a treaty with them and be protected. They should have already been searching for another planet to offer them protection, before the krelin decide to advance their plans for their currently slow absorption, takeover, of Estreldez. It was only a matter of time.

Somehow that became my business, and I even thought about how I could steal information from Necias to help protect Estreldez, help protect Luan.

"I know," Loric replied. That nonchalance made me turn to face him, unable to hide my agitation. If he knows then why was he still here with me, and not barging into whatever one-on-one Luan was having with that insect warrior? If he wouldn't do it then I felt compelled to intervene.

"You know?" My voice rose with ire. "You know, and yet you do nothing?"

Now it was his turn to glare at me, but he did not move to approach. He stayed firm and remained calm.

"That was probably why he was sent to participate. Almder saw Luan react to Trent, and a union between the planets would benefit us."

I couldn't believe what I was hearing, and he held a hand up as if to explain. "A union with me would also benefit Estreldez, and I have no intention of letting him take her back to Krelis. You should know it's possible her mating loh were released because of his pheromones, and even still he would not be in control over who she chooses to mark as her mate."

I blinked back my confusion. What was he trying to tell me? Lucky me, I didn't have to ask him like a dumb ass. He answered for me, finally taking a step forward, more brazen since he knew my interest was piqued.

"She doesn't need saving." Loric walked past me, and hovered in the doorway for one last remark, "Where you're from the females must be weak, but on Estreldez they can handle themselves."

"It must be lonely for her, knowing at all times she must be strong all the time with no one to share that burden with." I didn't know why I said it, but I understood Luan a little more. That fierceness about her, that wall she had behind those cold silver eyes. She relied on no one. There was no one coming to save her, and I was reminded of myself.

She'd be okay, but even I used to wish as I grew up that someone would help free me from Necias, from Jax, from my handler Carmen. I could have escaped Carmen, like I did the last handler, but that was only temporary.

An illusion of freedom, before Carmen entered my life and told me killing her wouldn't solve my problems.

It wouldn't, I knew that. But, I smiled at how it might have been worth the extra debt to have a few months before they sent a few war cruisers after me.

I could survive on my own, just as Luan would without me, but it was exhausting fighting alone.

Images of Luan by my side, that determination in her eyes as we fixed up the ship to prepare it for an inevitable fight for freedom against the necia. Jumping through hyperspace to reach a new star outside of the Trillome System together.

Why had I inserted her into my future? Why did it feel like such a lighter experience to fight with her by my side? It was dangerous, and I may not live, and yet the image excited me.

Loric was already out the door, leaving me to myself in the library. Luan's scent was still strong around me, I smiled down at my fingers that I had unconsciously pulled from my pocket to sniff her earlier arousal.

A warmth thrummed through my chest, and my cock grew hard again having not been satisfied from our last encounter. Fuck, that this woman's toxic radiation was addling my mind.

But knowing that didn't stop the possessive thought from entering my mind, she was mine.

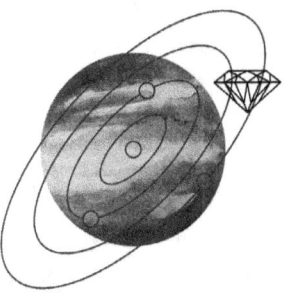

Chapter Eleven

Luan

My loh still glowed from the aftermath of those hot fingers exploring my body in the library. The bundle of nerves at my center were throbbing, making my thighs clench and shift as I walked towards the garden. Every brush of movement was sensitive, and I couldn't shake the image of Vareo's hooded eyes darkened with need, for me. No one has ever looked at me that way, and then he spoke of never letting me go.

I panicked, because the terrifying truth was that I wanted that. I wanted him.

But I had my clan to think of, and now it was more important than ever that I sneak upon his ship without him knowing. If he never let me go, then how was I to barter or steal the information from the necia to find that planet's technology. I had to know whether what Vareo said had any truth to it.

Tearing a piece of my long skirt, I wiped the juices from my thigh and threw the cloth to the floor before entering the garden. I'd pick it up later, but I'd be damned if I let Trent get any ideas by seeing my arousal drip down my leg while I spoke politics. Because that was all we would be doing, speaking, I assured myself. But part of me worried about how my mating loh responded to him earlier. The look on everyone's faces told me enough to know my mating display was more than the usual attraction. I refused to matebond with a krelin warrior. Mating was one thing, bonding was too risky. I didn't trust myself enough after what I allowed to happen in the library with a stranger, ready to throw myself at him just to relieve myself of this heavy feeling inside.

Mabel said it would be easier to control after I mated, but I came all over that bounty hunter's hand, and I still had an overwhelming sensation to have his cock fill my throbbing sex, and pulsate on my pleasure center. More than when I started. What would happen being alone with the male that ignited my mating loh to begin with?

I walked away from the bounty hunter. I could do the same with the krelin, I reassured myself.

I'd talk about our trade, and the increased demands on our jewels. That was all.

Then why was I so uncertain?

My heart was racing, and the heat within my loh was not normal. And he was waiting for me, there, smelling the buds from our rose algae, a hardy and sweet odored bacteria growth that only liked to grow deep in the tarnpul pits, but seemed to flower now that it's been transplanted to the gardens.

"You like the blackpul rose algae?" I asked him, and his back muscles rippled like his wings would emerge again.

"It's sweeter than Krel Nectar." He turned to face me, his honeyed eyes glowing and that blonde hair swept back. "I like it very much," he admitted.

"Estreldez has many types of algae plants," I agreed, "the blackpul is the sweetest of them, but not until they flower. Before that, they are quite bitter. They still smell nice, though."

"I can only think of a few things sweeter." A teasing tone to his husky voice told me he wasn't speaking of plants any longer. I pulled at my skirts as if to hide my scent.

Could he smell me? Somehow that felt much more invasive than I could have imagined.

His eyes, the color of the honey they bring to trade, followed the movement, and as they lingered I felt the growing need to move. I stepped forward, and continued the conversation to bring his attention back to a discussion less physical, something I was more adept at dealing with.

"Have you been sent here to discuss trade?" It was direct and to the point, but krelins were not usually ones to mince words. They took what they wanted, and assertiveness was the only way to do business with them.

"I've been sent to assess other assets that might be agreeable to Krelis."

I flinched at the way he referred to assets. That wasn't normal for me to be so on edge, and he made me that way. Instinct told me that he was again not referring to the various quarries our planet had to offer, but perhaps our clan itself.

"You wish for more krelins to participate in our mating ceremonies?" My throat dried anticipating his response. Did I want him to say yes, or was I nervous he would say exactly that.

"Your females are strong, and our males are fertile with more men than there are available mates," he said matter of fact. I appreciated that he thought my clan's females were strong, and that he worded things in such a way that implied he wished to help solve an issue of contention for Estreldez, but was joining our populations with more krelin wise for the future of our clan? I didn't know.

He saw my hesitation and continued, "Our warriors are harsh, they spend their time defending our trade, our planet, and fighting outlaws without the comforts of a clan to soften them. Entitlement has them rebelling, causing tension between our treaties. Something must change, and that change could be the Estreldez people that soothes the souls of our krelin warriors."

"Are you not a warrior yourself? You seem soothed enough to control yourself," I clipped, not fully believing his calculated words. How was I supposed to believe that the krelins wouldn't take mates and still extort our trades, and even worse than that... invade.

Take what they want when they have a firmer hold within our land.

His smile broadened showing the sharp row of teeth that lined his molars, and I knew they trailed down his throat to help mince and grind their preferred food, the bones of their very own people. I couldn't let his attractive exterior make me forget what the krelin were capable of. Before our trade for our jewels, they were a cannibalistic hive. There was no guarantee they weren't still.

"I am as possessive, and greedy as my hive," he shocked me with his ease of admission, "and I feel the restlessness within them even now, but I had something to focus on that they do not."

He stopped there, and it begged the question of, what did he focus on? But, I already knew the answer. His wings flared out from his back, leathery golden wisps that were majestic and sparkled in the light of the moons. My breath caught, and those honeyed eyes glowed as they stared into my very soul. My loh buzzed as he stepped closer, and my heart hammered in my chest.

I was in control, I repeated to myself, but I was anything but.

The only thing that came out of my mouth in a rasp was, "What do you focus on?" Say anything but me, I begged internally.

"You." His arms snaked around my waist, pulling me in. There was no resistance from me as I breathed in his heady scent. His fingers trailed my lower back and my mating loh burned to release. He was the cause for my display earlier, I knew he had to be.

"You only just met me..." my voice was barely a whisper as he pressed his forehead to mine.

"You are the Jewel of Estreldez, and the only way my mother will accept a union between our species."

He knew who I was and if he knew that then he must be one of the krelin generals or higher, only they have been under oath with the hive's queen to know I was the next almder. Why would they send him to be a delegate? Why would the queen want me to mate with him?

"Who are you?"

"I'm the warrior who found a solution to both our problems that doesn't involve bloodshed."

I shivered, understanding made me cold. The queen would invade, I knew that's where things were headed, but I didn't think it would be so soon. I thought I had more time. Time to find more support for our star system, for Estreldez.

"You mean to take me." My voice hardened, and any desire I had for him shriveled. My loh continued to glow, but it wasn't lust that powered them now.

"I mean to save both our planets," he corrected.

My muscles tensed in his grasp, and I stiffly replied, "Do you even have the queen's blessing on this, or do you think I don't know that taking me doesn't guarantee my planet's safety? Krelis could still invade."

"I'm not sure you understand the leadership of our hive. You could change everything. Mating with me will give us both the strength and influence within the hive to lead them. She would have no choice but to accept our plans for peace."

How was that possible? He was telling me everything I wanted to hear. A solution to our tensions with Krelis, and all it would take was a different kind of tension with this male. Could I trust him?

He saw my indecision and cupped the side of my face holding it to his own to whisper into my ear, "I will cherish you beyond all else. Not merely a mate, but a partner, a queen. Will you accept me?"

"Trent..."

"I like my name on your lips," his voice vibrated with a kind of buzz. He ran his fingers down my back loh, tickling my senses until my mating crystals grew, heating my skin. My skirt shifted as he pressed himself against me, his desire hard against my stomach. My eyes fluttered closed, but it wasn't his face that I saw.

I groaned remembering Vareo's fingers melting my insides, and my thighs squeezed at the sensations rushing to my core.

Panting I felt Trent trailing hot kisses along my neck, and Vareo's image blurred replaced with the fierce maple eyes of the male before me. My mating loh thrust out possessively as soon as I fell into the sensations Trent stirred in me. He could help my clan, he wouldn't leave once we were mated. It was nice to have a piece of that burden lifted from my shoulders.

He bent over to place kisses on my arm now wrapped around his neck, and I rubbed my nose into his blonde hair taking in his scent. Trent would take care of me. I sighed feeling more relaxed.

"I feel you," he moaned as he pulled me against his chest.

Oh my moons, I trembled in his arms knowing that if this continued I would do what I feared would happen. I would bond with him. This was more than mating, he sought to claim me, and my mating loh were seeking to do the same.

I wasn't broken.

If this is what it could be like with the krelins for my clan, then we would do more than save our population... we would be irrevocably bonded with the hive.

Spooked at making that decision too quickly, I tried to blink away the haze of his overwhelming presence.

"Not yet," I begged, as he rubbed himself against me only making my loh glow brighter. My hips moved against his muscled thigh, as he lifted me into his arms. My sensitive bud throbbed as I shuddered with the movement. Trent's strong hands gripped my ass, to help position me atop his strained cock, only his pants keeping us from uniting as one. His wings beat behind him, and I clung to his toned body with my own mating loh spread behind me. Neither of us cared that there were a few other couples wandering the garden, there was just us in our sights.

"Too fast," I tried to say again, but it came out heavy and full of lust.

He pulled back, his golden eyes laden with intense desire, but concern and confusion soon followed.

"Tell me to stop, and I will," his voice husky as he gave me one last opportunity to continue, because I knew he would not touch me further if I objected. How did I know that? Why would a krelin deny themselves what they want when they've taken from our trade forcefully many times over. His restraint was unusual for his species, and for what we've had to deal with from them regularly.

I placed a hand on his chest, and I didn't even have to say the words and he adjusted me back to my feet. Stunned, I stared at him still processing that he would be so gentle, so understanding.

Could all of Krelis be capable of this? Was I wrong about them?

"I need time, " I paused wondering if this was the solution I was searching for this whole time, "to think." He was so different from our other encounters with Krelis.

His face cleared of any signs of what we had been doing before, he nodded his acceptance before releasing me and taking a step back to give me space.

"Come to me during the ceremony when you've decided." His nostrils flared, then he rolled his shoulders for his wings to fold back.

Without another word he made his way through the garden, and before he was out of sight I called out, "There's no guarantee your plans will work. You'd still be mated with me... why?"

I was willing to risk it for my clan, but maybe he didn't realize the difference between mating, and a mated pair? When an estreld released their mating loh, it was for life. It's why I ran from the bounty hunter, and why I needed more time to decide.

My mating loh released with both of them... Either I had to learn to control my loh, preventing it from releasing during the mating ceremony, or I would surely bond with one of them.

Trent stopped, having heard me to reply, "I'm fully aware of what your mating loh means, Luan. We would succeed. Why you?" He repeated my question with a smile, and those golden eyes glowed when he answered, "because only a queen will do, and you're the only estreld who dared to research ways to destroy us should negotiations not play in your favor. You are kind, but you are also a warrior at heart. Even your mating loh are beautifully deadly in their pursuit of a mate. You are perfect."

While I clutched at my chest, he turned to leave me there, alone with my racing thoughts. My mating loh burned with their glow for him, for my enemy, for the krelin who was both passionate and patient. Then why was I so hesitant?

Because you haven't mated with anyone, let alone committed yourself to a single male ever. It was different when I thought it was only physical, a compatible chemistry for mating. Now that I knew I didn't have control over my essence, bonding was serious, it was permanent, and I couldn't take it back. Was this how the clan felt when they mated? Were the females that mated successfully with offworlders bonded and suffering from their absence?

Shame cooled the heat in my body, making me feel clammy. They did it for the future prosperity of Estreldez, and so should I. Trent was already gone, and I rushed from the garden to find my mother. I'd choose who was best for my clan.

But not before bumping into Bayle. He mumbled his apologies. It wasn't like him to be so flustered, then again neither was my haste. I looked around him for the mate he was assigned to, but found no one.

"Who is your offworlder?" I demanded, to turn the attention away from my own actions and on to his. I should have been more understanding, but I was about to give up my dream of traveling to be a hive mate.

Bayle stood taller and accepted his consequences for not being with his assigned male. "Vareo of Sholonus."

My eyes widened, and worry creased my brow. "Why are you not with him? Has something happened?"

Every muscle tensed up with a feeling I wasn't used to. Without thinking I grabbed Bayle's shoulders and itched to run as soon as he let the words leave his lips, but I forced myself to still.

"I left him to the transport terminal. He was added to the next ship for males without tarnpul offerings."

That was impossible, he was dripping in tarnpul from willing females. He couldn't be leaving. My loh flared to life behind me, rage burned through me that he would touch me and skip the planet without so much as a goodbye. Bayle watched me, stunned, but lucky for him did not say a word as I stormed off.

When I made it to the transports they were already headed to the moons where their ships orbited.

I entered one of the individual pods, and searched the available ships still connected to our moons. Placing my palm on the scanner to gain access, I flipped through until I found what I was hunting for.

The only ship registered from Sholonus, didn't even have a proper connection to our moon. Either the ship was old, or they were hiding something. Or both.

I didn't care.

The only thought on my mind was he would not leave me.

He was mine.

As I finally heard the words in my mind I stared at the blinking controls that waited for me to launch towards the ship before it was allowed clearance to leave thinking I had already chosen without realizing it.

I had chosen him.

Clicking the launch acceptance I strapped in and as the seconds dragged on I winced. I had chosen the one male that didn't choose me too. What was wrong with me?

I shook my head trying to convince myself this had nothing to do with being rejected. He was the only one I knew of that had direct access to knowledge which could save my clan. He knew of a planet that had science capable of answering our food shortages and our mating declines.

Chapter Twelve

Vareo

The dismay on her face when I mentioned never letting her go was enough to tell me that it wasn't my place to go help her defend against the manipulation of a krelin. Bayle only stayed behind long enough to see the shuttle ship launch off with the unaccepted males.

The very transport I was meant to be on. There were enough offworlders to disappear into, and sneak off. Loric was something else, being able to round up the mate candidates so quickly, he had this planned well before he informed me. Sneaky bastard, I thought as I made my way to the gardens I'd passed on the way there.

I'd laugh to myself, but didn't want someone to question why I was without my escort.

Luan wasn't hard to find. Her legs were wrapped around the krelin, and my temper flared imagining tearing him from her, and claiming her for myself in front of everyone. I stalked through the rock garden, hiding behind black stone, and easing my way closer before I stood off to the side glaring him down.

The krelin must have felt my invasion into their space, he peered from between her wings searching the garden before easing her down to her feet. His wings folded back, and he took a step away. I smiled victoriously, he couldn't know where I was, but there was a reason Sholonus was targeted all those years ago... shols were a natural predator to the krelins, he could feel it.

She called out to him, and when he replied Luan stood there stunned. They were too far away for me to hear, but she turned and clutched at her chest. Then I felt like an ass-hole for even attempting to help her when she was obviously choosing the krelin as her mate. Leaning my back against the rock I sighed staring at my hand that had recently touched her. Her scent was still on my fingers. I groaned, feeling my cock harden at the thought of what would have happened if I didn't pull away. Would she have stayed?

Distracted, I lifted my gaze up just in time to roll away from the krelin descending from the sky. My body hummed with the call of battle, a guttural growl coming from my throat as I crouched.

His horns protruded from his wrists ready to poison me. Then I saw the mark on him, his veins turned black up his arms, he was not a mere warrior.

"You're Prince Trenton," I accused, knowing full well a regular warrior didn't have the black poison in them. His planet hired Necias Delta Fal to attack Sholonus, and he may not have been alive then, but he led the armies that paroled the star system and was the reason why he couldn't search for any shol survivors.

"You're a shol," he replied amused, and his eyes lit up excited at that information. "My mother still hunts for your kind obsessed that too many were bound to seek revenge."

We paced around each other, circling slowly.

"Is Estreldez your next target?" I seethed, all of my loss and history surfacing to haunt me. All the years I've suffered under necia's claws sank into my flesh, forcing me to steal for them since I was a child.

"Not for the same reason as Sholonus," he denied, and retracted his stingers. "Estreldez needs protection. The necia have set their sights on this planet to control the quarries here then supply much of the fuel across the star system. If they gain that kind of power the whole system is at risk."

"So the krelins plan on taking the power instead."

That wasn't any better than having the necia in charge.

"I have no intention of misusing the estrelds, they may continue to have their autonomy."

It made sense now why he was here. The prince creating offspring here would bond the two planets.

"You're mating with Luan to force the Almder to accept a new agreement with Krelis, proving the compatibility–"

"Between krelins and estrelds," he finished but added something I wasn't expecting, "but I'm not forcing anything. Almder is fully aware of my intentions, and is agreeable should Luan choose me."

"You would take her back to Krelis..." I stopped moving to stare at him. This couldn't be possible. Leaving her because she was better off not following my dangerous life was one thing, but leaving her to be trapped in a hive harem was something else entirely. "She will not choose you."

"That's not your decision to make. We are compatible, and her scent is intoxicating."

He gave me a knowing grin, referring to the way she had clung to him earlier. I knew all too well how viral she was. So much so I was willing to expose myself to a krelin that would sooner kill me than talk to me, but here he was with his stingers retracted and... talking.

I didn't know whether he was trying to get me to punch him, or if he wasn't as mindless as the rest of his hive warriors.

"What can you offer her?" he asked, seeing right through me, baiting, and then hitting me with a waft of his damned warding spray. It was filling the air making my nose crinkle in disgust.

"How do females not smell that?" I gagged on the atrocious musk.

"It has nothing to do with gender," he mocked me like I was dumb for even suggesting his scent was deplorable. "It's about biological chemistry. It repels and attracts, and most don't smell it at all. It's shols who are particularly sensitive to the musk." His tone was filled with disdain that wasn't there earlier. "Your species are nothing but barbarians."

"Right, that's why the krelins have taken it upon themselves to eradicate all shols." How very unbarbaric of them, I thought with derision. I lifted a hand when he was about to explain. "If you're here for diplomacy, you won't kill me here. And if you're worth being chosen by Luan, then you'll wait to inform your ship about the shol you found on Estreldez until after the ceremony."

He lifted a brow considering my bargain. I could win a fight here, but there was no telling if the warship he came in would let me leave this planet without pursuit. And now that I have gained his attention, there was no option where I could take Luan with me and not have both the necia and the krelins after us. I need that dick, Loric, to bond with her, and for Trent to keep his word about waiting until after the ceremony to alert his ship of a new target. I trusted Loric to seal the deal in their one-on-one time in the grotto.

My chest tightened, and I growled my distaste at what I was going to allow to happen. She was mine, but she couldn't be.

"If I see you at the dance, then I'll assume you've changed your mind about our deal. I'm not a monster, shol. Your species has been through enough, and I only seek to make sure my own doesn't find itself in a similar fate, nor the estrelds." He stepped aside for me to pass him.

I glared at him for thinking this small act of decency would make me change my mind about the krelins. It may not have been him, but his mother was the reason I had no family, and was a slave to the necia.

His mother had many children, but he was the only one to inherit her black blood, making him a potential successor to the hive.

Leaving without the jewel of Estreldez would make the necia angry, and I'd still be in their debt, but there was no choice if I wanted to do my part to keep this planet safe, and Luan. The shuttle bay was empty when I arrived, save for the few attendants processing whatever authorizations and logs he had to go through before heading out.

One of the estreld techs scrolled through the list of males sent off like I couldn't be in front of him right now. "How did you miss your shuttle?"

"The female who offered me her tarnpul chose another," I clarified.

He didn't glance away from his screen to cluck his tongue like he was sympathizing. "The shuttle is a bit much for one passenger, you can take the spare pod, but they are slower. Might be just as quick to wait until after the dance when there will be more departing. Do you want me to call your escort?"

"I don't mind the time to think," I assured him. If I stayed for the dance, Trent might not keep his word to wait on informing his ship about what I was.

As soon as I reached outside of Estreldez's atmosphere, and near the moon my ship was orbiting I sent out the signal to Carmen that I was returning.

A few minutes later my comm was buzzing.

Carmen didn't give me the chance to say anything before she was ready to tear me a new one.

"Do you not care about your life? We've done nothing but bail you out since you were a kid and this is how you repay us?"

"The High Commander of the Krelis Hive was there, and if I didn't leave we'd have more trouble than not finishing a job."

We'd be dead, I thought, but I'd put up a decent fight. My ship was beat down, but I knew how to handle her. We'd damage their ship, and take out a chunk of their warriors by aiming for their water synthesizer.

Carmen took me out of my suicide mission thoughts. "You're in deep shit, Vareo. Jax already had you marked on the job with the client. You will have no support from the team should you require intervention with them not being thrilled about your pitiful performance."

"This is just another way for you–" The comm disconnected before I could finish my own rant about them tacking on more debt for 'protecting' me from a jilted client. This was what they would have tried to do even if I did get the jewel. Any excuse to keep me under their bone claws, and in service to bring them more credits.

I smashed my hand on the dash of the small pod. "Fuck."

This job was too good to be true, and now I was even farther from escaping this star system.

Chapter
Thirteen

Luan

T he pod opened to a disgruntled woman with black hair pinned back, and a scowl on a much too symmetrical face.

Words were streaming out of her mouth before she could process that I was not her shipmate, Vareo.

"Worthless piece of space trash. I should gut you for what I have to deal with because–" she cut off when her gray eyes met mine, her lips flattened before they curved up in a small devious grin. "Who do we have here?"

I might have been jealous of the beautiful woman on Vareo's ship, but the greeting she had intended for him told me she probably wasn't mating with someone that she'd termed trash.

Lifting my hand for hers, she automatically grabbed my offered hand unthinking before I pulled myself from the pod to stand before her. That was usually how I handled most situations, if you act fast enough people didn't have enough time to process their own reactions.

"Thank you." She was quite tall for a female and my head only reached her shoulder, which reminded me of how similar in height she was to Vareo. "I know this is probably a surprise to have me boarding your ship. I am a guest of Vareo, or should I say the space trash you might have been referring to earlier."

She stepped aside for me to enter, watching curiously as I looked around. This was a rather small transport deck, and I could hear the whiz of the decompression modules whirring in the background, hissing like dying glorbins. There were no overlay screens, just bare metals, and a strange smell that reminded me of the smelting farms where we brought our jewels to reform and package them. This ship was in need of repairs, I surmised.

"Tell me, 'guest' of the scum off the ship's haul, what business did you have to board today?" The woman sounded pleasant enough, but something told me she wouldn't be helping convince Vareo to return to Estreldez. I'd have to speak with him directly for that. Or at the very least find out why he left so suddenly.

"He was one of my compatible mates," I told her honestly, but I couldn't bring myself to admit to her that he had left without telling me after what we had shared together. I blushed thinking about his hands on me, and I couldn't hide the glow of my loh responding to that memory.

Before I could explain any more about how he had information I needed, she saved me having to figure out what to say by assuming what had happened.

"So, he thought he could bring his new fuck toy on our ship and what? Did he think Jax would be thrilled to have another liability on a job after screwing up?"

Pursing my lips in distaste at the idea of her calling me a liability I tried not to think about how that's what my mother and Loric would call me for deciding to leave the planet, even if it was only on an orbiting ship. Strange enough, I had no problem being called Vareo's fuck toy, because the way she said it made me think he didn't usually have that option. I was smiling despite myself, happy that he wasn't toying with other women, and it seemed not even the gorgeous and foul-mouthed one he shipmated with.

"What the fuck are you smiling at?" she grumbled while folding her arms over her ample chest, which was much larger than any estreld I'd ever witnessed.

"You have the temper of a hergslat," I said with humor. We often used hergslats to help quarry the stones and jewels because their anger made them perfect for smashing the rocks into manageable chunks, and we never had to mistreat the beasts because they were easy to migrate and raging helped them file down their claws. The woman stared at me, growing more angry as my smile refused to falter despite her displeasure.

"That must help you with your bounty hunting," I added, trying to explain it was a compliment. "It makes hergslats tough and, to be honest with you, they are quite sweet when you approach them correctly."

"Are you relating me to an animal that resembles a large rodent with many clawed legs, and tusks?"

When you put it that way, it wasn't the most flattering of compliments.

"Scary upon first impression, but a fascinating animal with many wonderful attributes once examined more close-ly." I tried to explain.

Her smile grew. "Don't examine me too closely, you pretty slice of pleasure meat. The danger doesn't disappear, it only becomes more apparent. Let's see what Vareo has to say for himself when his pod arrives."

Now, I was the one confused. How did I arrive at his ship before he did?

She sat down with a flourish, lifting her boots to prop up on one of the handles welded across the deck just in case the gravity simulators failed.

"Take a seat," she stopped, realizing she didn't know my name.

With a shiver I grabbed a handle to lower myself onto the cold ledge that doubled as a sliver of a seat. I was keenly aware of how underdressed I was for a ship that didn't have the latest technology to simulate the moon's radiation warmth. I'd have to rely on my loh activating to keep my body temperature up.

"Guess they don't need much clothing down there if all you'll be doing is fucking." Her eyes wandered to my gauzy skirts, and I clamped my legs together and gripped the fabric where the slit was to prevent her from seeing just how true those words were. My neck heated with embarrassment that I didn't normally feel about my body. Was that how off-worlders saw us because of our clothing? We kept our fabric light and sparse because we absorb as much of the moon's radiation as possible. Clothing only got in the way. Suddenly, I felt very exposed in front of her.

"It's uncomfortable to cover up our loh," I clipped back while squaring off my shoulders to hide how small she made me feel. In an act of defiance I released my grip on my skirt, letting the slit open up so the loh down my thighs weren't covered anymore. I leaned forward, forearms on my thighs to add, "And only I choose who will be doing any fucking."

She grinned at me, her gaze lingering on my hip where the slit ended. the very slit I had adjusted to give Vareo full access to tease my coiled nerves within my core.

Her eyes darkened like she knew what I was thinking.

"I can see why he'd want you. He likes a fight in his cock sport, but because I like you I'll let you know that I'm going to use you as leverage to get that boot slime to finish his job. Don't take it personally," she finished while using the heel of her boot to flip a switch.

Contraptions from behind the wall surged around me before I could think. Retractable metal straps wrapped around my shoulders, my ankles. The straps snapped, slamming my arms into the wall. My head cracked from the force of being sucked back into the seat, disorientating me while my hands were cuffed and latched to the armrests. This was a bounty hold for prisoners.

I groaned, struggling against the bindings but I felt the surge in static building with my movement until it released, shocking my body making me slump.

"Oh, right. If I liked you more I would have warned you that struggling only creates an electrical current that builds up and releases in a rather uncomfortable shock."

Uncomfortable was putting it mildly, it was downright painful and I felt my body numb where the metal made contact. The glow of my loh flickered and faded until another shock wretched through my muscles making me scream.

"Guess it works with whatever energy those jewels on your body were producing too. Better try your best not to activate those," she purred, amused by my suffering.

My head lulled against my shoulder as I slumped. My whole body was numb, unable to move. I knew as soon as feeling returned I would be in for a painful awakening.

A suctioning whoosh of air sounded through the transport deck signaling the arrival of another pod.

Vareo...

His voice echoed through the comms, "Open the fucking hatch, Carmen."

That's who was holding me captive. At least I could put a name to my tormentor before life as I knew it changed forever.

"Glad you could make it, you sneaky bastard. Thought you could get the payout from the job on your own did you? I'm not letting you out of your pod until we're at the dropoff and you have no choice but to give the client the jewel or die."

"Carmen, you psychotic bitch, what are you blabbering about?"

"Don't play dumb. I'll be back when you want to take your dick out of your ass and be straight with me." Carmen bounced up from her seat and sauntered over to me. She pinched my chin between her fingers and whispered, "Enjoy the ride." Her tongue licked up my cheek, tasting her victory, but I refused to show any emotion, not that it was difficult considering I couldn't feel my face.

"This won't hold," he growled through the comm.

"Don't take too long," she antagonized before letting my head lull back with a thunk against the wall and back onto my shoulder.

Seething I vowed I would repay her kindness as soon as I was out of this contraption.

With a swish of her hips, she left the transport deck and the automatic doors closed behind her.

It wasn't long before pain was shooting down my arms and spine as feeling returned to my limbs. I gritted my teeth, but I was unable to stop the scream that echoed from my throat while not being able to writhe around. The small jerking motion of my muscles built up that buzz within the bindings, and I stilled, hoping for it to dissipate before it ignited once more.

Chapter
Fourteen

Vareo

S creams of pain came over the intercom, and the shrill
sound made my very blood chill. I was already pulling apart
wires from the door panel to bypass the locks on the transport
deck, but a renewed vigor took over. I was only able to unlock
one of the two bolts, and I was much too impatient to think
straight. Feeling nothing but the need to get through the barrier
between me and the voice I recognized but never wanted to hear
filled me with agony. I slammed my fists in the small opening
creating a wedge for me to rip through.

My whole body pulsed with adrenalin and I tore through the top half of the metal. I needed to replace it anyway, the rust only helped my cause. This pod would stay attached to my ship until the door could be repaired. I didn't care, I kicked the panel and shoved myself through the jagged metal, scraping skin, and burning a trail of fire down my sides.

Her limp form was strapped into our holding stocks and I roared in an outrage I hadn't felt since finding out I didn't have a planet to go home to. Slamming my fist into the release lever, I ripped it from the wall tossing it to the floor, before rushing to grab her before she collapsed as the restraints retracted.

Breathing labored, I held her small form against my chest trying to calm my anger, but finding nothing would soothe me until I had my hands wrapped around Carmen's neck and snapped it in two.

Luan, what were you doing here? How did she get you? I had only just seen her storming from the garden. She groaned against my hold, but I didn't want to let go. I nuzzled my nose into her blonde hair, and inhaled her scent possessively. No one was to touch her.

"I'd rather a hergslat," she coughed out, her voice rough from the scream I never wanted to hear again. Was she relating me to a creature on her planet that she'd rather have been saved by?

"Sorry to disappoint," I grumbled, but still refused to release her.

"Carmen," she corrected.

It pleased me that she wasn't upset with me, even though it was because of me that she was hurt. I had left to protect her from this. Well, maybe not exactly this, but harm all the same.

Suddenly, the ship jolted and that could only mean one thing... Carmen was gearing up to exit this planet's orbit. Fuck.

"I shouldn't have come." Luan adjusted in my lap, but stopped when her muscles spasmed. Those restraints were designed for rough bounties, she'd be feeling sore for at least a day.

"Why did you?" I carried her to the open pod to strap her in for the ride. I'd have to get back into my own pod before the gravity fields disabled for warp, but I couldn't resist asking.

She leaned back and those silver eyes stared into mine only to wander over my body narrowing at the scratches I received getting into the transport deck to get to her.

"I didn't know if I could trust Trent to keep his promises, or even if he did, whether his word was enough to help my clan."

Hearing the krelin's name on her lips, I snapped back, "What does that have to do with being on my ship?" I regretted the outburst as soon as it came out and her features hardened, a steely wall between us despite just being in my arms.

"You're a bounty hunter, and I have need of your services." I imagined her core locking around my fingers, and all the other things that I could service her with, but then she slammed that thought down. "To secure the information about the technology that could help my clan. You weren't specific before, and the outlaws on Necias would use my vague understanding to take advantage."

They would swindle her without specifics. It was typical to give incorrect information then charge double for the information the client actually wanted to begin with. That cycle could stretch out without a clear agreement on expectations. She needed my help.

"What are you proposing?"

Gently, I transferred her into the pod's seat. This was one of her own planet's pods so she should be comfortable sitting in here instead of in the transport deck. At least, I couldn't imagine her wanting to sit in any seat on a necia ship after her experience with the restraints Carmen put her in.

Carmen was always a bitch, but even this was out of character for her unless she got something out of it. What did she get from treating Luan like a prisoner, and piloting the ship without me? She was more than capable of piloting, but she got pleasure out of bossing me around like a servant.

"I'm being taken to Necias, aren't I?" She wasn't afraid, and she was unfortunately accurate in her assumptions. Carmen would take her to Necias if she had a plan to blackmail me, or even Luan. Would she force her to be enslaved to the necia?

"It is where bounty hunters hang out, along with most of the people with a price on their head."

Luan nodded her understanding, accepting that fate before locking her silvery eyes with mine. A fire brewed within her as she bargained like she was always meant to be an outlaw herself, "There are only two of you on this ship. Carmen," she said the name with a hint of vengeance to come, " and you. I'd like to employ you to help me find the technology for Estreldez, instead of having her sell me to the highest bidder. We would have needed to go to Necias anyway, and you'll get more credits from Almder with the tech and me, than for whatever bounty might be offered right now."

Grinning at her I couldn't help but be fascinated at how dignified she was while outnumbered, and threatened with being sold to outlaws. I had no doubt that an estreld female would make a pretty penny on the market with how exclusive the planet's reputation was for being a destination for unbelievable sex. Yet she still held her chin high, and appealed to every bounty hunter's or outlaw's greed for more credit. She was smart, but I didn't want her credits and I wouldn't allow another male to touch her now that she was no longer better off without me.

"No deal." I turned to get back to my own pod. Somehow I had to get her back to Estreldez, but I'd use the lure of the technology to convince the Almder to allow Luan to choose to stay with me. It'd be a tough sell, my life was dangerous, and I'd probably never truly be free of the necia. Especially, not after what I planned to do with Carmen when I got a hold of her.

"What? What do you mean no deal?"

I glanced over my shoulder to see her seething from the rejection of her plan.

"I'll help you, but I need to know you're up for pretending to be an outlaw, and not a diplomat. What you're asking is dangerous, and I need to trust that you won't turn me in to the krelins as soon as you get what you need. You'll also have to help me get rid of Carmen." Leaning against the cold steel of the compression chamber I waited for her answer. I knew I had to get to my own seat and strap in, but I'd learned from years of negotiations you always strike when their guard was down. She was more focused on Carmen's betrayal than what my intentions were. Right now I was a way to get what she wanted.

"Bounty hunters are barely above an outlaw," she remarked, but she had a glint in her eyes like she was considering the deal. "But if you can help me get the..."

She was testing me, her brow lifted now waiting for me to fill in the blank.

"Scientist," I revealed that it wasn't merely a technology, but a person who was stolen from a different star system, and helped research the technology of the scan that detected anomalies for the necia. The same kind of person that would be needed to help pinpoint compatibility and discover how to solve their mating crisis on Estreldez.

It'd also be beneficial to return that scientist to their planet, and create a treaty with them to prevent the necia or krelins from invading. That planet is also rumored to be protecting the last of the shols from my planet. Win-win.

Not missing a beat she continued, "I refuse to hire outlaws to snatch a person from their home. We just need to know where they are so we can talk with them, or make an agreement with the leader of their clan."

"Not all species have clans," I mused.

"Then we will offer the scientist an agreement, personally."

The gravity simulator turned off, and I gripped the handle on the wall. It made me happy that she was so pure that she had no thought that the scientist wasn't already stolen from their home, but she'd find out soon enough the better offer was to steal Brinny from the necia, and find a mobile lab for her. Unless the Estreldez were prepared for a fight they couldn't bring her back to the planet or to her home planet either.

"We'll look into it when we get there," I delayed. There was no need to tell her Brinny has been part of my escape plan for a while now, she was only going to go back to Estreldez when this was all over anyway. I already had a deal with Brinny to have her remove my tracker, and with her access steal the data necessary for me to make my ship disappear from their database.

That would be it.

She'd get her scientist, I'd start a new life in a new star system.

Why did that feel so off now that she was here? I dismissed that sensation as a lack of gravitation steadying my stomach.

Luan bit her lip contemplating before deciding to ask, "Were the books about Necias correct? About there not being a moon?"

Why didn't I think about that beforehand? Of course she would be concerned about whether there was radiation for her loh to absorb. Would she be okay being away from Estreldez? There was no moon orbiting Necias... only many satellite docking stations, and even permanent mobile bases for various businesses. Necias was only thriving because of the constant trade, and fluctuation of outlaws and hunters. The planet was a mecha of all things technology, and had absolutely nothing going for it in terms of export, unless you counted being the hub of trade between black market deals.

"There are no moons there, but plenty of technology. Will you need a radiation pulser?"

She didn't know, it was plain as the moon's light that she had never left Estreldez before. Fuck, would I have to bring her back to her planet before finishing my escape plan or freeing the scientist?

How was I supposed to get her back without the krelins finding me? I'd have to send her back by herself.

"I should be fine," she clearly lied. That was good to know, lying wasn't in her skill set. I'd avoid putting her in a situation where she had to answer questions.

The ship jolted, and yanked me from my loose hold on the wall handle. I had been distracted, and jerked through the pod. It was Luan's arms that reached out and pulled me to her before I could grab for another latch to secure myself. Gripping the holds beside her seat, I didn't have time to strap myself in for the warp, and even Luan knew that as she squeezed me to her tightly. Her hold alone, even with the handles I clung to, wouldn't be enough to stop the warp from flattening me outside of the cockpit. The transportation deck wasn't designed with comfort in mind, it was for prisoners and securing supplies. We would both pass out from the constant spin of the ship without being in the main living quarters. Pushing my boots to the bottom of the pod, I activated the magnetic locking to secure my feet, and with one hand removed my belt to strap my hand to the other latch.

All of this extra effort, and bruises I'd get at the end of this to spend a few more minutes with her.

"See you on the other side," I joked, already feeling the strain of holding myself in place.

"How long?"

"Carmen might wait until we're passed out to transfer us, or it could be hours before we reach a satellite requiring her to end warp for long enough to gain access to the main cabin."

"Hours..."

"I'm sorry," I said sincerely as my vision blurred from the forces pressing me against the wall, and possibly suffocating Luan with my chest.

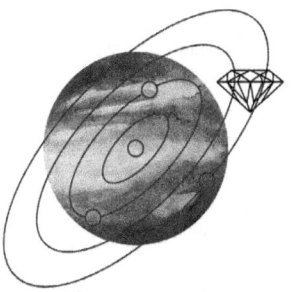

Chapter Fifteen

Luan

Vareo's large body pinned against me, and became heavier as his muscles stopped fighting against the warp's pull, his head cracked with a thunk as he passed out.

Now, that he was unconscious I wiggled against him to un-latch his hand from the belt securing his arm so he didn't drift along the walls bumping along when the warp fluctuated by degrees. I may not have been a pilot, but I knew enough through my studies to know hours of rotating around at high velocity was going to take time to recuperate from. Time we didn't have if Carmen didn't have to take the same delay to grab us. I also didn't like the idea of seeing him banged up when we woke.

Undoing my own straps I clung onto his torso, and shimmied down to reach the magnetic boots and deactivate them then pushed off to the center of the pod. It was barely enough room to stay in the center and not touch the walls, but I could do it. I knew I could. It would just take my reserved energy, and I had no idea what would happen to me if or when I no longer had the radiation of the moon inside of me.

My loh extended out from my back and in slow steady pulses I exerted the radiated light from my body to keep us centered within the pod and stationary as the it rotated around us. This wouldn't work if the gravitation simulator was on, but as long as we drifted I could keep us safe.

After a few minutes Vareo groaned, and I tensed up hoping he wouldn't move too much when he woke. I hadn't expected him to come out of his state so quickly. there wasn't much information on the shol from the one book I could find, but an estreld's loh have been known to help my clan withstand most pressure from space travel, for a time anyways. Until our radiation runs out.

But we've always had the moons nearby to recuperate. I had no idea what would happen to me without the moon's rays. This should have been one of the things I figured out before trying to form an offworlder diplomatic mission. It was always assumed we would be near a moon, or a sun.

My loh pulsed in slow waves to steady us, and when Vareo's muscles twitched in his back I thought for sure he woke up, but he remained still and said nothing.

"If you're awake, don't move. It's more difficult to keep us in position if you do."

He moved anyways, wrapping his arms around my waist and pulling the rest of me in closer to him.

"What part of don't move do you not–"

I pushed out a bit more energy to steady us, and found now that we were even more firmly held together it was actually easier.

"How long can you maintain this?"

His fingers traced along the edge of one of my loh on my lower back, and I wanted to adjust myself to look up into his face, in hopes of reading his thoughts, that they would be clear on his features. As much as I worried about what would happen if my light ran out, I equally worried about what would happen if I let him go.

"I'm not sure," I answered honestly. This was new to me, both the use of my loh without the moons and the man I held in my arms. I wanted him, I knew that much, but I didn't know him. Now, I was stuck with him until we distracted Carmen, and he was probably only helping me because I offered him a chance at profit instead of using me like a hostage.

And yet despite that I decided to help him during warp instead of only helping myself. It would have been easier to do this alone and then wait for Carmen to come back pretending to be passed out. Have her drag the unconscious Vareo out first while I used whatever energy I had left to trap Carmen in the prisoner seats and take over the ship. But there was no guarantee that my plan would have worked, and at least this way I'd have the muscle of Vareo to help take the ship back.

For some reason I trusted his word despite leaving the planet without telling me. He had no reason to inform me he was leaving if he decided he didn't want to mate with me. Was that why he left? I mean, I told myself the reason why I went after him was because I needed his help with finding the technology that could help our offspring rates, but then why did it upset me that he didn't want to mate with me after our time in the library? My cheeks burned thinking about the way his fingers moved inside of me, and his cock strained against his pants reassuring that at least his body wasn't rejecting me.

Get a hold of yourself, Luan, this was business nothing more.

"What should we do?" I asked, wondering if he had a plan for Carmen when she came back.

I had my own thoughts about strapping her into the prisoner seat like she did me, but needed to know where his head was at.

"The warp drive makes the time inside the ship slow down." We kept our eyes closed to avoid disorientation from the walls spinning around us. "We'll have to wait it out."

"That's not what I was asking." I knew how a ship's warp drive worked. "after that."

"Right... I was going to sell Carmen to the traders."

I gasped, unable to stop myself. That seemed too far to take revenge, even if she was a bitch.

"She'll be fine, she's necia they'll check her tags before she's actually sold off and they'll release her," he assured, while his hands absently stroked my hair.

"Oh." I was relieved to hear that, but something about being tagged seemed off. Did all necia tag themselves like supplies?

That seemed like something only done in the black market, and my lips flattened remembering that Necias was an outlaw planet, of course they tagged their people.

"How long will it delay her?" I asked instead.

"They don't scan until the very end of processing when they are about to brand the slaves." His voice was cold when he explained. "The processor will toss her to the side to blackmail her boss for a payout, and she'll be held in the Lord Zorn's office, humiliated, but no worse for wear. It's after the scan when things get personal."

There was a sadness in him that was palpable as he spoke. Like he knew exactly what being processed by the black market felt like, not just a bounty hunter that was tasked with saving a slave, or taking down a trader that went too far for even morally gray outlaws.

"Was that where Carmen was going to send me?" The reality of how close I probably came to being a slave hit me hard. I squeezed Vareo's hard torso, like that would keep the out-laws from kidnapping innocents.

"It doesn't matter what her plans were. Our plans are to find a scientist."

"Once we have the planet's location, we can head back to Estreldez and send a diplomatic ship over to seek their assistance," I agreed.

It wouldn't solve everything, but maybe Krelis would be open to the idea of a mating treaty to stop their trade hostility? Trent had mentioned they needed to find compatible females for their hive, but only if our clan agrees.

The scientist would be able to help both our species. Perhaps we could develop a pre-screening technology to see who would be more likely to bond with krelins? I shivered, and Vareo held me closer. I had to resist nuzzling into his chest.

We waited in silence for what seemed like hours holding each other, before my loh starts to flicker from exhaustion. My muscles strained trying to force out more radiation to steady our bodies floating within the pod. The pulse stopped, and we drifted until my loh scrapped against the metal as it spun. I bit down hard on my lip and my whole body clenched against the pain of feeling my loh being torn apart until it caught on a piece of metal and we both turned with a yank and were tossed through the hatch, my back loh bouncing against the surfaces breaking away as we flew. My screams silenced as my throat became raw and I felt my grip on Vareo slip until I slumped in his arms unable to move.

Everything went white.

Chapter Sixteen

Vareo

We were thrown into the main transport deck, and Luan's screams filled my ears, chilling my blood. My eyes focused only on her, and her small frame went limp in my arms

Fuck.

Her gorgeous diamond wings were shredded, floating around us in shards mixed with a disturbing amount of blood streaming through the air like a morbid snow globe the ancient artifacts dealers tried to pawn off. The bright light around her faded, and what was left of her loh retracted into her back. As I held her to me, I couldn't prevent us from drifting closer to the walls that circled us, but I'd make sure it was me that bounced around the walls this time.

My hands were sticky from her blood, and I could see her loh were cracked and broken along her back, some jewels completely missing, creating large craters of open flesh wounds. My whole body grew cold, and detached from itself like I had lost a very piece of my soul.

I swore into her silver hair, wet liquid dripped from my eyes, and I hadn't known that was still possible. "You are not fucking dying on me."

My shoulder hit the wall and I grunted, tucking her in my chest to make sure she didn't get clipped again. She didn't need to protect me, my body would be bruised, but I'd survive just fine. She'd pushed herself for too long making sure both of us didn't suffer, waiting to come out of warp, and she didn't need to. It wasn't the first time Carmen held me in the transport deck for warp, they were well aware of how sturdy shols were.

But apparently Luan didn't know that, and she was tougher than most necia warriors I'd seen. This wouldn't end her, I repeated that over again until I believed it.

An unusual feeling was building within me that I couldn't explain. Pressure grew within my chest the longer I held Luan in my arms, unable to do anything to help. I felt more helpless now than I did the day I realized I was nothing more than property.

She was mine, I growled, and I did nothing to protect her.

That was it, I realized as soon as I said it.

She was mine.

And I failed her.

The walls were getting close again, and I was prepared to take another blow before I felt the gravity field activate around us, and I landed crouched with Luan sagging against me.

I gently placed her against the wall, away from the door to the main ship. Brushing a stray hair away from her face I felt her breath against my fingers, still alive.

"This won't take long," I promised. When I took in the transport deck, my anger grew seeing her blood splattered across the surfaces, and her diamond loh shattered like glass. Was she still bleeding?

My fist smashed into the med kit hidden in the wall and I pulled out the clotting spray. She moaned as I moved her as gently as I could. I sprayed her whole back to seal it up until I could do a more thorough patch job. Then I scooped her up, and rushed her to the med unit.

I slammed the button, and yanked the pod open to place her inside the gel bubbling up from the bottom. Closing the pod I rushed for the command chair to secure the ship.

I roared, not even caring about letting Carmen know that I was coming for her. This was my ship. She was responsible for harming my mate, and no matter how many scars I got subduing her she'd pay.

When I reached the command deck, Carmen was waiting for me with her arms folded over her chest. I didn't stop to talk, I grabbed her neck in my grip and squeezed. My eyes wild with rage.

Shock had her padding at my arms like a defenseless swarm-pel, not even bruising me with her weakening strikes. Those gray, soulless eyes widened, not expecting me to truly harm her. I wasn't a monster. I wouldn't kill her, but giving Carmen time, enough time to release her sharp bones from her flesh to skewer me, wasn't an option. I had to knock her out before her exoskeleton sprung out like a vicious dagger cushion.

Gasping for air that I wouldn't allow, she finally stabbed me in the gut with her claws before she twitched into unconsciousness. Her bones stayed where they were when she slumped, telling me that her ability to manipulate her bones was not instinctual, but a conscious effort. It might not be comfortable for her when she wakes to still have her bones protruding from her skin.

Sharp spikes were peeking out of her shoulders like she was a pin cushion, and was about to have those killer bones stab me in more than just my side.

I brought her back to the transport deck and locked her in the prison restraints, though I knew she wouldn't wake right away. She was still breathing, but she'd be sore when she came to. If she was anything like the first necia that I choked out in my first escape attempt she'd only be out for five minutes. Three of which I already used to bring her to the transport deck when the comms sounded.

Jax didn't trust me with an upgraded AI assistance ship, or voice command. I'd have to go to the command deck to answer.

Who answered wasn't Jax, as I expected.

"King Sylve," I addressed and bowed my head. Keeping him waiting was not ideal, he wasn't known for his patience, nor forgiveness. Commanding a planet of outlaws didn't require those traits.

"You've secured the jewel?" He was ignoring my delay to answer his vid comm, and I didn't know if that was a good sign or not. I'd never spoken to him before now, but he was smiling, which was disconcerting.

Dressed in his finest armor, and not a hair out of place. He'd never had to do a job himself, but he didn't become the King because he was born into it. He was ruthless, and he'd slaughtered his way to his position.

I cleared my throat, he'd find out sooner or later that I failed to retrieve the jewel, and now it made sense why the job was too good to be true, and had a ridiculous amount of credits to its name.

Was he the client?

"Didn't Carmen fill you in before we warped?" I tried to avoid saying the words myself, if she already broke the news to him, I didn't want to disappoint a second time.

The King's smile widened and a gleam filled his green eyes.

"Why else do you think we would be talking? I've already sent another ship to meet with you at the satellite station XVR-8-7. Your ship is not ideal for protecting the package."

I blinked at him confused. Did he think we succeeded in obtaining the jewel?

"King Sylve..." He wasn't much older than myself, but if I didn't handle this right I'd have more to worry about than kidnapping a scientist and escaping to a new star system. He'd put a bounty on my head, and I wouldn't have the element of surprise to get a head start in disappearing.

"I ran into the Commander of Krelis on Estreldez, and as you are aware they have a deep hatred for my species. I barely had time to leave the planet before he informed his war ship–"

The king dismissed my explanation.

"What do I care if the mission attracted the attention of Krelis? That's why I sent my own war ship to meet with you, the Viper Raul, to ensure your safe return to Necias."

Shit.

The Viper Raul was his personal war ship, the deadliest of his enforcers. There was no way my ship would make it into warp before they destroyed us, or latched on to stop warp altogether. They were that fast, and equipped with grappling arms, among other offensive technology.

"Operative Carmen already reported on the krelin's involvement. You'll hand over the jewel, and report to the CO of the Viper Raul."

"I believe there has been some misunderstanding," I tried to explain now before he figured out that we didn't have the jewel and think we stole it from him. Then again, there was no guarantee he wouldn't already think that when I was through explaining.

His face hardened, a firm set of his jaw as he stared me down through the feed.

"Do you not have the Almder's daughter, Luan, in your custody?"

I straightened at the mention of her name, and schooled my shock into a mask of indifference at hearing that Luan is the Almder's daughter.

"Operative Vareo," his voice was cold as he commanded my response. "I've already verified that Estreldez has prepared their own warship, and teamed up with Krelis in search for her. If you're trying to bargain for more credit then you'll be detained instead of promoted, so choose your next words carefully."

This wasn't happening.

Luan was the Jewel of Estreldez.

And I would be handing her over to the very man that I was spending my life trying to escape, even if he was the newest successor to the throne.

"She came willingly." If she was going to be captured, the least I could do was make sure she was treated well enough until I could figure a way out of this mess.

The king lifted a brow curiously, waiting for me to continue.

"She believes that you'll assist her planet with researching solutions to their population crisis."

"A diplomatic offer? What does she think she is trading this research for?"

He leaned in with a mischievous grin. King Sylve didn't have any reason to agree to a trade when he already thought he had what he wanted, but he may play along with pretending she'll get what she asked for a time.

"She would not presume what kind of trade would be suitable without meeting with you first."

He wasn't a dumb man, I couldn't come up with a valid trade agreement from a planet I didn't know enough about to even know the jewel was a person.

I was so certain she was my mate, despite her not being shol, but there was a difference between fooling around with me during a mating ceremony, and accepting me as her mate. I was a slave, an outlaw, and soon to be the most wanted in this star system for not only kidnapping a future leader of Estreldez, but being tracked down by Krelis, and eventually on King Sylve's shit list when I found a way to get her back to her planet and disappear from this system before my expiration date.

"Bring her to the command deck."

I should have expected that.

"Carmen has done some damage to her since boarding, she's in the med pod."

I needed to end this conversation fast and make sure that her vitals were improving. Being away from her was making me anxious.

"You'll send the data to this link immediately, and if you haven't already, make sure Carmen is unable to damage her further. You understand?"

"Taken care of," I replied, trying not to sound too pleased that I wouldn't have to explain her condition to the CO of Viper Raul.

The ship jolted as their grappling hooks attached to the docking mechanism. They would board soon.

"Oh, and Vareo." His tone was deceptively calm. "I'm aware of your record, if you show the slightest hint of insubordination you can say goodbye to your hunt status, and your new accommodations will not allow you the freedoms you've enjoyed so far."

Freedoms, I'd scoff if it wouldn't get me killed. I kept my face neutral, and nodded my agreement.

There's no way in trill I would let him have Luan without a fight. But I had to be smart about this. I needed more information. What was King Sylve planning?

Chapter
Seventeen
Luan

Unfamiliar sounds filled my ears, but for one. Vareo.

"She's not ready to be moved," he insisted, a stubbornness to his tone that made me smile.

"King Sylve has reviewed her chart personally, and believes your med unit is not capable of completing her recovery without the upgrades provided on the Viper Raul."

"It'll have to wait until she can be transferred without further damage incident," Vareo was firm in his denial of whoever was trying to take me. Me, I repeated. They were trying to move me from a med pod?

The images of flying through the transport deck while in warp reminded me that my loh were badly injured. And with no moon around, I had no idea what the repercussions would be. The liquid gel I floated in numbed my nerves, making my skin tingly.

"We can't stay near this station for long, and your med pod has been known to fluctuate during warp. We'll have to risk it," the other man argued. "Her stats are stabilized."

I heard the beep of a mechanism turning, and I felt cool air on my forehead as the gel receded. They were releasing me from the med pod.

Wiping away the goo from my eyes I coughed up the gel as someone used a suction device down my throat to get the rest of the fluids out for me to breathe.

My hands flailed to swat at them, and as the muscles in my back stretched from the movement I screamed, the pain returned in full force.

"It's too soon," Vareo said as his hands grabbed me and pulled me to him. I found a small comfort in his arms and weakly whimpered.

"Then you best hurry to bring her to her new med unit." The other man didn't seem to care one way or the other, but it was clear he didn't want me staying here.

"The king will replace you with another looking for a quick promotion by murdering you if she is harmed by this," Vareo snarled at the man, who didn't seem fazed by the threat. A growl vibrated through Vareo's chest and I gripped his shirt to gain his attention.

His blue eyes met mine, and I smiled.

He didn't appear harmed from the warp, and we had survived.

I'd done it.

I lasted long enough.

Then I thought about his words. King, and murder. What went wrong?

"Carmen?" I questioned, worried for him.

"She's detained," his voice was reassuring, and less gruff than normal, "but we can't take you back to Estreldez to heal without running into the krelins, and you have a diplomatic meeting with King Sylve of Necias."

I practically flung myself from his arms right then. No one had a 'treaty' with Necias. They were bullies that took what they wanted and had 'agreements' in place that benefited their black market trade. A treaty with them was just an understanding that you worked for them, and they owned you.

What diplomatic meeting could I have with the king that would result in anything but blackmailing my mother to hand over the freedom of the clan, enslave my people, and steal our jewels?

"Calm down." Vareo adjusted his hold on me, and I cried out from the sharp jabs within my back loh as I moved.

He could shut the fuck up with his calm down.

He whispered, "We are boarded by the Viper Rual, the king's personal warship. You will meet with him and discuss diplomacy."

The other man was listening, I doubted Vareo's whisper went unheard.

That was who Carmen was in contact with, and where we ended up outside of the warp. I thought we'd have more time to get lost into the fray of the outlaw planet to hunt for information before necia tried to intervene.

"She doesn't seem 'willing' like you claim."

I stilled, trying to ignore the raw pain surging through my body, making my eyes water.

"She's in shock, and you would rescind your willingness to meet if you were attacked after boarding."

The man seemed to be placated by this explanation, and gave a curt nod as we walked. Vareo's strides were becoming more brisk and hurried as we went, making the journey more uncomfortable but also stirring concern about how he felt my health was doing.

Was I going to be okay?

I'd never been away from the moons when I needed to heal before.

I couldn't die like this.

I had to help my clan.

Gripping Vareo's collar I rasped out, "Comm the king." I was worried I wouldn't have much time to bargain with him.

If anything, me dying would only help negotiations with him. All I had to do was convince him that I could ensure my mother wouldn't call for war upon hearing of my death.

I could give him that, if he gave my planet peace, and the technology they stole from the scientist and their location.

"What are you talking about?" he hissed between his teeth. "You are going straight into the new med pod."

Glaring at him I repeated with all the authority I could muster while being held like a babe. "Contact the king, now."

They both exchanged a concerned look before the slender man tapped his wrist comm, but they both kept moving.

"Xan," was all the king said through the link in a demanding tone.

"My king, you told me not to bother you unless the jewel was awake."

"So, she's recovered?"

"Not exactly."

"Do you value your life?" He said almost too sweetly for threatening his man.

Without another word he angled his wrist in my direction, and then a screen projected of the king's face. He was younger than I had thought he would be. Toned, and chiseled features with perfectly groomed brown hair. His green eyes lit up upon seeing me before narrowing.

"What is the meaning of this, operative?" He was speaking to Vareo now, but that wasn't the point of contacting him.

"She's being transferred to the new med pod per your–"

I interrupted Vareo from taking over. "You'll be addressing me," I croaked. My voice raspy from screaming, and my teeth still gritted from the pain coursing through me as Vareo jostled me through the corridors.

The king's hand swiped through the air dismissively, before his features became stone. "What is she doing awake, and obviously still injured? Are you both incompetent? Did you not think to sedate her so she would be transferred without pain?" Though his tone was still even, the underlying threat was clear, if not more frightening to witness.

"King Sylve," I strained to speak, gripping Vareo's neck and huddling into him for support. "I may not have much time. My condition changes our negotiations for both of our planets. If you do not wish to go to war, we must discuss a solution before I'm dead."

Vareo growled at my admission of what state I believed myself in. If I were home, I'd probably heal from this in a matter of days with my mom's help. But I knew well enough that outlaws weren't going to be willing to give up their collateral.

"We can discuss this when you arrive." The king didn't seem convinced that I was dying despite my haggard appearance.

"If you are not taking me back to Estreldez, then there is no guarantee that I will make it. And I will not die without offering you and my clan a better solution to war. I'm willing to linkcom with Almder with a treaty that includes forgiving my death if you provide Estreldez with the technology and means to implement research that will allow my clan to make headway in solving our mating decline."

"Are you in such a position that you believe Estreldez can win a war against Necias?"

"Do you wish to see a decline in business, and a loss of your trade, and assets by going to war with Estreldez?"

We may not be in a position to win, but they would incur devastating casualties if Krelis was involved, making them susceptible to being taken over by the hive.

I knew enough to bet that as soon as Estreldez fell, Krelis would swoop in to take the victory themselves, and push back- if not destroy- Necias in the process.

Neither of us wanted that outcome.

"I will consider it. But should you live, the terms change. I did not take you from your home, you willingly came to me begging for my assistance. I magnanimously agreed to help you, but you were attacked in transit. As you recovered, you found you no longer wished to return, seeking to become my adviser and diplomatic advocate staying on Necias. Should you die, I will still uphold our bargain to assist your planet under this story. Should you live, you become a permanent resident here, where you can continue to sway my good graces towards your clan."

"And you will give Estreldez the technology and research they need?"

"Yes."

"What assurances do I have?"

"The same assurances that I have in your word that you will not attempt to flee Necias should you live."

"That's not good enough."

"There are other ways to solidify cooperation," he offered with amusement.

"There are," I agreed, trying to think of a way to let my mother know there was another path besides war or submission.

I was done with this conversation.

The king noticed my change in demeanor even being carried by Vareo and barely hanging on to consciousness.

"Connect the Jewel with the Almder before the sedatives of the med pod take effect." He spoke to Vareo this time. "If she doesn't uphold our agreement on what to say then remind her that I already have every station within warp of Estreldez equipped to handle even a Krelis warship should war be the option she chooses."

How was that possible?

There would be no way he had the time to coordinate such a feat in the time it took to warp here. That could only mean he'd been planning to attack Estreldez regardless of my recent absence. Did he really want a war?

Would anything I said to my mother make a difference?

The transmission ended with the king, and Vareo placed me in a standing chamber, much more advanced than the med pod I had been in before. He held me to him before the gravity field within the chamber activated and he reluctantly released me to float there.

With nothing touching my back anymore the pain was more manageable, but there was a coldness to my skin where Vareo's touch used to be.

Then, instead of a gel, the chamber filled up with an invisible gas that smelled of fruit and flowers, numbing my nerves. It felt heavenly. My muscles relaxed before my mother's face appeared, giving the illusion of comfort.

Chapter
Eighteen
Vareo

The Estreldez Almder appeared on the vidcomm, and I could see Luan visibly tense up even after the pain relievers that should have made her whole body feel like a cloud. It was the good stuff, the kind of med treatment never afforded to me except when I was a kid and they feared their investment would die too soon.

I wanted to reach out for her, but there was no way I was showing my face to her mother while she saw her daughter in a med tank.

"Almder," Luan spoke first.

"My Jewel, you've troubled my heart with your reckless behavior. I know you took the transport pod to a mate's ship without consulting me. If you had wanted to mate with him, all you had to do was say so, I would have negotiated his return."

I grinned to myself, letting myself believe for a second that Luan had come onto my ship to mate with me, and not to convince me to help her clan. The idea that she could want me as I wanted her, made my blood heat, but images of her with the krelin shut those feelings down as soon as they rose.

"One of my mate's crew members betrayed us," she explained, and I nearly rushed to her at the sound of her calling me her mate. Did she mean it?

I needed to hold her, to have her say it again to me directly. I needed that melodic voice of hers no longer strained with pain to say my name, to call me hers.

My body pulsed, and it urged me to complete the mate bond with her, despite her current state. Or perhaps because of it. If our mate bond was consummated I could share my strength with her, be there to help her heal.

My thoughts were interrupted by what she had to say next, bringing me back to reality, "She didn't agree with my request to get an audience with King Sylve."

It was Almder who spoke now, "What on Estreldez would you want to do that for?"

"Because they were planning on forcing us into an agreement whether we talked with them or not. We are much too isolated and rely too heavily on the words of our treaties. We should have been sending diplomats, and not just having them come to us during our mating ceremony."

"We have many diplomats," she disagreed with Luan's assessment.

"All of them speak with our trade partners when they visit and through vidcomm. How are we supposed to verify information?"

I could tell Luan was tiring, and even without the sedative she didn't have much time left before her body needed to recover.

She was right, plenty of their traders could have been coerced into lying to the estreld diplomats through vidcomm. Without a diplomat on site to check on things, there could be broken relationships.

She'd make a great leader one day.

Without me, I thought sadly, but dismissed it.

"I send out a team of diplomats regularly to our partners, My Jewel, but there have been other priorities," her mother explained.

"I know Almder. That is why I needed to leave to help with those priorities."

"You don't look well, what kind of damage have you sustained by the traitorous crew member?"

"It isn't good, mother." Luan's voice grew softer, more distant.

"Come home immediately," she demanded.

"I won't make it in time. My fate is in the hands of this med pod."

Luan lied to her mother, we could make it on time if King Sylve demanded it of the Viper Raul. It was the fastest warship with the latest technology, both legal and black market. I'd try my hand at subterfuge taking this ship's command and take her myself if her reports declined.

The Almder finally showed some emotion on that hard face of hers. She took off her crown and held it to her chest while shaking her head in denial.

"My Jewel," she choked out. "The Krelis Prince has sent his warships in search of you. Just send your coordinates and I'm sure there is a fast ship nearby. Loric is also eagerly awaiting your return, he has offered to be sired to you and any offspring you may have with the Krelis Prince."

Of course Loric would be diplomatic enough to know Luan would need to mate with another for their planet, but he still wished to be her mate. I had once thought I could be okay with leaving her in Loric's care... How stupid had I been?

"Almder, we are on the brink of war, how can you speak of mates? I do not wish for our clan to suffer. I've made an agreement with King Sylve that as long as they provide Estreldez with technology and research to assist with our clan's needs, and leave our planet unharmed, then we will not go to war with them, and I will stay on Necias to be a diplomatic liaison."

Almder froze on the screen so still I almost thought the connection was lost.

"Necias has every incentive to keep me alive, but if they can't, I need you to promise me you will take the technology and research they offer. If they back out of their deal, make a trade agreement with the Krelis Prince. He seems to want to invest in our planet, and may seek to protect it."

"My sweet Jewel, I can not promise you that. Not when the prince has made it very clear that he'll have you as his mate or he'll find another planet to fit his hive's needs. He has mobilized his entire fleet to retrieve you."

It was like having daggers thrown into my gut, and my own injury from Carmen's claws throbbed hearing about Prince Trent throwing his whole hive into a war with Necias outlaws to save Luan. All while I stood here powerless to help her and I was just a few feet away.

I didn't deserve her as a mate.

Even if the krelins were on my shit list for genocide-ing my species, Trent was strong, decent enough to give me a head start escaping his warship, and worthy of a mate like Luan. But not Luan, I thought darkly.

If he had killed me instead of being merciful, Luan wouldn't be where she is right now. She never would have escaped onto my ship, Carmen never would have warped away from Estreldez because his warship would have got to her before she knew that the krelins were on to her, and Luan would be safe.

I saw the way her legs wrapped around Trent in the garden, and the way Trent looked around knowing someone was watching. If it weren't for me, she'd be at a mating ceremony right now. Not dying in a med pod.

My fists clenched at my sides. She would not die, I had to believe it, or I might just space myself.

"You'll have to talk with Prince Trent, then. Tell Loric that I won't be able to take him up on his offer, and that I'm sorry he wasted so much time waiting for me. To the moons, my Almder." Laun's eyes fluttered and I snapped to see C.O. Grear was administering the sedative into the chamber.

"To the moons, My Jewel."

And the transmission ended.

Grear walked out of the med deck leaving me staring at the floating form of Luan, her silver hair pooling around her face behind the clear chamber. Tiny microbots filled the med pod, glinting like she was floating off into space, and all I wanted to do was join her.

She'd survive this, but would she come with me when I finally freed myself from the necia?

Or would she risk a war between her planet and the outlaws, making her the newest slave of King Sylve?

Chapter
Nineteen
Luan

I could only hope my Almder got the message. The outlaws couldn't be trusted. To the moons was something
I used to say as a child, and it would always be followed
up with an explanation that the moons provided us with
radiation, but there was nothing else there. At least not until
my mom outfitted our biggest moon with a research facility.

If King Sylve already had warships out-posted around
Estreldez, then he already had his mind made up to come
after us.

He wasn't going to stop his plans just because I asked him to, or give us technology or research data to avoid a war he was already planning to start. At least with my death he'd look bad to other planets, possibly cause other leaders to increase their defenses or even retaliate to secure the balance of power dynamics.

To the moons was my way of telling her to take the research if she could, and take her own advice that there was nothing on the moons unless you made it yourself.

The King would betray her.

And whether Krelis was or wasn't sending their whole hive of warships after me was of no concern. It was tactics to let it slip that we had Krelis's support. Perhaps King Sylve would fall back long enough for us to have an advantage, if only a small one.

And if the Krelis Prince did support retrieving me, then maybe not all things were lost after all.

But the very idea of mating him somehow repulsed me now. He was an attractive man, and powerful. He led his hive, he was a prince. And even with the time that I spent with him in the garden... I had no desire to feel his touch again.

Instead it was Vareo's hands that filled my mind, and those very fingers that I imagined plunging into my pulsing core.

I gasped clenching my thighs together, and then my eyes opened, remembering where I was. Inside the med pod, floating like a pretty display, and still alive.

And awake?

155

"There isn't time to make this pleasant," Vareo's voice was strained as he pulled me from the chamber and the ache of gravity beared down on me once more, "We're docked at Necias' Station TF-9W and there are only two ways off this rock. As slaves, or stowaway outlaws."

He was carrying me against his firm chest, and I groaned as we made our way to the transport deck of the Viper Raul. The pain relief gas was wearing off, I could feel my back loh throb.

"Why not just leave me?" I was an inconvenience for him to escape from King Sylve, an extra trouble to account for.

"Stubborn woman," he grumbled. "I've been monitoring your vitals, you aren't healing properly without your moons, but you are out of critical danger. You might have eventually recovered in the chamber after a time, but we don't have time. And if you stay here you'll be used against your own planet."

We made our way through the airlock attaching the Viper Raul to Vareo's ship.

"How is no one guarding us?"

This was much too easy, if his assumptions were correct.

"Where would we go? I have no access to the Viper's transport deck codes, and according to the med bay chamber you're stable, but showing no signs of improvement. And they have a hive of warships making their way here to worry about." He made it a point to emphasize the Viper's transport deck when explaining the absence of any necia being around to stop us from what appeared to be a frivolous escape plan.

I glared at him, and he seemed to sense my agitation. He eased me to my feet and cupped my face in his large hands while his blue eyes pierced into me, making my heart thrum. What was he doing? The ache in my back seized like we were suspended in time.

The longer he stared, the more ragged my breath became, and he leaned in. Lips nearing my own, I could feel the draw of closing that gap between us before he pulled away so I could think of it no more.

Uncomfortable with what passed between us, he cleared his throat and averted his gaze. "Can you walk?" His hands dropped from my face, and grabbed my shoulders making sure I could stand, even though I had been mobile without his assistance since he propped me up.

"I can manage." Twisting to turn from him made me clench my teeth, but I was made of sterner stuff than he realized. If we were within the moon's rays this wouldn't have been an issue. My other loh would have compensated and repaired my back in no time.

"You're in pain."

He recognized the twitch in my muscles as I moved. I was hoping I had hidden it well enough.

"You've seen my med pod reports, that shouldn't be a surprise to you." I lifted my chin and kept my tone even. This wasn't the time to worry about my comfort. If he had a plan to get us out of King Sylve's clutches then we needed to hurry.

He nodded, accepting my confidence in my abilities as good enough to continue. I was thankful I didn't have to labor on the topic long since I could feel my back loh strain with every muscle twitch.

When we made it to Vareo's transport deck, Carmen was still strapped into the prisoner bonds. Her hazel eyes lifted to meet mine, and she grinned at us both.

"It's about time you came back for me, Dick head." She was still ever the diplomat.

"I didn't come for you," he didn't sound pleased to see she was awake. "You're lucky all I did was detain you."

"That's not all you did," she said with a bit of sultry implication that sent a pang of jealousy through me despite her being the one locked up.

"You knew King Sylve wanted Luan," he accused.

"Of course I knew," she spat. "You should be thanking me instead of risking your life to save her. She doesn't need saving. She's going to be the Fucking Queen of the Trillume System."

That didn't make any sense.

She was talking like King Sylve knew he would have me captured. I cocked a brow at Vareo who was averting his blue eyes in guilt.

"What is she talking about?" I asked him.

Carmen beat him to it, "I'm saying we were hired to bring you to King Sylve."

And I was dumb enough to follow him into the trap. Went right onto his ship.

I laughed, causing my injured loh to burn. I was never allowed to appear weak in front of people, so laughter was my escape. But none of it was caused by happiness. I steeled myself against the hurt.

"I can explain," he urged, and I shook my head.

"No need." I waved him off. "I don't care how I got here. I care that you'll keep your word to get us out of this. Can I trust that your interests are aligned with my own?" For now, I thought ruefully.

Carmen made it a point to tell me that he was why I was here, and all that made me do was believe that Vareo had intentions of backing out of his agreements to whoever he was employed with. Whatever bounty was on my head he either had a conscience or thought my Almder would be a better long-term benefit. There was no telling whether King Sylve would keep his word about paying him, and he didn't seem to know that's who had hired him before now, he seemed genuinely upset by the idea of working a bounty for him.

I'd like to think that I wasn't gullible enough to be fooled another time, but I had already acted rashly in boarding Vareo's ship to begin with, thinking he was something more than a male my loh wanted to mate with.

I didn't know him.

And I had misinterpreted the energy my loh had given off. Now that the light of the moon's radiation had left me I couldn't be fooled again.

He was handsome, and there was something comforting about his presence but I was more clear-headed without the interference of my loh.

Vareo could tell I was all business and his seduction antics wouldn't work this time. His jaw clenched as if holding back what he was about to say, in favor of a simple nod of agreement.

"Perfect, then we should figure this out before whatever distraction has the king and his henchmen occupied is resolved."

It was Carmen who spoke next, "Fuck, why do you have to be so damn poised and admirable even while practically collapsing in front of my eyes?" She stared at me, and I tried to see what she had to gain from complimenting me, but she bit her lip, irritated with herself or me? It was difficult to figure her out. My loh was wrong about her too. I had felt too comfortable around her, and she had taken full advantage of my belief that she was good by nature despite her bark. I was mistaken then too.

"Worry about yourself," Vareo gritted through his anger. He blamed her, when it was no one's fault but my own that I was in this situation. If I had stayed on Estreldez, none of this would have happened.

Sure, they pulled me through the threshold, but I had been opening the door to that danger before they added their parts.

King Sylve would still be surrounding my planet, but I would not have been aware of it.

On the other hand, there might have been so much more damage done if I hadn't left my planet when I did. So, even if I had made a poor decision for myself and this situation was not ideal, this outcome was not the most devastating of the possibilities. Was it?

Vareo stepped toward Carmen with promises of retribution.

"Wait! Hold on. She was never supposed to get hurt." She pleaded with me next. "You were never supposed to be harmed. The bindings are horrible, I get that, but that isn't lasting harm compared to Krelin hoarding access to the jewels from Estreldez. King Sylve needs a strong queen to hold off Trillume forces from claiming this star system in more than just name. Do either of you know what kind of ruler the trill command is? This star system needs Necias."

The trill forces were what the whole star system was named after. They were said to be a strong race that helped keep order and created the accord between space traveling species. They were who we'd try to contact if King Sylve crossed a line.

Like attacking Estreldez.

But there was no evidence of that yet.

And like Carmen, I had my reservations about asking for help from someone powerful enough to defeat an outlaw outpost without help, leery they might decide to stay and assert their power over this sector.

"What does Estreldez's exports have to do with Trillume?" I took a step towards her, but mostly to prevent Vareo from doing something rash before hearing what she had to say.

"Tarnpul is a strong alloy used for many ships, but that's not what they are after." It was as if she read my mind that I had expected our most valuable rock to be what they were after, and to hear that it wasn't... Well, that was a shock that I kept guarded under a mask of indifference.

I waited for her to continue. When I didn't say anything she bit her lip and groaned.

"Your mineral deposit of Globin Flower has been found to be the most efficient fuel source for space travel, and fuck it... it's basically the most sought after fuel source for the planet Trillume and any other dipshit that wants to upgrade their machinery."

Globin Flower was a food source on our planet, we hadn't even considered using it for fueling anything else other than living organisms. How it was hardy enough to fuel a ship, or machinery, was beyond my knowledge, but I wasn't a scientific engineer.

This was troubling news.

"So, the trill wish to have the Globin Flower for themselves?" I contemplated how this changed King Sylve's actions. Was he being pressured to take control of Estreldez or risk the trill invading? Or was I giving him too much credit?

"They call it Ordin Crystal," she corrected.

"Does it matter what it's called?" Vareo interrupted. "How does keeping Luan keep Trillume from taking the planet for themselves?"

"If you weren't so cock struck then you'd see that joining the outlaws with Estreldez, and then striking up a deal with the krelin queen would protect this star system from going to war over the Ordin Deposits. If we don't unite this system, we're going to end up like the Shol."

Carmen was glaring at Vareo, and as much as I wanted to stay angry with her, her words struck me.

Was she implying that the trill were responsible for destroying the shol?

And that we would end up like them if I didn't stay with the necia to find a common ground?

King Sylve was trying to prevent an invasion by invading us first, and subjugating us onto his side. I shook my head.

This wasn't the way.

I finally saw the rigidness of Vareo's spine, and the hard set of his dark eyes.

He was shol.

"You're lying," Vareo's voice was cold, and threatening.

Carmen sighed. She had every reason to lie to us, anything to have us release her from the restraints. To trust her.

And it was working.

On me at least.

Vareo was another story.

"Yes, we took advantage, and profited from what the trill did. King Sylve even took credit for your planet's ruin as a means to gain respect and be feared by other outlaws." Carmen was now watching me with frustrated watery eyes, pleading. "He's an asshole, but he isn't the horrible guy that his reputation demands of him. Have you never once asked why he didn't kill you after your first attempt at leaving the organization?"

"No, he just hunted me down like a trophy, and found every credit I saved to make sure I'd never leave again. He's a saint," Vareo mocked with venom.

"For fuck's sake, Vareo!" Carmen struggled and her muscles tensed, feeling the sting of the restraints shock through her. Luckily for her it seemed the shock didn't affect her quite as badly as it did me. "He was protecting your life. Why would he spend so much credit on an insubordinate ass like you? He does give a shit about an entire species being eradicated. He's even been searching the star system for a shol female for you."

"And I'm supposed to give a shit that I'm some sort of science initiative?" He was obviously unmoved by her speech, but I was more riled up by thinking about him mating with another woman. Even if it was to continue the integrity of his species DNA, I didn't like how it made me feel.

Jealous. Of a man I was still debating on whether I could trust him or not. It was ridiculous.

"He can keep his fucking protection to himself," Vareo said and slammed his fist into the release mechanism for her bonds.

He was freeing her? Carmen rubbed at her bruised throat, and when their eyes met they stared at each other with an intensity that made me feel embarrassed to be watching them.

"Get in the pod," he demanded.

Carmen stood with shaking legs, not from fear of Vareo, I could tell that much, but from her body still recovering from the shock of her restraints and whatever altercation led to her bruises. She was a strong woman, even when the credits were against her. Her hips swayed as she gained her bearings, and she teasingly taunted him with a glance over her shoulder.

"You know, if I didn't believe in what King Sylve had planned for you and your species I would have given you a different kind of bruising all those times you eye fucked me." She licked her lips and entered the pod, walking backwards so her eyes lingered on Vareo, who appeared more pissed than flattered.

Why did that relieve me?

"What exactly do you think you're doing?" I folded my arms over my chest, expecting answers. Vareo lifted the latch for sealing off the pod, and then slammed the button underneath. The whizzing sound of the pod closing around Carmen, and pressurizing for preparing its departure made me wonder if this was our way to freedom and Carmen was the test subject, or if he really was letting her go?

"The only thing Carmen cares about is what's best for Carmen," he answered with his eyes closed, and his fist still clenched over the button.

"She's going to the same place we are, the one exit out of Necias space that isn't monitored by King Sylve himself or his army." I continued to stare at him, scrutinizing.

"And where might that be?" What I didn't ask was, what were we going to do with Carmen when we got there?

"To Genbi's, the Solbin Traders." The slave traders he meant to say. That was the one being I was most afraid of being caught by when coming to Necias to begin with. Being caught by Sylve was one thing, at least my mother would know where I was. Being caught by the Solbin Traders was another thing altogether. I could end up anywhere... and it wouldn't matter that I was the future heir to Estreldez.

I'd be a slave.

Doubt crept in, and I found myself glancing back over my shoulder the way I came, contemplating going back into the med pod and awaiting my fate with King Sylve. The evil I knew was easier than the evil I didn't. Then Vareo held out his hand to me.

"Trust me," he pleaded, and before I knew it my hand was clasped within his, and he was leading me to the pod I'd used to come to this ship. I bit my lip. Was I really going to trust him?

"You have a plan?" I hoped to the goddess he had a plan to prevent a life of servitude, and then I closed my eyes realizing that that's all Vareo knew. He was King Sylve's slave. He knew what was at stake and he was risking it for me.

"Lord Zorn doesn't answer to King Sylve, they merely co-exist and deal with each other. That gives us leverage, that leverage being your planet's wealth. And the fact that Lord Zorn has been denied access to your planet's mating ceremony every season."

My mouth fell open. Of course he wouldn't be allowed to taint our ceremony with his foul genetics, he was a slave trader. No female would ever choose him. Was Vareo suggesting that I convince my Almder to allow him on our planet? I paled at the idea.

"You can't be serious." Pulling back on his grip, I stalled from entering the pod. His blue eyes turned away, ashamed, and did not reach for my hand again. The cold air on my skin frustrated me.

"His business is disgusting, but he keeps his word, and he would not harm the estrelds. He doesn't seek out his slaves, they are brought to him." Grinding my teeth I glared at him. It was like he was excusing Lord Zorn's behavior, like what he was doing was somehow an honorable way of conducting bad business.

"You know him," I surmised.

"I grew up with him." He nodded his agreement.

Chapter Twenty

Vareo

The steeliness of Luan's gaze tore at my insides, making me feel even more guilty for being responsible for her even being here. Let alone the washed out pallor of her condition that led me to using my one favor with Lord Zorn to escape now instead of when I could grab Kensie, the scientist. I'd be caught again by King Sylve without the scientist's help to reprogram my chip, but not before Luan got back to her moons, and the safety of her people.

The pod docked at Lord Zorn's personal loading station on planet Necias. Every other transport off the planet had been locked down since we arrived. When the deck was depressurized, the hiss of the oxygen being pumped into the tube between the pod and the trader processing center signaled we could exit. The pod opened, and unexpectedly Lord Zorn was there to greet us personally. His long brown hair was braided in many strands and tied back with his species' traditional bone adornments that made his hair look like a spine. On his neck was the bird brand of the Zorn, the mark of the slave, and through its heart was a sword signaling his rise to Lord. From slave to Lord, Zorn knew of this life more than most.

Luan may never agree with me on trusting Genbi, but he really was the best thing that had ever happened to the slave trade when he became the next Lord Zorn. He brought order, and a semblance of morality to the business, as gray as it was. It was a step in the right direction. I wouldn't fault Genbi for the choices he had to make. He was more a slave than any of us, with no hope or dream of escape, because escape for him would mean someone else would fill his position and in all likelihood it'd be someone a lot less kind.

Kindness, I thought, would be the reason why one day Genbi would groom someone else to take his place, the same as had been done for him.

"Lord Zorn, I didn't think you'd greet us personally." Quickly, I unstrapped and scanned the walkway into the transport deck for threats. His guard was nowhere to be seen, he came alone. This didn't bode well. Genbi smiled, and reached a hand out in greeting, I couldn't refuse. He was an unGor, and even if he wasn't Lord Zorn of this ship, offering his hand was an honor to his species. As his grip slid up my forearm to my elbow he pulled me in and patted my back twice before releasing me.

"You used the codes I gave you, and knew you were calling in your favor to leave. I would not have you disappear without a proper farewell." Genbi peered over my shoulder to Luan and lifted a brow. "This surely isn't your scientist?"

My mouth went dry, I hadn't told Luan about the scientist, not exactly. I tried to steer the conversation away by admitting as little as possible and moving on. "No time to get in touch with her," I tried to keep this line of conversation short. Genbi could see the urgency in my cold eyes, and nodded.

"You've done something stupid again, no doubt. You don't happen to have anything to do with the Krelis's warships heading to this sector, do you?" Genbi asked, but he had already - correctly - assumed the answer.

"I've something extra to ask of you." I paused and tilted my chin in Luan's direction. "I need you to get this one back to her planet. I promise you it'll be worth the effort."

"I'm listening." His dark eyes lit up with anticipation.

"She's your ticket into the next mating ceremony of Estreldez, and whatever else you think you can negotiate for," I bargained.

"Excuse me," Luan's voice shrilled behind me, unhappy with that last bit, but probably both options, including inviting Genbi to the next mating ceremony.

"I've acquired many 'tickets' but because I'm recognized for my position as Lord Zorn, those tickets have all been denied. How is this ticket any different?" He was right to be cautious about such a claim, the only reason why I had been able to get into the mating ceremony myself was because I was a nobody, and could easily manufacture a past to meet their screening tests. Even with a manufactured past, Lord Zorn was always found out before he made it past the medical examination.

"I am no one's ticket! I refuse to accept a smuggler of lives to be anywhere near Estreldez. I will sooner die," Luan proclaimed indignantly.

I shook my head, if she kept this up she would get her wish. She nearly sacrificed her life to make sure I was okay, when my skin would have borne the abuse much more easily than her own. She was dying, and she needed her moons, her own lands, to heal. I would do what I had to do to atone for my carelessness. Her voice seemed to trigger recognition by Genbi, and he took a step back for us both to pass him, stunned.

"You have the Jewel of Estreldez with you, you could have led with that, my brother." Genbi smiled and bowed to Luan with a flourish.

I found myself stepping between them possessively.

"How do you know who–" Luan stopped herself from confirming his suspicions but it was too late.

"Your voice has been heard on captured communications, and your beauty has been talked about across the star system,"

Genbi touted, and then added with his hands in surrender, "I do not mean to offend you. You'll be safe in my care. I'll see to it personally that you are returned to your planet."

"At what cost?" she growled back at him.

"None," he replied, and I was just as shocked as Luan was. As much as I believed Genbi was a good guy at heart, he had to do unspeakable things to run his business, and the years must have tainted him in ways I couldn't imagine. Asking for nothing was too good to be true, and had my instincts tensing up for a fight.

"Feel free to return to your pod and go back to where you came from, I will not stop you." Genbi turned his back to us, and kept walking while adding, "I am an unGor of my word, as Lord Zorn, I am the only one with ships capable of leaving this planet. That is the deal I have with King Sylve, my business is my business. If he breaks that bond, well," Genbi trailed off unconcerned by that potential outcome.

If anyone could challenge the king it was the Lord Zorn, he was the one with the most connections to other planets, and trading lives was not the only transport he did. It was his ships that hauled all manner of trade in and out of Necias.

"What do you get out of helping me?" Luan snuck her way around me, and was now within reach of Lord Zorn. I quickly stepped behind her to make sure I could swipe her first should Genbi seek to grab her. Genbi didn't turn back to face us, he had no fear that I would attack him, because it wasn't in my best interest to. I needed his cooperation. But he didn't seek to intimidate us either, allowing himself to be in a perceived state of weakness by giving Luan his back, he was showing her his respect, as the future Almder of Estreldez.

"I am a businessman, and even if you abhor me in this moment, you will know that I keep my word when I give it. One day you will trade with my ships, and I will free your planet from dependence on Krelis for your resources, without needing to be controlled by the Necias."

"So you seek the Ordin Crystal as well," Luan sounded exhausted. We needed to speed this along. The sooner she reached her moons, the sooner she could heal.

"A wise leader." Genbi turned, and kneeled before Luan with his long braid held aloft for her. "Do you accept my proposal? I will not force your trade agreements. Only a fair, and reasonable exchange of goods. Your lands can heal, and we will both profit. A percentage of the profits will be given to Necias as a tithing for crossing their planet, but they will not pressure you to give more than your planet can give, nor will you be forced to mate with me or any other, you have my word."

"How do you know so much about what my planet needs? And how am I supposed to trust a smuggler of your repute?" Luan was unconvinced, and folded her arms to restrain herself from doing something she'd regret. As someone brought up to be diplomatic, she was probably unaccustomed to the feeling of wanting to harm another person for dealings that were not within her moral compass.

Genbi remained still while he replied, "I deal with many of questionable repute, and as such they test my Lordship of Zorn, when given the opportunity. Keeping my title has been unpleasant at times, Princess. Change does not come as quick as one would hope. Darkness does not live without the light, nor does light live without darkness, and there is always someone who seeks to tip the balance."

Luan scoffed, but took Genbi's offered braid in her hand. Being a future Almder she probably learned about the un-Gor customs. "My planet is not defenseless."

"And there are worse threats out there than Necias, Princess. King Sylve is merely trying to protect our star system, as much as I am, but in his own way."

"The trill..." she huffed out, and I couldn't let this drag out any longer. I wrapped my hand around hers as it clutched Genbi's braid loosely. My skin tingled at the touch, and I snapped my hand back.

"We should get going," I suggested.

Luan pressed his braid to Genbi's chest, and released it. "I, Luan, future Almder of Estreldez, open discussion of trade with only you, the current Lord Zorn, should you return me and Vareo to my planet unharmed." My face went blank with her adjustment to the terms. She included me in her conditions.

"You can't," I tried to prevent the agreement.

Lord Zorn accepted, before I could say another word.

"Undo it," I pleaded with Genbi, "She doesn't understand what she is asking."

Now, Luan was staring at me confused.

"You weren't planning on coming with me?" she asked absently, a hollowness to her tone.

I shook my head. "I can't stay with you, if you are to be safe. I am, as King Sylve stated before, one of the last of the shols. He won't allow me to leave. My only escape is to disappear from this star system. If I go with you..."

She finished my thought, "The king will come for you, and demand your return." Luan nodded her assent. "So be it. As I said before, my planet is not defenseless, the moons will defend us, and King Sylve already has Estreldez surrounded. You staying out of it doesn't do either of us any good."

Lord Zorn stood tall, and smiled at her. I felt like punching his teeth in, but it was Luan's words that finally processed in my mind, stopping me from doing something stupid. She was willing to fight for me, for my freedom, and keep me close. Was this the reaction of her loh drawing me in? As damaged as they were, could I still be affected by her radiation?

The warmth that filled me to my heart would say yes, and this overwhelming urge to have her claim me as her customs suggested, had me smiling instead of fighting my old friend. Would she do just that when she was healed by her planet's moons? The thought reminded me of how much she looked like a goddess with her mating loh fully extended, and if she were to show them only for me I would not care that this was all because of her radiation spreading through me, as long as this feeling never ended. But, I couldn't let her put herself in danger for me.

"You must let me leave this star system, if for no other reason than splitting King Sylve's attention, and resources."

Genbi watched me curiously, and placed his palm on the door's scanner before deciding to give his unsolicited thoughts on the matter, "You'd only be a small distraction, and without the scientist you told me about, you'd be back on Necias before long."

"Not if–" I began, only to stop myself immediately. Genbi lifted a brow, and I realized I had almost given away what I was planning for myself, in front of Luan. She'd never accept it. The only way to disappear from King Sylve would be to join the slaves, but I couldn't be sure I'd ever escape, or find another way to be free. At least I wouldn't be used against Luan, nor would I be a weakness in her upcoming fight against the Necia.

I couldn't keep my promise. The scientist, Kensie, was still with King Sylve, and it would be up to Lord Zorn to help both Luan and Kensie escape.

"Not if what?" Luan was glaring at me, and I didn't like seeing her upset. The weariness of her injuries were more prominent when she narrowed her silver eyes. We had delayed long enough.

"Not if Lord Zorn can arrange for the scientist to join me, and safely remove my tracker bots." I hoped Genbi understood what I was asking of him, without spelling it out. He knew I would join the slaves, and wouldn't want Kensie to follow that path.

"This scientist can't be the only one capable of removing your tracking device, or blocking its signals," Luan wasn't buying it. She spun on Lord Zorn and, like the ruler she would become, she faced him down and threatened his pride. "Are you to have me believe you are incapable of blocking his tracker, or removing it, when you are in charge of smuggling lives?"

Instead of being offended Genbi laughed and smacked me on my back in a brotherly manner. "Stop your foolishness, Vareo. Your mate has spoken, and she will not be swindled by your misplaced sacrifice."

My mouth flattened into a blank expression. He had called her my mate. the very thought had my insides warm, but she had not claimed me. So how did he know my feelings so clearly? More importantly, Luan said nothing to dissuade him from his assumptions. I brimmed with temporary contentment at the acceptance.

We passed by Genbi's guards in the hallway, and he led us towards his personal offices, away from the processing centers. Luan wouldn't wish to see those, and I was still thinking about what he had said, watching Luan as she followed him ahead of me. Not once turning back to glance at me. She did not agree with Genbi's assessment, and my stomach twisted with a cold sensation as my doubts grew, knowing she would eventually correct the mistake.

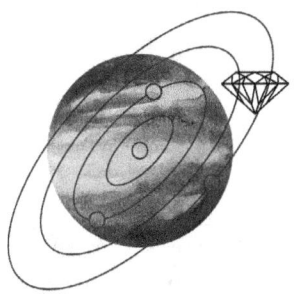

Chapter
Twenty-One
Luan

My mate, the words repeated in my mind. I had thought if I mated with him my loh would calm down, and we could both move on from this draw he had over me, but his face fell into a stoney wall when Lord Zorn mentioned it. I couldn't face the rejection I knew I would find there, so I pushed past him, and followed Lord Zorn closely.

No matter what Vareo thought of us, I wouldn't let him become a slave to someone else in a fruitless attempt to save his female scientist. Female... Why hadn't I seen it sooner? She was the one he cared about. Vareo was always bringing her up, and he called her by name, she wasn't a stranger to him. Kensie, she sounded beautiful. Her name had the root of 'sie', the sweet sap from the blackpul rose algae, and 'ken', the fibers of the kentos trees which are strong and soft. Which was more than I was. I was stubborn, and weak.

All of my radiation was gone from my loh, I could feel the emptiness of death looming in the path ahead of me. I wouldn't make it home in time to survive, and I wouldn't let Vareo sacrifice himself for life in vain. For a moment when Vareo took my hand, I thought I felt life again in my fingertips, as if a glimmer of radiation still existed deep within me, and his touch could draw it out, but he retracted so quickly, I knew that was only false hope. The will to live could play tricks on the mind.

"I can remove Vareo's tracker," Lord Zorn admitted as we entered his office, which looked more like a bedroom. Pillows, drapes, and rugs covered the room as if preparing every space for the possibility of mating in comfort. I felt the 'but' coming in his next words. What would he ask of me for this favor?

"It's dangerous," he continued, "normally I have someone reprogram their chips, but Vareo's tracker is unique."

"How so?"

It was Vareo who answered from behind me, "King Sylve spared no expense when he implanted a self-replicating nanobug into my blood cells. There is no guarantee of removing every nano bug even with a full blood transfusion." Without meaning to, I reached out to him, gripping his hand and pulling him forward to demand Lord Zorn fix it. He had to have another way or he wouldn't be smiling at us like he was one agreement away from getting whatever he wanted from us.

"You know another way, tell him," I ground out.

Lord Zorn nodded. "There is always another way. A costly way, of course."

"What is it? You are aware my planet has plenty of valuable resources, expense isn't the issue."

Lord Zorn was pressing my buttons, and if we were on Estreldez right now, he wouldn't be wearing such a smug expression with the full power of the moons at my disposal. The ache of my loh flickered on the top of my hand that held Vareo's, and I stared at it, wishing for it to flicker again. To tell me that I hadn't just imagined a spark of power there.

Wishful thinking again, I knew it, because Vareo's focus was on Lord Zorn, and he felt nothing of the fleeting radiation of my loh. It was nothing, but I continued to stare at our hands, squeezing his fingers in an effort to bring that spark back.

Lord Zorn answered then, "We inject another nanobug into the blood transfusion that will proliferate his system before any remaining previous bots from the king have a chance to replicate again. Nanobugs working against the code of the originals."

"So, basically you'd be able to track him, but King Sylve wouldn't."

Lord Zorn laughed again. "You've chosen well, Vareo. Though, I suspect she had more to do with it than you did. She's smart, but," he turned his attention back to me, "On my word, the only thing the bots would be tracking would be other bots. Consider it an anti-bot protection. Even I use the same technology for myself."

I would have never guessed that Lord Zorn was the kind of male that would laugh so heartily, or seem so easygoing. It was almost comfortable to speak with him, with how charismatic he was. The longer I was with him, the more difficult it was to imagine all the horrible things he'd been known for. Suspicion made me narrow my eyes, but Lord Zorn's humor didn't waiver. And I followed his attention back to my hand still holding Vareo's and he hadn't pulled away from me yet.

Distracted, I looked up into Vareo's blue eyes, and we stayed there for a moment before he cleared his throat. "Genbi is true to his word." He squeezed gently in reassurance.

"I owe my life to Vareo," Lord Zorn lounged back onto a couch that looked more like a throne with how big it was.

"That has long past been paid," Vareo denied, and I found myself yanking on his arm to keep his mouth shut. If the Lord Zorn thought he owed him his life, then so be it. Don't go giving him any reasons to sell us off to the market instead of keeping his word. Lord Zorn patted the couch, offering for us to sit with him at any number of the available sitting cushions.

"Brother, this will be the last time I can spar with King Sylve for you. He's grown more suspicious over the years, and there is only so much I can do before he decides to hire people to create a mutiny within our ranks."

Over my shoulder I could see a few guards within hearing range standing alert at Lord Zorn's office entrance.

"Only my most loyal guard my office," Lord Zorn noticed my hesitation. "They share my plans for the Zorn legacy, and would die for the cause if need be." One of the guards was glancing back at us with a smile, her teeth gleaming in a mischievous grin. I felt Lord Zorn was underestimating the commitment to only their own death, that one made me think she'd shank me given any perceived threat.

"What plans might that be?" If I was going to potentially be opening up trade with a trafficker of lives, I had to know if I was doing more good for my people at the expense of an unseen bad to others. My mother would never accept it if I didn't think several steps ahead, and project possible outcomes. I was surprised I was even contemplating the deal.

Even more so when it was Vareo who answered for him, "A path to freedom, true choice." There was a longing in Vareo's eyes, and I knew then that there was more to this story, and I wanted to ask him about it. Instead, I found myself leaning into his chest, and trying to comfort him. His secrets would have another day to live.

"Not everyone agrees with my plans, which is why it's best to keep them between us. For now. Even my path is not perfect, but it is mine to take."

I could respect that, even if I didn't respect his business. He seemed trustworthy, which was a dangerous prospect. To think that I felt any kind of trust forming with a trader of lives like Lord Zorn was a sign of how easy it was to be complicit with evil deeds as long as the perpetrator was affable and giving in select kindnesses.

"Any business conducted with you would come with conditions," I remarked knowing the conditions would go both directions. Hardness remained in my tone despite my waning resolve to stay objective when he had the means to help cure Vareo. "One of which is all labor must be paid for, and your labor must choose to work for you uncoerced. No one in connection with the transport or trade is forced to be there. Do you understand? No parsing my words or intentions."

There was a twinkle in Lord Zorn's dark eyes, and he pushed himself up from his cushioned throne in a swift yet smooth movement.

"Consider it done," he agreed with a toothy smile as his eyes glimmered in a way that made me think I'd been swindled in some way.

"I haven't agreed to anything yet," I said, taken aback by his quick conclusion, nearly dropping Vareo's hand in the process. He wasn't letting me go so easily, and I warmed at the thought that perhaps he didn't want to let go of the comfort of that touch just as much as I didn't. In that moment, I didn't want either of us to separate, because like this I didn't have to think about whether he was only protecting me, or whether he actually cared.

"Lord Zorn," the same guard interrupted, "all clients have been transferred to the planet base. We're ready to disembark."

"Excellent." Lord Zorn collapsed back onto the throne, and used one of his rings to unlock a chamber in the armrest. A rug slid across the floor, and a table command center lifted from the ground. "Vareo, you know where your rooms are, unless you'd like to stay?" The gleam in his eyes told me that if we stayed nothing good could come of it. Lord Zorn laughed, and waved his hand dismissing us.

As we passed the guards in the hall, Vareo waited until we were out of ear shot, and whispered in a deep voice, "He will keep his word."

"You were going to have him send you away with the rest of his slaves..." I wasn't going to bring it up, but it came out before I could stop myself.

"It would have been better for you."

We turned down a corridor , and my anger bubbled up.

"That is for me to decide!"

"And you've done such a great job of that so far?" He raised his voice an octave to match mine, and I was clenching his hand so hard my knuckles were white. I hadn't realized I was still hanging on to him this whole time. We squared off, and I felt my chest heave with irritation. He had no right to judge my choices. Even if my choices were the reason why I was stuck on his ship, damaged my loh, and lost all my radiation all to be near him, and protect him.

Why was I acting this way about him?

We stared at each other for a long moment, our breathing heavy with emotion. That warmth from within me tingled, and my loh on my hand glowed.

I wasn't imagining it.

He had to see it too. His blue eyes drifted to where I stared, and he pulled me to his firm chest, and wrapped his arms around me. The tension between us snapped, and the memory of his hands all over my body had me gripping the back of his head, and tugging him down to me. When our lips crashed into each other, electricity coursed through my limbs. Everywhere our bodies touched it was like he was recharging my loh, and the radiation within me returned slowly bubbling up within. But that couldn't be possible. Without the moons no one had ever gained their radiation back through self regeneration.

Was there an artificial radiation field close by? He said my name in a husky moan between kisses. Vareo's hand was rubbing up my thigh, and then gripping my ass to hold me closer. I knew we should stop, but everything in me kept urging me to continue like my life depended on it.

And perhaps it did.

Chapter Twenty-Two
Vareo

I could feel her hesitation as Luan's hands trembled, and I forced myself to pull back, brushing a few strands of blond hair behind her ear. My shoulders tensed, she was so stubborn, and when the look in those silver eyes changed from irritation to lust I acted before I thought better of it.

But she responded to me, touch for touch.

My skin was on fire, I wanted to be in our rooms already and remove the leather compression shielding from my chest, and shoulders. Anything between my skin and hers was too much.

But I stilled, staring into those deep-in-thought diamonds of hers. What was she thinking to stop the storm that was brewing there moments before?

Threading one hand behind her head, I squeezed her ass in the other, pressing her hips against me. Her breathing was still as heavy as my own.

"Will you leave again?" My heart clenched within my ribcage at her words. She was in my arms, and her touch searched for mine, but there was doubt I didn't know how to ease.

She bit her lip, and I wanted to devour them again to express to her how much she meant to me, but actions alone wouldn't be enough, not when I'd already proved capable of disappearing on her. Even if it was better for her to not be involved with me. I couldn't deny what I was feeling anymore.

Whether it was her radiation or not, didn't matter to me as it once did. Not now that I knew my body was responding to her, claiming her as mine. Lifting her up, she gently wrapped her legs around my waist, and I steadily got us to our room before elbowing the button to close the doors behind us in silence. She waited patiently for me to answer her, and I set her down on the table just in case she changed her mind after I told her what needed to be said.

This was more than a one-night decision. And she needed to know. Undoing the straps of my compression guard, she licked her lips, and I grinned. Chemistry was never the problem. As soon as my top guard was off, she gasped. Stepping up to her, placing myself between those still open thighs, I grabbed her hand to guide her finger over the newly developing tattoos on my chest.

"These are for you, and only you," I began to explain before my breath caught when she placed her palm over my heart. Her touch was only speeding up the bond and my skin burned to finish that claim once and for all.

"These are—" she stopped before finishing her assessment.

"Mating runes," I growled out as I gripped her thighs with both hands. My cock was hard, pulsing against her. She had to know that if we did this, there would be no one else. I would never leave her, and if she didn't let me stay by her side it would break me.

Her loh glowed again, this time the jewels that sprinkled along her inner thigh like freckles warmed the front of my pants, as I strained against the fabric.

"How is this possible?" she asked in a hushed whisper. I could sense the vitality returning to her and it made me happy and relieved to know that even if she didn't choose me the med pod had saved her life.

"You hardly know me," I admitted, "and I've already broken your trust." I leaned in, nuzzling into her neck. "But a mate bond of the shol is for life, and my essence knows you are my perfect match. If you'll have me, I'll have the rest of my life to fall in love with every part of you, and to prove to you every day that I choose you." My muscles tensed at the possibility that she would reject me right here and now.

"You do?" she choked on her own words. Her eyes watered, and I gathered her into my arms, pressing her cheek to my chest and stroking her long blond hair to sooth her. I had upset her already, and this was not how I saw claiming my mate. At this rate, there would be no claiming at all, and my heart stilled, silently breaking.

"You were giving up your freedom to protect me. If it wasn't for me, you wouldn't be in the middle of a brewing war," she lamented and shook her head in my embrace. I felt her push away from me, but I held firm. This would not be the reason I lost her.

"The war would have happened whether you came aboard my ship or not, but it is because of your sacrifice that your planet and all estrelds have a chance at coming out of it more or less unscathed. You were able to warn the Almder, and even gain the support of the Krelis Horde."

"You make it sound like all of that was intentional," she scoffed at herself, the compliment buried.

"Does it matter if it wasn't?" With my thumb I dashed away a wet tear from her cheek.

"All because of who I am supposed to be," she mumbled, a sadness laced in her words. She still believed she wasn't going to make it back to her moons in time. I gripped her shoulders and pulled back a bit more to stare at those beautiful eyes. I couldn't be distracted by being between her legs when I tried to convince her of the truth before her.

"Because of what you represent. Possibilities. A future. Freedom."

She smiled weakly, cupping my cheeks in her small hands before lacing them behind my neck, rubbing her thumb against my ear. The soft touch made me close my eyes and suppress a moan. Luan was the one pulling me back in, her legs pressing the back of my thighs to close the space created between us.

The loh on her arms glowed faintly, giving the room a hazy blue glow, scattering around us mingling with the dust in the air that hadn't been filtered out of the room yet. Her fingers stopped moving against my skin, cold and prickled where her hands hovered.

Luan stared at the glow, and her mouth hung open, before the room darkened again, only lit by the small orbs in the ceiling. Whatever she was going to say caught in her throat.

"Don't stop," I pleaded with her.

Hesitantly she stroked one of my mating runes that ran up my neck, heat rippled down to my fingertips at the contact, and when I opened my eyes the faint glow had returned to her hand, traveling up her own arms.

"How is this possible?" she repeated to herself barely above a whisper.

Pulling her in closer to me, I whispered back, "Does it matter?"

The important thing was that it was possible, and her loh were healing. A vitality was returning to her, and everything inside of me needed to touch her, and never let go. I didn't care how she was recovering, only that she was.

My hand warmed as it held her thigh. We both glanced down, and saw the loh glowed beneath her gauzy skirts. I moved along her skin, and her loh ignited everywhere I touched. Her body shivered, and I smiled into her hair.

"It's you," she said between heavy breaths, finally realizing that her body was responding to my ministrations

I needed my name called out from those lips, nothing less would quench this growing desire within me. Leaning down I held her against me, groaning as her hips moved up to grind against my cock.

Chapter
Twenty-Three
Luan

With every touch a soft hum of my radiation returned. Starved for the contact I pulled his neck down to meet me. My whole body hungry for more, I crashed my lips against his, and immediately a jolt of energy surged through me. I didn't know how it was possible, and like Vareo said, did it matter?

Faintly, in the back of my mind I nagged at myself that I should slow down and think about things, but it was like an animal took over within me. My hands pulled, and tugged at him to be closer. Legs wrapped around his waist, I squeezed to feel the pressure of his firm muscles against me.

There were too many layers, too much between us. I tugged at his strained pants, reluctant to release my hold on him to allow the leather to be removed properly.

Vareo grinned against my lips, and a low rumble vibrated in his chest as he hoisted me from the desk to the much softer bed, larger than I would have anticipated for a guest chamber on a ship.

He stilled above me, and I tried to pull him close again to keep my loh glowing, to feel the warmth of life that he offered me, but his arms locked in place, and he steadied himself.

"Luan," his voice was husky, strained to keep himself under control to speak, "tell me I'm yours. That you accept me as your mate."

I blinked up at him. I knew he had said these mating runes were mine, but I couldn't help thinking about the scientist he was willing to be a slave for, and how much I still didn't know about him. Where his skin touched mine, I could feel my loh healing, and faintly warming from the contact. His touch would save my life. I wasn't thinking about what this would do to him.

His words came back to haunt me, a mate bond with a shol was for life. Then his next words had stung as he admitted that he didn't know who I was. Could I do this to him? Have him bond with me to save my life, and risk that he may get to know me and regret this decision a million times over when he thought about his scientist?

I closed my eyes, flushing with embarrassment that I had let my instincts for survival overshadow what I was doing to him. Nervously I gnawed at my lip. The glow of my loh faded, I could feel the heat leave my body, and my skin go cold once more.

Then his mouth was on mine before I could say a word. The fire ignited, and all thoughts left my head as my arms wrapped around him pulling him close. My hips moved against him, and his hands moved up my thighs between the slits of my skirts. He roughly brushed the fabric out of the way, and his mouth seared a path down my ribs, and kissed at the top of my hips. Those blue eyes filled with need searching my own for permission to continue.

I couldn't deny him, not when everything felt so right, so perfect, and with every feeling I felt farther and farther from the grip of death, from being drained of my moon's radiation. As if my hips had a mind of their own they thrust up, begging him to continue, and he did.

His thumb circled the nub at my center, and he lowered himself so his tongue did deliciously amazing things that made me arch up to grind into his mouth. With both of his hands, he lifted my bottom up, to gain better access to his meal. My whole body trembled, and hummed, the glow of my loh brightening with every minute.

Calling out his name, I needed more. When I opened my eyes again, his mating runes were glowing the same color as my loh. Those blue eyes watched me as he licked my juices from his lips. My breaths came out in rasps, and I stared at how beautiful he was. The ache within me needed him. He stopped too soon, I needed more.

But questions haunted me.

Would he stay with me like he said?

And if he did, would he regret being mated to me for life, when the heat died down?

Was it okay to be selfish like this?

"Vareo," I panted and felt my eyes prickle with moisture. "How do you claim a mate?"

I couldn't let him do this, if it meant he was bound to me for life. Deep down I knew that if I did survive, and made it back to Estreldez I might not have the choices for mates as I once did. With our planet surrounded by King Sylve, and the threat of the trill after the Glorbin Flower, I would be indebted to the Krelins for their horde ships' protection.

Claiming Vareo as a mate, would not stop an arranged mating with the Krelins should they demand it. And for the sake of the estrelds... I would be forced to accept. I couldn't do that to Vareo, not when there was another female out there for him. Another shol to continue his species.

I needed to know that if we continued, he'd survive if we were torn apart.

I couldn't be his mate... not when everything was so uncertain. But I needed him, needed his touch. My eyes pleaded with him to tell me what I needed to know so I could accept my fate either way. My loh pulsed begging for this to continue, and the longer he stared in contemplation of my question the softer the glow became.

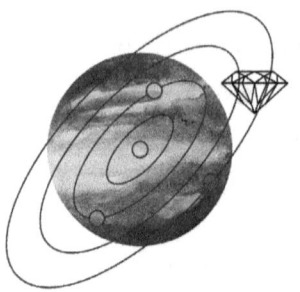

Chapter
Twenty-Four
Vareo

Something in Luan's demeanor changed drastically. I knew in my bones that she was going to reject me, and I couldn't let her. It was wrong of me, but I did everything I could to steer things back to where they were before. Even if it was the last kiss I would ever receive from her it would be worth it.

I couldn't tell her what I already knew in my heart.

It didn't matter if she accepted me as her mate.

It didn't matter if she let me finish claiming her as mine.

I was already hers.

My mating runes were complete.

I was mated to her for life.

If she rejected me now, it would change nothing. All I could do was try to convince her to let me stay by her side. It would be the least painful. Being separated from her would be devastating. Some shol have been known to die from the separation from their mates. Not that I ever believed those tales, since I never grew up with my kind. But, with how my chest felt near to exploding in agony at the mere thought of rejection told me they were more than stories. It felt as if I would die on the spot. As soon as her words hit and solidified that decision of hers, I would be done for.

Then she asked how my species claimed a mate. I didn't want to lie to her, tell her that I hadn't already bonded myself to her, but the estrelds were different; she wouldn't be bonded to me just because I claimed her as mine. According to the mating manuals given during the Moon Ceremony, sex didn't bond them to their mates. They could mate with many males.

The idea of her with someone like Trent made my teeth grind, but I had to say something.

I had to be honest with her.

Rolling slightly to the side, with my elbow propping me up to stare down at how beautiful she was, even with that concern etched in her brow, I smiled at her while running my other hand over her jewels shaping her hips and growing smaller as they reached just under her breasts. I needed to keep the glow from fading from her soft skin.

"Nothing I do will force you to claim me as your mate. That decision is yours alone," I told her as honestly as I could without scaring her with the reality that I was already mated.

I imagined escaping in my ship with her, finding another source of radiation, and never returning her to Estreldez. We could both find the last of the shol, and seek vengeance on the necia together...

It was then that I realized I saw her by my side always, but that my vision didn't include letting her become the next Almder of Estreldez. I was such a visp, the greediest of the parasites on Estreldez.

"You said the shol mate for life..." My jaw ticked at the fear I heard in her voice.

Was I so miserable of a being that the idea of a life with me was terrifying?

My fingers stilled in their ministrations, watching as her jewels lit up as I touched them. The glow faded the longer I stayed away. Her loh slowly turned a dull gray, a stark contrast to the brilliant silvery blue she had before. Almost as if I would lose her if I didn't hold her close.

And maybe I would either way.

The thought tore through my gut.

I was right the first time when I told her that she was better off without me. Dragging her away from Estreldez wasn't an option. She was the future Almder, and her species was approaching war soon. As much as I wanted her to myself, I couldn't let another planet come to the same fate as my own. Destroyed by Necias. If I stayed with her I would be putting a larger target on her and her planet. King Sylve would come for me, adding a legit claim to his reason for surrounding Estreldez with warships should Trillume investigate.

I focused on things I could control in the moment. I was already mated, my fate sealed to her. The least I could do was make sure she healed long enough to survive the transport to her planet, without burdening her with the full truth.

"When a shol mates, it has nothing to do with what I plan on doing with your body." I traced the loh beside her breast, and trailed down watching her skin illuminate as I went. Her breath caught with a small gasp making me smile as I stopped to give a bit more attention at her hip bone, where a loh nestled pointing to where I wanted to bury myself in pleasuring her. Her butt lifted trying to get my hand to move farther down, but I stayed firm not wanting to continue until her mind caught up with her actions.

"Mmm," she moaned with heavy-lidded eyes, tempting me to finish what I started.

"Let me do this for you," I begged, but it wasn't just for her. With my mating runes fully formed, everything in me craved to be close to her, to feel her, and give her what she wanted. Even if what she wanted was never to see me again after she's healed.

I would accept it.

Even if this was the only rotation I had with her, I could die happy.

"Vareo, I can't—" her voice caught as I let my hand wander farther down to cup her entrance in my palm, touching, but not letting my fingers move or probe. Her chest lifted and fell in rapid succession as her hips wiggled, trying to get me to do more. More is exactly what I would give before she could deny me. I didn't want to hear her finish her thought. I already knew she wouldn't claim me as her mate. She was a leader, a princess, a catalyst of change, freedom, and hope. She wouldn't give me her heart, but I'd take what was offered. I was a criminal, and in this instance, I accepted that label with open arms if I could have the jewel that was lying before me.

Just for the rotation.

She was mine. And I would always be hers.

Her fingers gripped into my hair, and pulled me to her lips, but in those last seconds she stopped just short of our lips meeting. She sucked in a breath as my palm lightly grazed her bundle of nerves, her hips lifted up. Fuck. I wanted nothing more than to help her release all that energy, and heal her wounds.

"No more games," she hissed. The loh on the top of her palm lengthened and curved down like a saber cutting through the closure that held my pants together. The layers of her own skirts were spread out around her, displaying the nectar of the sweetest flower that I would take my time to enjoy before I gave her what she just released from the confines of my own clothing.

The estrelds had it right, wearing loose-fitted cloth with no obstructions to their instincts. Women wore flowing dresses, barely a wisp of coverage, and slits so high that it was merely a matter of arranging the pieces out of the way. Even their males wore billowy skirts that tied back at the ankles with overlapping strips that could easily be parted to join with their counterparts at any given moment. What once seemed impractical, I now understood as a difference in priorities. Mine were rightly aligned now that a feast was waiting for my exultations.

Her hand clasped over my dick, making it vibrate and pulse in her care. I groaned into her hair before I let my finger trace up and down her slit, teasing at her entrance. The sounds my gentle stimulation emitted from her made it so damned hard not to move my own hips on top of her eagerly parted legs. Her grip on my cock moved up and down making my finger slip and press into her slit to prepare her for my own entry. In time with her strokes I pushed in and out with one finger, then two. Her hips thrust up to meet me, and her hold on me stilled as she moaned.

Her ecstasy was my own, and my need grew with every delicious sound.

The little pebble of nerves glowed like her loh, filtering out through the cracks around my hand and it elongated, a hard nub pressed against my palm. Removing my fingers from her sheath I circled the eager bud, only gently passing by, grazing it lightly a few times. Her hand wrenched from my cock to dig into my arm as she panted. She pulled on my bicep, writhing beneath my hold, trying to force me to have a firmer hand with her. I captured her moans with my lips. Her mouth opened as I deftly played with her tongue as if I were teasing her clit before I noticed fangs biting into my lower lip drawing blood.

My body hummed and shivered, my shol heritage took her aggression as a strong female claim and my mating runes only glowed brighter. I didn't want to wait any longer to have her. Adjusting from her side I moved atop her. For a moment she whimpered at the loss of my touch on her pulsing need, but I wouldn't have her wanting for long. I was so hard with anticipation and my cock throbbed ready to release my seed.

Without entering her, I pressed myself against her sensitive flesh, the scent of her reminded me of the Yhel flower of my home planet. She was my new home. My cock vibrated on her extended nub at the bottom of her inviting petals, and she screamed out, grabbing around my neck and clawing at my shoulders to pull me closer. My name in those howls of pleasure had me brimming with pride. But what brought more happiness was the loh on her shoulders pulsing, no longer cracked or dull.

This was healing her.

The pleasure I was giving was healing her, generating radiation that pulsed off of her in heady waves. My mating runes responded in kind, warming my body in a bright blue haze.

"I need you," she pleaded between the play of our lips moving together.

I rubbed my cock against her opening, easing away from the pulsing need of her bundle of nerves that felt like heaven against me. The absence of that touch was only momentary before I slipped up between her wet folds. Her bean pulsed against the underside of my cock making me still in pleasure before I tremored inside of her in measured thrusts. As I slowly released myself from her hold, the nub pulsed along my length as my tip rubbed at her entrance once more. And as she whimpered I too couldn't stop myself from shivering at her touch.

I needed more.

Gruffly, I grabbed her ass, and pushed into her hard and was happily met with equal vigor in return. With each thrust I felt her radiation pulse out from her extended bud gliding against the underside of my hard length. Her legs wrapped around my waist, her heels pushing my ass in time to our rhythm to force me deeper inside. I didn't know how much longer I could last like this. I wanted this feeling to go on forever, but with every shudder I had to force myself to hold back.

My eyes grew heavy with need, and I felt like her hands were touching more of me than two hands could possibly cover. I forced myself to tear my eyes from the lusty silver ones below me, and the air sparkled with radiation, surrounding us. She was brighter than any sun, but I was not blinded.

I never wanted to look away.

Her loh pulsed, and just like our time in the library of her palace... her wings grew.

Chapter
Twenty-Five
Luan

With every sensation from his touch, my body hummed, and my mating loh ached. Vareo's runes glowed bright blue, and it was like his energy was connecting with mine on a level I never expected. I'd had sex before, but that was with estrelds that were known to be sterile, and my mating loh were firmly under my control. This was anything but that.

I felt liberated, and every nerve was on fire. The kind of heat that pooled deep in my center, and hummed a beautiful song that tingled as it played. My most sensitive loh beneath my nectar glands, settled within my wet folds, extended out to him, seeking out his touch pulsing with need, creating small little nubs that only served to stimulate my flesh more. It was still a wonder his cock remained outside of his body at all times, unlike the estreld who kept their mating cock sheathed within a slit between their legs. Fascinated with his cock, it vibrated against my core, sending shivers down my spine that made me arch up to rub against him. I needed the friction, the pressure or I would burst.

Then he slipped inside and we both stilled in unison. His cock filled me so completely that my muscles clenched to keep him there, like he was never to leave. Those blue eyes closed before burying himself into my hair with a groan. Like my loh had a mind of their own, no longer in my complete control they sought him out, and rubbed underneath his cock sheathed to the hilt inside my warmth. He nuzzled into my ear, and I squeezed the back of his head closer to me as his hips thrusted up and out of me painfully slowly.

The absence of him was torture, and yet added another sensation I couldn't put a name to. It was everything but unpleasant as the head of his cock stilled just within my entrance, stretching for him, and my hips bucked, seeking to return him to where he belonged. He stayed there, teasing me, and I whimpered. If he didn't finish what he started, I would be flipping him around so I could have my way with him.

As if timed perfectly, my final attempt at thrusting my hips up to fill myself with his thick shaft, I pulled him down simultaneously as he slammed into me. I shivered at the hard impact, shock rippled through me at how much deeper he got with a bit more power. I needed more. A hunger consumed me. And each stroke of his cock had to be harder, it had to be faster, and I wouldn't accept any less. At every timed thrust my loh vibrated, and rubbed against him in a delicious euphoria. His runes glowed, and my loh matched his excitement until I convulsed around his cock, every muscle tightening.

I screamed out his name, and a wave of more pleasure shattered through me, aching through my back, and I needed to touch more of him, until I felt like everything was on fire.

Then I opened my eyes, that I hadn't realized I had closed in that moment, to see my mating loh had fully healed, and my wings wrapped around him possessively. Like they had a mind of their own, they rubbed down his arms, his back, his butt, and even pulled at his thighs to go deeper still. I was so royally screwed.

My heart swelled, and I could feel the moisture leak from my eyes.

If my people needed me to leave this man... a part of me would die.

I had chosen him as my mate.

And it was now as my legs wrapped around him, and my loh shrouded the room in a radiation that shouldn't have been possible with no moons, that I realized this was what it felt like to truly be compatible.

How had my people been able to let their mates leave off-world after they shared this? I clung to Vareo and pressed my wet cheeks into his neck, hoping he mistook it for the sweat of our current embrace. What was I allowing to happen to Estreldez?

His arms wrapped me up, and his movements inside of me stilled, making me ache for him to continue.

"Don't stop," I pleaded with him. But the sob was evident in my raspy voice that couldn't be shadowed by lust.

I was healed, I knew that. I had generated enough radiation between us that I could last until we reached the moons of Estreldez. He didn't need to continue what we started to save my life. Whatever this was between us... he could stop, and I knew he should.

Letting my planet suffer wasn't an option, and I'd do whatever it took to save them.

Including mating with a krelin if that's what it took.

He pulled away from me, the glow from our mating faded. The lust-filled eyes of a man in the throes of passion was gone, an unreadable mask shrouded his features.

A chill shivered through me.

"You're healed now, you should get some rest," he monotoned.

His cock slipped from me, still hard and slick from my nectar.

Then he pulled me against his chest, and I stared at the steel confines of our guest quarters on the notorious ship of the smuggler Zorn with his arms wrapped around my waist. My loh still buzzed from his touches, but there was something different now. His cock remained hard against my butt, evidence that he was yet to be satiated from our coupling, but he made no move to continue what we started. He simply stopped, and squeezed me to him, with his face tucked against my shoulder. Hot breath lightly tickling my loh, uneven from the vibrating heaves of his chest rising and falling.

"I thought I could do this for you," he whispered into my ear sending shivers all the way to my toes.

There was such a strong chemistry between us, but I'd ruined it with my tears. And he was already preparing to tell me what I already knew... that this was temporary. The very thought of having to choose another mate besides him filled me with dread. I grabbed his hand and pulled it up to my face, holding his arm to me as he wrapped me in his warmth. Was there another way to help save my people without using the Krelis fleets? The radiation of our moons was strong, and we could hold off an attack for a time, but Necias's forces were many and likely to overwhelm our defenses.

"Luan," my name soft on his tongue, distracting me from my thoughts. "When you return to Estreldez—"

"Enough," I stopped him from finishing that line of thought. He was speaking as if he wasn't going to be joining me, and I couldn't bear to hear it. "If you're going to say something about how being on my planet gives King Sylve an excuse to attack me, I think we're past that. The absence of evidence doesn't constitute proof of your stay on my planet. With or without you, he will attack us." I took a breath, and refused to turn to stare into those eyes that seemed to capture the vastness of the universe in their depths. Forcing myself to continue I added, "You're right though, it's dangerous for you to be on my planet, but not because you are a target."

Vareo pressed his cheek to the back of my neck and spoke softly in my ear, "A queen doesn't need a warrior to protect her people. She needs a leader with an army at their disposal all willing to destroy her enemies. I'm nothing but a bounty hunter."

I shivered, then twisted in his arms to face him, wrapping my arms around his neck. The hurt in his eyes wasn't something I had noticed before, but I was looking now, and my chest ached at the sight. He had spoken in passing about having a past with Lord Zorn, and he didn't explicitly mention anything, but I saw the scarring on the back of his neck, barely covered by his growing hair. He had been a slave once, or perhaps he still was. Trapped by King Sylve.

"Your title isn't who you are. King, warrior, hunter… slave," my mouth went dry and it was difficult to continue. I couldn't begin to imagine the kind of life he's had to push through being the last of his species, his homeland destroyed, traded through slavery, and forced to work for an outlaw. Then he just had to meet me, only to throw him in the middle of war all because I was selfish. He had answers about a scientist that could help my planet, and if I was honest with myself none of that mattered as much as my need to be near the male that triggered my mating loh.

I chuckled to myself in uncomfortable clarity at my disgusting disregard for what was truly best for my planet. Someone capable of such actions was not worthy of ascending to Almder, and I was undeserving of even the shol male before me. Tears prickled at the edge of my eyes, and I turned away incapable of facing my truths reflecting in his eyes any longer.

He pulled me back, preventing me from escaping the ugliness of my decisions.

It wasn't just my planet that I was failing. I was failing him.

He was the last known shol male, and if there was even a chance there was another female that survived his planet's destruction he would have the weight of his species on his shoulders. I would be violating system law to prevent his species from continuing undiluted. His kind mated only once.

The tears I should have been shedding for my selfish decisions and how they affected those around me were not dripping down my cheeks for any other reason than the hurt inside my gut at letting go of someone I wanted.

Even now, I was only thinking of myself.

Vareo wiped away a tear with his thumb, and lifted my chin.

"Nor is it who you are," he threw my own words back at me, and it felt like a blow to my throat. He was right, I was not defined by being a future Almder. My actions were far from what was to be expected of a leader.

I couldn't do this to him.

I had to let him go.

His forehead gently tapped against mine, and I stilled, holding my breath.

Chapter
Twenty-Six
Vareo

The strong, feisty queen was crumbling before my eyes. Luan's shoulders were shaking, and a viscous clear liquid slid down her cheeks that smelled like flowers. As I wiped a tear away, my thumb heated at the contact. Everything in me wanted to protect her even from pain I couldn't reach. My mating runes glowed, and as my forehead touched hers, I wished to take all of that pain through osmosis if I could.

She was more than a title of Almder of the Estreldez, she was the future of this star system, even King Sylve knew what her future held before her. Her planet holds the rarest of minerals that every star-faring vessel will fight for, and she's the only estreld in history to survive this long away from her moon's radiation. But what's more is she is the rare kind of jewel that is willing to sacrifice herself to protect her clan.

It was a suicide mission to leave King Sylve, but as long as he had her as leverage, her planet was in danger. However, neither of us had known she would generate her own radiation and heal her damaged loh before we even got close to returning to Estreldez.

I was less than a slave, I was scum from the bottom of the waste dispensers for thinking I was saving her by removing her from the med bay in the off chance I could get her home before her light faded from this world. I had had no assurances.

"This life is all I've ever known." I frowned at her tears as they kept on flowing, and so I did the only thing I knew how to do in such situations. I shared what Zorn used to tell me when we were younger every time I mentioned my family, my planet, and my fate as nothing but a tool for those with power. "It is useless to think on what might have been, or a life that isn't mine.

"Those who seek to control us will give us the illusion of limited choices, but there is always a path untold. A path that may not solve all our woes, but gives us options that weren't there before. Eventually even the impossible can be probable once more. War may loom in your future, your clan may be facing a threat that can not be overcome by force alone, and you are one estreld against an army." I sighed realizing I had stuck my fist in my mouth as her tears only intensified.

"I mean to say," I tried to remedy my misstep quickly, "You may feel trapped by the choices you are confronted with, but there is always a path not readily given. You will find that path, because a light like yours could outshine the vacuum of space itself."

"It's not light," she corrected me with a trembling smile. "Our loh don't 'produce' light, we stabilize and store energy. The glowing is the act of stabilizing a decaying atom. Without radiation, our bodies try to stabilize the energy inside our cells that aren't meant to be used in such a way. Our metabolic loh system that protects us from our planet's radiation is the very reason why we can't sustain ourselves outside of the moon's rays."

The tone in her explanation sounded less like she was telling me for the sake of why it was remarkable that she recovered, but more to convince me that she was less than radiant in her own right.

Her body attacks itself to re-energize, but without the radiation, the only energy for it to consume and stabilize is her own cells. That's why the estreld can't heal themselves without radiation. There is no energy to use to rebuild her cells, and in order to rebuild decaying or damaged cells, more radiation is needed. but none of that depreciated the fact that she put herself in harm's way to protect me. She almost died so that I would be saved from even the smallest of pains.

Luan didn't know enough about the shol to know that my body would have sustained the damage of being tossed against the metal of the ship's interior haul with much more resilience than an estreld.

"Not light," I agreed, but it didn't change the sentiment for me. She was still bright enough to blind the darkest of black holes in space. "Luan, even the stars do not light every particle of their surface, it does not make them any less capable of incinerating a ship."

She had to remember the fiery sun within her was capable of defending her planet, and finding a way to stop King Sylve, and I would remind her of that as many times as she needed to hear it.

My heart stilled at the thought.

I had meant every word.

But, it confirmed I had no intention of allowing her to take the easy way out of this war. I couldn't let my mate choose another for their... hive of warriors, and fleet of ships. If that Krelis Prince touched her I would start a war of my own.

Every mate rune on my body glowed more brightly with my realization.

Would I truly risk everything to selfishly keep her for myself?

Her silver eyes stared up at me, and my resolve only grew. Fuck, I was going to owe Lord Zorn more than my life for what

I was about to ask him to do. I knew tasting her when I was fully mated to her was dumb. Pumped with endorphins I wasn't thinking clearly, and in the back of my mind I knew I should walk away, let her save her people by mating with another male, but that voice was faint now. A whisper of a conscience describing the probabilities of success not being high enough to risk Estreldez's freedom. I wasn't much for mathematics anyway, and a much louder voice was reasoning that neither King Sylve, nor the Krelis Prince cared about killing anyone. The Glorbin Flower was what mattered, and the lives on Estreldez were more valuable alive to harvest it, so my actions weren't risking lives... not really.

It was a stretch, and a deeper part of me knew that, but that part was too quiet to hear as my mate bond demanded I protect Luan... but more importantly protect our future together.

I lifted my head back from hers to press my lips to her forehead, closing my eyes to relish the moment before the storm. If we survived this, she might just murder me herself. But, none of that mattered because she was the only one I'd allow the privilege to do so.

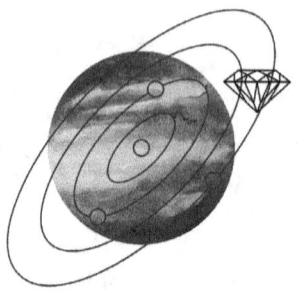

Chapter Twenty-Seven

Luan

My skin still tingled where Vareo's lips had touched my forehead. It wasn't the steamy touch we had shared before, but it left me speechless, and warmth pooled in my belly.

His words lit a fire within me to find that unseen path towards scorching the forces threatening everyone I cared about. Be the sun, I thought before he suddenly unwrapped his arms from my waist and stood leaving my skin cold.

"Get some rest," he offered with a tenderness that stopped any stubbornness from rearing at being told what to do. He tucked a piece of my hair behind my ear, which served no purpose but to expose more of my face to him. Saying nothing more, he steeled himself and left me there staring after him. His back turned to me, a scar I hadn't noticed before pulled my attention to the back of his neck, partially hidden within his dark hair.

A blackened leaf, or wing that didn't blend well with the rest of his tattoos. I'd felt the raised flesh of scarring when I threaded my fingers along his scalp minutes before, but I had been distracted. And now he wasn't here to answer my curiosity.

That's what I wanted, wasn't it?

For him to live his life, find a shol female, and survive outside of this coming war, away from me?

Then why did I feel so miserable at the sight of his shadow disappearing behind the sealing doorway?

I clutched at my chest, there was this tug I had never felt before urging me to right myself and stand. Before I knew it my feet were padding across the borrowed quarters of this slavers-owned vessel. When I thought about it that way, the small ray of light I felt being in this bubble with Vareo disappeared. This wasn't merely a transport ship taking us back to my planet. This was a vessel, possibly filled with slaves who had no choice but to do whatever it was that Lord Zorn asked of them.

An image of Lord Zorn's tattoo with the burned bird wrung through with a sword flashed in my mind. It was the mark of a slave killed and in its place a lord reborn... My heart stilled. Lord Zorn and Vareo knew each other... and Vareo had the mark of a slave still. It was not removed, like those who had escaped their fates.

It was the first thing any freed slave would do, find a way of removing that which claimed them for someone else.

I wasn't dumb, I had realized he had been a slave, but not the potential that he still was one.

And Vareo's absence took on a whole new meaning... and that tattoo on the back of his neck reminded me he might not be free at all. Did Lord Zorn say something to him? My whole body tensed as I waited with my hand near the door's sensor. Was Vareo even free this moment? Was this all a trap to have Lord Zorn gain access to Estreldez? Was I leading a monster into the heart of my clan?

I froze.

With a shake of my head I couldn't fathom Vareo betraying me like this, even if he was still under Lord Zorn's claws. I was just being paranoid, I thought, while staring warily at the metal pad next to the door.

Vareo had saved my life only moments before, I felt it in my soul. If it weren't for him I didn't think my body would have found the small amount of radiation it did. Somehow he generated exactly what my body needed to heal itself, it was unheard of. And if anyone on Estreldez caught wind of what a shol was capable of then his species would be even more sought after aside from being nearly extinct... to imagine the shol were capable of generating the same kind of radiation produced by our moons, it could change everything.

His species was more valuable to my planet than a lost heir to the Almder could ever be. No one could know what happened between us only moments before. Not if Vareo, and whichever other shol out there wanted to have a semblance of a normal life focused on rebuilding their own species.

I pressed my lips together at the thought of Vareo being with any other female, the tips of my ears burned with jealousy. And in the same thought I realized my trust in him was so fragile, thinking he could still be under the influence of the slave trader, Lord Zorn, and this whole thing could have simply been trading one captor for another.

Hovering over the sensors that would open the door, I paused, needing to be wrong. Needing that feeling of betrayal and the sadness in Vareo's eyes to be in my imagination. I closed the distance and pressed my palm firmly in place to leave this room and chase after him so I could tell him I didn't want to push him away.

His absence already caused my insides such turmoil that I never wanted to experience again, but as I stared at the unmoving door my panic only grew.

Nothing happened.

I lifted my hand and slammed it back into the sensor pad, not even a scanning light lit behind my touch. The door stayed securely where it had been before my assault.

I was locked in.

And I was fuming.

Chapter
Twenty-Eight
Vareo

"Shouldn't you be with your mate?" Genbi asked without even turning to see who I was. He had always been more intuitive than me. His eyes were still focused on the screen before him, and his guards let me pass without a word.

"You know why I'm here," I spoke softly, still debating about my decision.

Lord Zorn finally turned to take a look at me, and his usual grin didn't grace his features when he said, "If you had half a brain you wouldn't be. Any reason why you would be in my chambers instead of your own, burying yourself into the folds of your mate leads me to believe you haven't one."

I narrowed my eyes over my shoulder as his guard chuckled at my expense.

"Don't take your decisions out on Pri-Re, she simply agrees that you're not in your right mind and if I were a better man I'd be turning you around and shoving you back the direction you came from." Genbi sighed before waving me forward. "But, for you, I'll listen to why you are doing something against the wishes of your mate."

"How do you know—"

He lifted a hand to cut me off.

"As feisty as that one is, if she agreed with what you're about to ask of me she'd be at your side."

Sinking down into the cushions of the chair next to Genbi, I buried my face in my hands before running them through my hair in frustration.

"She's not shol, she doesn't understand what she is to me. She's the very air I breathe, and I barely know her, yet I know everything about her at the same time. The more I get to know her the more I love, and I can't let her go. Not now."

"You intended to," Genbi added gently, but allowed me to finish.

"Of course I fucking did, she's meant to shine brighter than what I could ever give her. She's facing a war on two fronts, and only a political match would help save her planet from what is coming. What is probably already there."

My best friend merely nodded and leaned back in his chair, saying nothing.

I punched him in the gut, making him lurch forward with a chuckle, as I didn't put my full force into the action, but needed him to give me something besides his indifference. "Just tell me what you need from me to convince you to join this fight. To give her planet time to defend itself. To make sure she isn't forced into mating a krelin!"

He lifted his hands in mock surrender. "You've made your case, but your mate will not like the cost." With a shrug, Genbi pushed a button that revealed a large vial and syringe. "This is my high-profile slave tracker, and I guarantee it will overwhelm whatever nanobots King Sylve has in you. It's only used on our most valued slaves. That is merely the first step of the request you're asking for."

We both knew the cost of what I was asking. It wasn't just about my freedom from King Sylve, though I guesssed that's a side effect. I took the offered nanobot injection, twisting the syringe into place within the vial. All I would have to do is jab it to my neck and press the button.

"You need an army, and the only one that will follow you into war for the rights to protect your mate, seize control over a planet with Globin Flower deposits, and fierce enough to rival that of King Sylve and the Krelins is that of Lord Zorn. Do you understand what you're committing to?" Genbi shook his head, but pushed a brand into the searing heat of a chemical reactor at his station.

Pri-Re and the other guard, who I recognized as Hod-Kar knelt at the entryway with their weapons thumping against their chest. They'd overheard everything and made no objection. They knew who I was and somehow their acceptance made this decision all the easier.

"For Luan, I'd do anything." Sliding from the cushions I took a knee at his feet.

"Right, brother. So be it." Genbi took his dagger from his sheath and carefully cut back the hair from the right side of my head down and revealed the tattoo beneath my hair. "All those who see this mark will know what you have done here, and will follow you as if it has always been. You can stop now, say the word or complete the vow."

He stopped with his hand holding my head steady, and the branding iron in his other, the heat steaming close to my skin. "From darkness we are born, in heat are we forged, and on this day I take my place as lord to those with no voice but my own."

Genbi held my head taunt, gripping my hair as he pushed the brand into my skin. Searing pain blinded me as my flesh melted for a second time. I gritted my teeth and hissed as the smell assaulted my nose. Jamming the vial of nanobots into my thigh I pressed the button to release the tracking serum, starting the process of cleansing my system from the virus left there by King Sylve.

Genbi smacked my head and lowered his own at my feet. The sound of metal clanging against armor from the two guards quieted.

"Lord Zorn," he addressed, lifting his braid in offering.

I clutched his braid, placing it to my heart, and then stood. The brand on my scalp still throbbed and a small trickle of blood dripped behind my ear where it didn't fully cauterize before the brand was released. Probably from my own instinct to pull away from the heat.

"Brother, we must prepare the warriors," I offered him my hand to rise to his feet alongside me.

He shook his head, and did not take my hand. My chest clenched at the sight of defeat in his eyes, of a resolve I hadn't seen there since our childhood.

"For you they will fight, they will fight for the Zorn that refused to rise at the cost of their life. For their lives were always in your hands."

"I left them," I disagreed.

"Did you?"

"I wanted nothing more than to disappear and have my own freedom." I watched as Pri-Re and HodKar stepped forward, their fists at their foreheads in reverence.

"Lord Zorn," Pri-Re addressed and her fist jutted out and back to her side. "True freedom is when we are released from

229

this realm into the next. Anything else is but an illusion. But life, My Zorn, can be fought for. And there is no life under the control of someone that does not see the lives beneath them."

HodKar stomped the ground to mimic her statement while adding, "Lord Zorn, see us."

Genbi repeated the phrase, "See us." He stood stomping his feet.

Joining in, Pri-Re stomped and said the same in a reverent chant, "See us."

A few warriors on patrol stopped at the doorway, listening to the commotion. Their feet stomped as they clanged their weapons against their armor plates.

"See us," they shouted while one tapped their visor in place to display the scene across the ship. The video surveillance popped up on Genbi's command station, and one by one crew members stopped what they were doing and stomped their feet, echoing the phrase until it was all I could hear.

This is the choice I made to save my mate, to give her the option to choose her fate. With the forces of Lord Zorn at my disposal, she wouldn't need the Krelin fleet. There was a reason why King Sylve did business with Lord Zorn, and did not seek to control it.

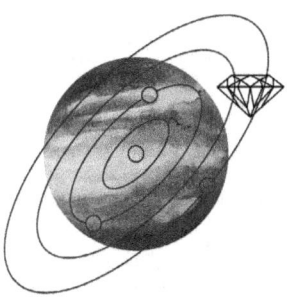

Chapter
Twenty-Nine
Luan

Thunderous vibrations quaked through the haul of the ship in a rhythmic pulse that could be felt to the very bones. I was done being a captive, and I risked depleting my loh to burn through the locking mechanism of the door with what was left of my radiation. I tugged and pulled to slide the door out of the way manually before I saw a screen with Vareo's face in the hall and a few guards stomping their feet in front of me. Making myself small, I squeezed against the wall hoping they wouldn't see me, but they were too enamored with the viewing screen to have noticed my presence.

"See us," I could finally make out what they were saying before they stopped, and waited in silence. Not even I could pull my eyes away from Vareo's stern face, but the screen panned out to see Lord Zorn beside him with his head bowed. I blinked my confusion.

"With your help, we will stop King Sylve, and give the Krelin's pause before they have a chance to defend themselves," Vareo spoke confidently to the crew, and I wondered what he was talking about. This was a slaver's ship, not a war vessel... Doing anything more than dropping me off at my planet would put everyone in danger.

Too distracted with watching Vareo I didn't notice when the two guards patrolling the halls had came upon me. Their brutish hands grabbed my arms and lifted me from the ground as I struggled, but unable to stop them with so little energy after using it to break my way out of the locked room.

"Let go of me!"

The taller one grunted, while the woman scoffed.

"You'll go swear your fealty to Lord Zorn or he'll have an uprising from some of the dumber crew members seeking to gain power themselves. I do not wish to have another Zorn, and I'll hardly get another chance to freely harm the Necia who traded me here to begin with."

"I'll die before I swear fealty to anyone other than my people, least of all a vile trafficker." I pulled my arm from one of the brutes only to have him clamp down harder. The other let go without much fuss as I rubbed my arm. She didn't leave my side though, and the taller guard did not release me.

"You will not speak of Lord Zorn with such filth on your tongue," he gritted while hefting me forward.

"Aren't you a slave, why do you follow so blindly?"

It was the female who answered, "Aren't we all slaves? Even you, princess of your own planet, must fulfill your duty to your people even against what you may want for yourself. Even those paid for their services in credit, are they not slaves to how much that credit will purchase them? How much time must they sacrifice to the will of others to have food, and a place to sleep? Do they work less than us?"

I pursed my lips, unable to reason with someone as resolute as that, but I had to ask, "Are you freely working here? Can you leave whenever you choose?"

"We do not seek death, pale one," the deep grumble of the taller guard replied.

I shook my head, stilled by the knowledge the only exit most slaves had was death. This was no freedom.

The female chuckled at the seriousness of her partner. "It is easy to believe that the threat of death brings loyalty through fear, but that is not what he is saying. He means, there are more ways to die than our bodies, and we've earned our rights to seek 'employment' elsewhere, but we'd be trading our lives for the illusion of freedom."

"Have they all brainwashed you?" I asked while stumbling over my own weak legs.

"You should be asking if you're the one that's brainwashed by your society, believing that many of your own people have a choice in the way they survive their lives on your planet. Do your females like being broodmares in a mating game each season to bolster their birthrates and protect the continuation of your species?

"Do your miners choose to spend day in day out to gather resources for the people? Do your animals choose to push heavy rocks and smash them on command to reach your Glorbin Flower? Yes," she watched my shocked expression, "I have read your planet's file as soon as you boarded this vessel. We, slaves, are not banned from knowledge."

"Estrelds are free to choose whatever profession they want," I defended resolutely.

The guard lifted a curious brow as if in defiance of my statement. "So, you are to tell me that how many loh your spawn are born with does not dictate what options are available to them?"

I frowned at her accusation, but I couldn't outright deny it either. Those with more loh are seen to be blessed by the moons, and have more radiation absorption, making them ideal for different tasks.

"Do you not have spawn with less loh managing the mines and doing 'menial' tasks?" she pressed further making me scowl, only for her to continue, "Are they included in the mating games, or are they deemed unworthy of being spawn makers?"

Snapping back, both guards stilled at my outburst, "You know nothing of my people! You see your data sheets about my planet and you think we are anything like Lord Zorn, you are wrong. I have seen the miners, took part in their jobs and shared meals with the Hergslats while they roam. Our females are not broodmares, and none are forced to participate in the mating ceremony..." my voice dropped at that last declaration, as for most of our people, they are free to choose, but I was not.

Understanding crossed the guard's faces and they gratefully said nothing to the tears threatening to draw from my eyes. I had spoken with many of the estreld females who were ready for mating, and all of them were nothing but excited to participate. All except for me, and I was the one with no choice to join, as I was to be Almder one day, and it was my job to lead by example. Though we did not force estrelds into any position, many knew what was at stake should they decline to be scientists, or... broodmares. The survival of our species.

Was that any kind of freedom at all?

I sulked alongside the 'slaves' that I might have misjudged as they might be more free than I, or my people, ever were. What kind of Almder would I be not to encourage the things that would help us flourish, help our spawn rates, our food imports? What kind of Almder would I be if I didn't?

"State your business," the guard that glared at me from before halted our progress. Her scowl, ever the present reminder that she'd kill me if she thought I was a risk to her Lord Zorn.

"Commander Pri-Re, we found this one wandering the halls and believe her royalness could help encourage support for Lord Zorn's new initiatives." She bowed slightly and then stood at attention.

"In requiem is the voice heard in the darkness, at ease," Pri-Re pounded her forehead with her fist and I winced. Her attention went to me. "Future Almder of Estreldez, our Lord Zorn will speak with you."

"Luan?" Vareo's voice flooded my ears from within and I walked past them both to see him.

"Expecting me to stay locked up, were you?" I brushed back the moisture from my eyes not wishing for him to see the weakness I had almost shown the guards in the hall. My voice was hard, the betrayal burning up my throat.

"You needed an army," he stated simply, like that explained everything.

I glared at him, waiting for more.

He cleared his throat, and it was Lord Zorn that answered beside him, "All of Zorn is at your service, and you'll be pleased to know that the fleets are willing and uncoerced into their efforts to protect Estreldez from King Sylve or any political arrangements with the Krelins."

That didn't make any sense. There was a price to be paid simply to convince Lord Zorn to give Vareo an anti-nanobug serum, let alone a fleet of warriors at Estreldez's disposal. I narrowed my eyes at the tall, confident Lord Zorn with his braids dangling with bones about his exposed chest. Those mischievous eyes twinkled in return.

"You're joining this war?" I asked incredulously at this turn of events. What exactly did Vareo say to him? And why did he do this on his own? Was this another betrayal, a trap?

It was Vareo that answered this time, but he walked towards me extending his hand, "You stood in this very spot, defiance on your tongue, seeking to battle whoever would come should they seek to retrieve me from your planet upon our return. You said with a fierceness I keep replaying in my mind, you are not powerless to defend against threats against us. We were an 'us' before you had ever labeled that which stirs inside. To repeat your wise words, me staying out of it doesn't do either of us any good."

His hand reached my cheek and cupped it gently as he forced me to look him in the eyes.

"I meant that you shouldn't be making deals with slave traders when we would figure things out when we got to Estreldez. My planet is not defenseless, and doesn't make deals with—"

Vareo lifted my chin up, and stilled my breath with his nose trailing from my forehead down the bridge of my nose to reach my lips as his mouth crashed into mine. Uncaring of our audience the pressure between us built up until his tongue sought refuge within to taste more of me.

Sensing the heat of need pulsing from his skin made my eyes grow wide at the realization that he was once again producing radiation that my loh responded to the more his mating runes glowed a bright blue, illuminating the room in a haze. My back loh pulsed until they grew, bursting in diamond-like wings behind my back as he deepened the kiss further.

I bit his lip, tasting the tang of iron in his blood, but he did not flinch from me. Nothing but a low possessive growl tore through his throat encouraging the untamed want within me to take what I desired. And I desired him.

He hadn't betrayed me, but somehow gained the army of the Lord Zorn to help my planet, and all I had done was doubt him. Guilt made me pull back from him, panting, but his arm grabbed my waist and tightened his hold on me, making my thighs press together to ease the throbbing at my core from being denied finishing what we had started earlier in our room.

Vareo whispered deep and husky into my ear, "I will not be kept away from you, My Sun. Tell me that I am yours and you may have me."

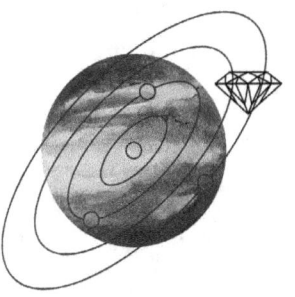

Chapter Thirty

Luan

M y throat was dry, and my lips ached to have his mouth on me again. He was agreeing to stay with me despite what may come for us when we reached Estreldez. I couldn't deny that in the moments I had resigned myself to letting him go, my whole body had wilted in pain. Could I have this one truth? Was I allowed this one pleasure?

I nodded up at him, lacing my hand behind his neck and he flinched. making me pause before his eyes warmed and he pulled me into his arms before I could change my mind about what I was agreeing to.

"Say it, My Sun, My Moon," he growled into my hair.

"You're mine," my voice soft but filled with lust at the admission.

"Louder," he said while nipping at my ear, making me gasp.

"Mine!" I claimed while he lifted me by my bottom to wrap my legs around his waist. His external cock was hard against my warm core already seeking the mating fluids my body prepared as his hands squeezed my ass. A few of his fingers moved underneath to rub at my entrance, making me squirm and my back loh protectively closed around us shielding us from prying eyes.

Vareo muffled my moan with his hungry lips, and his finger slid up and down my pussy teasingly avoiding my clit as his other hand gripped my ass pulling me harder against his shaft secured behind too many layers of material. I tugged at his vest clasps, needing to feel his skin without interference. My fingers stopped again remembering that we were not alone. Noticing my hesitation he pulled away slightly and the cold air between us made me whimper in protest.

"As much as I am yours, you are mine, and I will show them all how brightly you shine only for me. Do you understand, My Sun, My Moon, My Mate?" With each title he nipped at my lip teasing a moan before licking one of my fangs, sending a shiver down my spine.

My mate... that was the one that truly had my loh humming in response as I pressed myself against his cock straining between us, digging my heels into his firm ass as I clamped around him.

Slowly, one of my back loh lowered to find Lord Zorn rubbing his trousers with hooded eyes. Even Pri-Re gripped the side of the entryway panting with her mouth slightly parted and her eyes staring at us with need. I blinked in my confusion at what was happening. I was no stranger to watching the mating ceremony on Estreldez every cycle, but I had never participated, nor had I felt any urges while watching pairs choose a mate beneath the moon's rays.

"Ah, trill," Pri-Re grumbled with a moan as she finally gave in to unstrap her briefs, plunging her hand between her legs to relieve the pressure brewing there. The haziness of my loh's radiation pulsed through the room, and I watched as the runes peeking out from Vareo's clothes matched in rhythm.

It was as if we were under the mating moons themselves, within their thrall.

Vareo guided my eyes back to him, nudging me with his nose, his voice gravely, "Only for me, My Mate." I had no desire for the guards, or Lord Zorn around us, but there was something primal about claiming Vareo in front of their eyes, letting them know he was mine. Was this what my people felt when they mated every cycle? I shook my head of the thought because I couldn't imagine feeling this way for any other mate.

This was different, I assured myself.

My loh flexed outward from my back, no longer hiding us from view. Vareo held me with one arm, a finger pushing up into my core past the feathered out skirts as I clenched him, wrapping my arms around his shoulders. I never appreciated my planet's clothing as much as I did in that moment, nothing preventing his touch except his own ludicrous space suit. His mouth sought out mine as he gently moved his finger against my walls, eliciting another throaty groan.

I grabbed for his trousers to release more of his body to me, but he shifted my weight to stop me from my pursuit. "Vareo..." I practically begged him to give me what I needed. He had said he was mine, that I was his, and...

He eased me down, his finger slowly releasing from my core, and I tried to cling to him with my legs so he simply bent to his knees and lowered me to my back with my loh spanned around us. A lusty grin on his face he demanded, "Burn for me, My Mate." Trailing kisses down my throat he slipped from my leg's hold to lick the loh under my breast, sending tingles through my muscles, heating down to my center.

Every touch searing, every lick purposeful, until his tongue flicked around my nipple, enveloping it within his hot lips. Sucking and then lightly tugging for just a hint of pain within the pleasure to blind me from the desperate future that awaited us for this decision we made to be together.

Nothing but pleasure radiated from us, and I did indeed burn for him. For the release that he offered that I'd never felt before him. Uncaring of who witnessed what he did to me, and what I did to him. Our audience was forgotten as his mouth reached my entrance, teasing his tongue between my folds protecting the bundle of nerves eager for his ministrations. Flinging my head back I moaned, and thrust my hips up for him to feast upon my juices.

Wrapping his arms beneath my legs, he pulled me in so my knees draped over his shoulders and buried himself between my thighs, freeing his hands to slip near my vibrating clit. A finger tapped softly around the sensitive tissue around my swollen gland, then pressed down and rotated up and around the nub expertly drawing out the sensations and building up the pressure I couldn't describe other than sublime. I gripped the cushions beneath me, remembering that Lord Zorn's office was littered with cozy spots to sit on the ground, and a sudden awareness struck me that we were not alone.

My eyes panicked, searching the room and more guards had gathered around us, watching in various stages of unrequited need filling their hooded eyes. Vareo clamped down on my clit, sucking it into his mouth and flicking it with his tongue to regain my attention.

"Oh, moons!" I squealed with his renewed vigor.

He released me only to lick his lips, and those dark eyes melted me with the words, "Have you forgotten my name? Let me remind you the only name you should be screaming is mine." Vareo delved back down, and plunged a finger into my core, then another, and then a third with the next stroke stretching me to take the one thing he has yet to give me and I needed more than anything.

My core tightened around his fingers as my body spasmed a pleasure-filled release leaking fluids down my cheeks lifted in the air, my back loh fluttered behind me, and I screamed. A whimper escaped as he removed his fingers and a cold air touched me as he lowered my limp legs to the ground. Rubbing my thighs together to ease the absence of him, he stood back to watch me.

"Do not close yourself to me," his voice lowered, a sinister quality that sent shivers down my spine. My eyes fluttered as I saw behind him the room was filled with voyeurs crowding the space, their excitement at what they were witnessing building as they watched. Some touched themselves, others fisted their hands delaying their pleasure. "Luan," his voice husky, "I will not repeat myself."

Something about this demanding side of him made my insides tingle with warmth, because I knew he would not force himself on me. This was my choice. It was always my choice.

I opened myself to him, one knee out, then lifted my foot to the side spreading my other, leaving my throbbing sex on display for him. Vareo groaned in response, but kept himself held back, tantalizingly removing the visages of his pants down his legs until his cock sprung forth eager to be free of the restrictions that bound it not moments before. Ridges pulsed on the sides of his shaft, and I bit my lip, drawing a drop of blood in my anticipation that I licked up, watching him stalk forward at a pace that was twisting my insides in knots.

Drinking in every inch of his muscular body, my core leaked in preparation for our mating. My hand reached down to rub the ache building within, needing to be touched. His dark eyes roamed over my exposed folds leading to my matehood, and his nostrils flared as what was left of his patience withered along with my own. As my fingers stroked faster, he quickly kneeled between my opened thighs. Leaning forward, his cock was as solid as rock, and pressed against my entrance giving my fingers pause to slather the pulsing beast with my slickness. I guided the large head of his cock up and down the length of my wet folds heating me up from the inside.

My hips ground up seeking to fill the void there, and my clit hummed with appreciation, making him grow feral with need, yet he stilled himself. Those dark eyes watched me.

"Mine," he gritted, waiting for me to deny his claim.

I simply nodded and lifted my forehead to touch his. His mating runes glowed, creating a blue haze around us and it was like being surrounded by the moon's radiation, so warm, and all mine.

"Forever," he added huskily.

I gasped, and remembered that his species claimed only one mate, but everything about having only him felt right. He was home. I nodded once more.

"Say it," he begged as his cock pressed against me making me moan.

"Forever," I agreed as he wrapped me up in his arms pillaging my mouth, his cock stretching me to meld around him more and more with each stroke of his hips until he was seated to the hilt within me. Then we both stilled as my loh throbbed, and his cock pulsed in sync. Waves of sensations coursed through my body to the tips of my ears and curling my toes. I moaned into his hungry kisses, and then he slowly eased out and then back in, pooling energy at my core with every stroke.

Chapter
Thirty-One
Vareo

Pulling Luan tighter against me, I smothered my face in her hair and inhaled the sweet scent of her and still smelled the scent of her arousal on my face when I drank her in. To hear those words that she was mine, and she accepted me as hers burned deep in my belly, warming every limb and muscle.

My mate.

Everything about her was perfect, like she was designed by the gods for me alone. And everyone in this room and across the Zorn fleets knew that she was mine. No one would hope to earn the look in those silver eyes that was given only to me, and all those who even thought to try would remember this cycle and know to touch her was to seek my wrath, and the wrath of all those who followed me.

Did they see me now?

See what was mine and mine alone given to me freely.

I growled into her neck and licked the sweat from her skin before kissing one of her jeweled loh, granting me another sweet moan from my mate's lips before I plunged hard into her welcoming core. Her heels dug into my ass seeking to be filled completely, and there was only one way to fulfill that final wish.

For a shol to claim an estreld, it had never been done before, but I had no fear that it would work. We fit perfectly together. Her clit vibrated along my shaft as I groaned once more. I couldn't hold on for much longer, everything in me wanted to finish my claim. My mating runes were brighter than I ever thought would be possible.

Luan's hands reached to cup my cheek and guide me back to her lush lips that I had no qualms plundering once more as I buried myself deep within her. Breathing heavy, she watched me with lust filled icy eyes, so cold they were hot.

"Vareo," she gasped my name as her body quivered beneath me. I slowed my rhythm down to let her ride her wave of pleasure with my name in the air for all to hear who she calls for.

"My Sun, My Moon... My Mate," I growled, lifting her up still riding my cock before I released her. The absence of her warmth was excruciating, but it wouldn't be long before I returned to the new home she's made for me between her legs. I eased her around, and slid my cock along her entrance once more, wanting all of our spectators to see my claim as her diamond-winged loh fluttered behind her. She was a goddess. An angel from the heavens.

I wrapped my hand around her front to replace the hand she was using to pinch her own nipple, massaging the loh around her soft mounds. Her fingers laced with mine, guiding me to where she needed me, our hands sinking down together as I nibbled her ear.

"I need you inside me," she panted.

Sliding my fingers along her folds I stuck one finger within and spread my hand out to angle her ass up. Her core clamped down around my finger and I pressed myself against my hand to ease myself back inside, feeling the tightness of her resist my head from reentry. She rocked her hips back and forth, my finger slid in and out, making her shiver and release just enough for me to press the head of my cock in next to my finger. Rubbing my finger against her wall my cock stopped at one of my ridges until she slammed her ass back, filling herself to the brim with my shaft and my finger stuck underneath.

"Fuck," I moaned as her pussy gripped me so tight that it was near milking my seed right then.

She wiggled her ass against me as she glanced over her shoulder at me. "That's not my name, my mate."

Say it again, I needed her to say it again. Call me her mate. My runes warmed all over my body, sending waves of pleasure through every muscle.

"Luan," I rasped out huskily and her loh glowed at her back, spreading out to wrap around me.

She grinned and I slipped my finger out from her pussy to grab her chin. Undoing every ounce of civility within me as she wrapped her tongue around my finger. I leaned over to devour her cheeky mouth with mine, needing to taste her juices myself.

Her clit vibrated against my balls, and I held her close to my chest as she sucked on my finger and I kissed the loh on her neck as my cock increased speed within her. Both our breathing was labored as I felt the energy of my mating runes coil and brim with need.

I grunted into her ear, nibbling at her lobe, "Forever, My Heart."

My seed spilled within her, and Luan spasmed around my shaft, milking every drop in time with her own pleasure. My ridges spiked, clinging within her, and I stilled, kissing the side of her forehead. She wiggled at the sensation of my cock marking her and I groaned.

"What is that?" she asked while her hand laced up into my hair to pull me into a kiss which I gladly partook.

I sighed nipping at her lip before replying, "You've been injected with the same cells that make up my mating runes."

Her spine went rigid against me, and I tried to explain in a more eloquent way, "You'll bear my very essence within you. A shol is only able to claim a mate once, and the cells will allow me to find you to protect you if you're nearby, but it also means only the one with my mark will draw my seed. Only you." She shivered.

Hesitantly she whispered realizing we had an audience still, "Will your cells influence my biology?" Concern laced her words, and I realized what she wasn't saying, will my mark influence her feelings for me? Are her choices her own? Is she still free?

A pang touched my heart that she would want to be rid of me, but I tamped that feeling down to hear her out once she knew the truth of things.

"No, My Sun. You are still you, but the mark will enhance your pleasure when you are with me as the runes are best when they are united. The mark does nothing to hinder whatever choices you may make, only my own," I admitted the last part reluctantly. The very idea of someone else claiming what is so clearly marked by me jarred my very soul and hot rage sparked within me before her soft cheek rubbed against my chest and I felt her smile. My cock pulsed within her, our bodies still linked together.

A shyness overcame her as she blushed, witnessing our audience's arousal in the aftermath from our display, and now that we were finished many were rushing out to do the same amongst themselves. I kissed her temple and eased my cock from her, even that, was a feeling like no other. The glow of our bond. Already I felt myself hardening once more for another round, but knew there were things to address, and our whole lives to show each other more pleasure.

"There are some things I must tell you," I rubbed at my neck where my brand had already healed during our love making. Her silver orbs followed the movement and lingered where my hair had been shorn.

Chapter Thirty-Two

Luan

I adjusted my skirts around myself and lifted a few strands up to lace them around my neck to cover my breasts to some degree. Vareo appeared very serious despite standing naked for all the ship to see. He was a vision, confident and poised even with his organs hanging down his leg. I smiled to myself, clenching my thighs together at the thought of his cock ramming into my core, filling me so completely only just moments before. It was so strange that it wasn't long ago that I thought it absurd to have one's reproductive organs on the outside, but now that I see them displayed for me I wouldn't have it any other way.

The people had fled the room, I didn't even see Lord Zorn around since we'd started, and I now knew how my people felt after the mating ceremony. There was no shame, only a glow of knowing this was my mate, and everyone knew he was mine. I brimmed, feeling my loh brighten as if I'd spent the night under the moon's rays.

What could possibly be on my mate's mind that he would look so serious, I thought for a brief moment before reality reminded me my entire planet was staring down war.

I gulped, uncertain of which disaster he would speak of first.

This was not the afterglow of our mating that I was anticipating, but he was right. There were things to discuss.

I nodded for him to continue, watching as his hand lifted to a newly shaved half of his scalp which made him look quite rugged. As he moved his hand I saw the start of that brand I had been curious about not that long ago. Though it was different even from the one I saw on Lord Zorn himself. This scorched bird, he turned his head more knowing I needed to see the whole of it, revealing a sword inked over the bird, but also freshly pinked flesh in the shape of a heart. I searched Vareo's dark eyes as if they would hold the answers without a word, but I couldn't read more than the guilt as he closed them to me with a sigh.

"You've been branded once more," I said hushed like that would make it less real. If I said it soft enough that it would disappear and fly from here taking with it the implications of the words I've released.

I raised my voice, "You've committed yourself back to slavery in exchange for the fleets, haven't you." It wasn't a question. I knew there was a price, and the look on his face said enough. "Take it back. We do not need them. We will face our future together."

Vareo smiled and cupped my face in his large hand, not even bothering to cover himself.

"Spoken like a true leader, but even a blazing sun like you needs planets to rotate around your beauty. You see the reason in needing your own force un-reliant on the krelin."

I bit my lip, and grimaced. "Not like this. Is this force any better than choosing to align with the krelin?"

His lips pressed gently to my forehead and he breathed in the scent of my hair deeply. "The Slaves of Zorn are at your mercy, My Queen. Do with them as you will, but know that the fleets will not demand a single return from Estreldez."

"Why would they do that?" I shook my head trying to comprehend what he was trying to tell me.

"Because I was the one who defeated my Lord Zorn when King Sylve sought to teach me a lesson for my behaviors. Genbi took my place to reform the business in my absence."

"That would mean..."

I gaped at him in panic, not wanting what he was saying to be true.

"I am the true heir and rightful leader of the slaves, Lord Zorn."

My mouth dried, tasting of sandpaper, and in need of water immediately after hearing those words.

"Lord Zorn," I nearly choked. "So, when you said you would join the slaves before you meant—"

"To take up my title, yes."

"Lord Zorn, I mean Genbi, he said it was a high cost, he meant—"

"Being Lord Zorn is a tainted commitment and once I've claimed it, it can't be undone. I've already forfeited my rights to Genbi before finishing my brand, that isn't an option again. There are things I will be forced to do that I won't be proud of, and the road to saving the slaves is covered in the grime of decisions that will alter my soul, but with you I know I'll be strong enough to overcome the darkness."

I pushed him back to glare at him. "You could dismantle this all!"

He lowered his eyes in disappointment. "Only to have it rebuilt by someone else. Would you give their lives to someone else who doesn't see them, who wasn't them?"

The chants from earlier all made sense now, and my heart broke at the vulnerability in Vareo's eyes. He needed me to tell him that his choice was okay, that I accepted this darkness within him.

"Is that why you need the sun in your life? To help you burn away the darkness?" I stepped forward, perfectly aware of what I was committing myself to. I wouldn't let him fall into the clutches of what his title would demand of him. We would run this trade together, but they would not be slaves anymore. If what Pri-Re said is true, then when Lord Zorn purchases slaves they will have more choice than they ever did in their lives before.

These fleets can be used for more than simply protecting Estreldez, but for protecting life in this system.

He searched my face for confirmation of what I was saying and I continued, "If all of your slaves are more free than any estreld faced with tough choices about preserving our future, then why can't Lord Zorn be a protector instead of a trader of broken lives?"

"I would love nothing more than to have you as the protector of my soul, My Sun."

Vareo pulled me into his arms and my back loh wrapped around him, still extended despite our mating having finished. It was unusual for loh to not recede back when not stimulated. Even Vareo's mating runes were black, only faintly glowing as I trailed my fingers over them.

"We'll face the darkness together," I said, lifting myself onto my tip toes to touch my lips to his.

The seam of his mouth parted for me to enter and our tongues pushed against each other vying for more pressure as

257

our kiss deepened. My heart fluttered knowing that for once I'd be able to keep what I wanted and make a difference that saved people's lives. My mother would not approve of settling for one mate, but something buried within me wondered if perhaps estrelds were always meant to feel what I was feeling now wrapped within Vareo's embrace. Complete.

Whatever war awaited us when we arrived at Estreldez, we would face it together.

Chapter Thirty-Three

Epilogue- Luan

W e would have to return to Estreldez soon. As much as I didn't like to admit weakness to myself, I had been naive about traveling the galaxy without a way to sustain the radiation provided by my moons. Having more loh jewels to absorb the moon's rays was a blessing, but I'd come to understand from the medics aboard Zorn's ship that it was also a curse. My loh were dependent on radiation to sustain my life, and relying on Vareo to generate what I needed was taking a toll on him.

His mating runes barely glowed anymore when I touched him. I was draining him. His life...

The hard lines of his jaw were softer as he slept beside me. My fingers trailed over his moving mate marks, blackened with only a faint blue essence as I touched them, some spots didn't light at all. Even the blue I'd become accustomed to in his eyes was gone, only the dark brown from his first holo-images remained. They were mesmerizing no matter the color, filled with a sweetness held only for me, but the reason behind the change was disconcerting.

"If you stare at me much longer, I may burn for your attention," he lazily mumbled, half asleep still, but awake enough to grab my hand from his shoulder and pull me astride his waist with little effort at all. I could feel the hard length of his interest, and he seemed unconcerned with the consequences of bonding before the ship made it back to Estreldez. Did he even know what might happen to him if the light of his shol runes faded completely? The loh on my back were shrinking day by day, and though claiming him as my mate healed me when I was injured... this was not sustainable. We knew returning meant running into King Sylve's warships, but did I have a choice?

We hadn't even attempted to contact my Almder or the Krelis warships, not wanting to be traced by our communications, losing any chance of a surprise encounter when we made it back to our sector. I didn't want to ask to return to Estreldez without knowing we were prepared for what awaited us either. Sending the Zorn ships into an ambush was not an option for the sake of my health. I was only one life, but with Vareo as my mate... that made it two, because I knew he would sacrifice himself to save me. He would be ruined regardless. A shol mated for life, and without their mate... they'd go insane... or join their mate in death.

I couldn't let that happen.

"I don't know what to do," I confessed, about to slip off the side to lay next to him once more, but he gripped my thighs, and stopped my retreat. His dark eyes were focused, more alert, and the sleepiness faded as he prepared to once again reassure me that we would get through this together. For someone with the history he had, he was much more optimistic than I was.

"Luan," he said my name with a sternness that demanded I pay attention to his next words, "Fear stops leaders across the galaxy from admitting they have any weaknesses or that they even know what the fuck they're doing half the time. They don't. I don't. And you certainly aren't required to know the future either."

"But my," I corrected myself, "our decisions will affect people's lives, and whether they have a future at all."

His black eyes glowed slightly, creating a ring of blue around them as they softened into that look that made my insides warm.

"That is why they can trust you to lead them, because you care that they have one, and you'll work hard to make sure they do."

I frowned, merely shaking my head in denial of his statement. How could I be trusted at all when I'd hardly call what I was doing hard work. I was safely protected by the guards of Lord Zorn, and this ship was avoiding the scouts sent after us by King Sylve. It wouldn't be long before tactics would change, and he'd make an effort to destroy an easier target to lure me out of hiding. I was easy to predict, because I couldn't live with myself if my life was put above the millions of slaves under Lord Zorn's command. Slaves... the word brought a bitter taste to my tongue and curdled my stomach. I felt sick accepting that they would fight for a cause that I couldn't be sure they agreed to support.

"Work hard doing what?" I snapped, and I regretted my harsh manner as soon as I saw the way the cold hardness of his jaw set in. He was retreating within himself, as if he were an offspring once more, and I were his master. How could I lead anyone when I was capable of making him feel so small, while he was merely trying to encourage me. I was nobody's light. I was darkness itself hiding behind the stars.

"This isn't a fight for one estreld, or one shol. Your insecurities are nothing to the fate of all those who are under Zorn's protection, under the Almder's protection. It isn't weakness to accept your uncertainty. It's weakness if you do nothing about that knowledge." His hand lifted to my cheek to turn my gaze back on him, making sure I'd listen. "You don't have to fight, clawing at your enemy's eyes, to be doing something. I thought I'd failed finding the Jewel of Estreldez, only to find I'd had her in my grasp all along, and she'd given me her heart. I didn't fight anyone at all. I ran. Do you think me a coward?"

I shook my head once more, fresh moisture brimming at my eyes. "You know I don't."

"We won't run forever," Vareo promised. "My Mate, sometimes the mere threat of defeat is enough to win wars. King Sylve is outnumbered between the Krelis warfleet and Lord Zorn's network of outlaws."

An idea suddenly brightened in my mind, and my mouth fell before sputtering with excitement, "That's it! You're a genius!" I squeezed his hand to my cheek and smiled.

His toothy grin was skeptical of my pronouncement, and he chuckled, "And what do I get for being a genius?" He shifted his hips, and I felt his hardening length beneath me, keenly aware that I was still astride him in that moment. I had grown used to sleeping in his chambers with nothing to cover my sensitive flesh, and as he adjusted, I felt his cock slip between my wet folds, already prepared for him. The tip of his girth prodded at my entrance, and I mewled with delight, but I had to tell him my thoughts before they were lost in pleasure.

"We need to make him think he's won, that we've given in to the threat of defeat. And find a way to advance the trill fight to happen here. We'll have a common enemy to focus on and he won't have time to think of another way to survive without joining with us. The war is coming regardless, we might as well face it together with all of the sector's force, including King Sylve."

"I like it when you talk tactics to me, My Burning Sun." He smiled up at me before he lifted me by my ass and rotated to grip my hips to grind my clit against his shaft. My insides clenched and the vibration from his ridges made my mind clear of any thoughts of the future. I lived in the now that begged to have him fill me, but thoughts of his fading mate marks stilled my response.

"Vareo..." I grabbed his hand from my hip and lifted it to my heart. My finger trailed down his forearm to show him the changes I've been noticing. The faint blue from my touch was scattered, and some spots didn't glow at all. He gave me a lopsided grin, dismissing the issue. "What happens if the mating glow is gone?"

He shrugged but let his grin fade to one more befitting the seriousness of the matter. "There are no elders to ask about this. And even if there were, it's doubtful they'd know anything about a fated mate that wasn't shol."

I pressed my lips together as I watched the contemplation play across his face and it grew into one of sadness. The loss of his heritage, his own clan, his species, his planet... it weighed on him. I was still determined to get through this war, not just to be free of this burden, but so we could find what remained of the shol. It wasn't even fathomable to me that Estreldez was very much next in line to become a blip in history, gone the way of Sholonus, and countless other species before us.

A large hand cupped my cheek and rubbed at a tear that had dropped unknowingly from my eyes. I had been staring off, lost in my thoughts, and he brought me back. "What I do know is being near you is the most complete I have felt in my whole life. And when we're together you regain your strength, and my engineering crew has told me to keep you occupied and far away from the engine core from now on if we want any chance of returning us or the crew back to civilization, no matter the planet."

I flushed of color at being caught sneaking into the engine bay, but I grew irritated and snapped in defense, "I had to find another way to charge my loh. I did it for you!" It was the only source of radiation that felt like it warmed my loh at all, and I figured it was safe enough since engineers wore protective suits when in the engine bay, and I only planned on absorbing what was residual in the room.

He nodded. "I know, but I'm telling you I'm fine, and whatever you did to our engine core had the whole ship panicking. We'll use your other plan. Set up a lure for the trill to meet us at Estreldez, we'll be back soon enough, and I've got what you need right here." Vareo smiled and moved his hips under me while his cock buzzed, sending shivers to my toes. My loh ached to feel the heat of him inside of me, and I wanted to believe him when he said he was fine.

"That's right," he cooed, as I rocked back and forth, allowing my clit to hum up and down his length. The more I moved the more my inner walls flexed and throbbed, until the head of him seated in the nook of my entrance, catching as it sought purchase within my folds. I was wet for him, and the ridges of his shaft hardened. I adjusted to apply pressure, seeking to have him sink within my welcoming core, but he moved his hips at an angle to have his length slip between us. I groaned in both enjoyment at how delicious he felt rubbing up against my sensitive flesh, but also in annoyance at the loss of the expectation that there would be nothing between us as he thrusted into my heat.

"Tell me what you want," he demanded, while I moved to capture his cock once more. His hand reached to grip the base of his shaft, and he agonizingly tortured me with languid strokes passing over and around where I needed him the most.

I should be using this excuse to stop myself, to stop us from merging once more when I had suspicions about what it was doing to our mate bond. But I was as lost to him as he was to me. Resisting this magnetism between us was like asking the moons to stop warming Estreldez. It was against everything it stood for, to ask the moon to stop radiating would be asking it to die.

Lunging forward to take his lips with mine, I moaned into his mouth my desires. "I need you."

"Take what you need, my mate," he said with a husky growl, his fangs nipping at my lower lip.

I wrapped my hand around his, guiding his cock through my folds. As the head of his hardened length sunk in, I closed my eyes with both relief and a delicious ache as I stretched for him. I clenched, stalling as I flexed around his thickness, enjoying the warmth and pulses that shuddered through my muscles before I relaxed enough for him to slip a little deeper.

"More," I panted as I worked my tongue into his mouth and sought to remove all semblance of distance between us that it felt like I had to devour him to feel whole. Thrusting my hips down, I clenched as I took all of him and felt the subtle vibration of his ridges setting my nerves on fire. My fingers dug into his arms as I bent over, my eyes clenched shut as my inner walls throbbed and pulsed with a sudden, quick release. The sensation so fast I gasped and panted against his chest before he chuckled and began moving his hips against me once more.

"For you, I will give everything," he said as the blue from his eyes shone brighter than I had seen them in days. The glow of his mating runes comforted me that he would be okay, that our bond would be okay. My skin hummed with the contact, and the pain in my loh released as he filled and moved within me.

He was everything, I thought as his arms wrapped around my back and glided down to grip my ass. Vareo's hands kneaded and guided my hips as he pulled to add extra pressure with every stroke. I felt my orgasm build again, and the achingly slow rhythm we had was like riding a wave of pleasure that I wanted to stride forever and yet also be completely consumed, drowning in the inevitable break when it crested. It shouldn't be possible to feel this whole, this addicted to a single spec of beautiful existence within such a vast, dark universe. Yet, here I was seeking to merge in the vacuum created by this magnificently resilient creature.

We moved together, our bodies in a synchronized poem gifted to us by the goddess. Rocking back and forth, in and out. His thrusts became more frenzied as our breathing quickened. The whole room filled with a hazy blue created by his runes and my loh, pulsing as one. I slammed my palm into the wall behind his head and moaned into his pointed ears. His cock pumped inside of me, tapping furiously at the back of my core, sending shivers through my arms, touching a deep part of me that only he could reach. With a scream, I shattered in our otherworldly glow.

As I opened my eyes all of the blue in Vareo's eyes was gone, and the bright glow of our mating bond clung to my skin. I smiled into his neck, and played with his ears as I panted, still feeling my folds throb and ache around him. His shol heritage fascinated me. Even the tips of his ears were made to help him hear things farther away than most, and it was always a shock that he could handle how loud we were when we mated.

"Are you sure you're okay?" I asked, shy despite our current position. What was the point of asking it now that I'd taken what I wanted already? What was done was done, and I couldn't undo that I'd ignored my instincts that without my moons I was broken somehow.

"There is nowhere else I'd rather be," he assured, but as I touched the mating runes on his neck with my nose, there was no response on his skin for me. My heartrate picked up for an entirely different reason, and I clutched at his chest, then scrambled back to touch more of him. Nothing, I lamented with shame.

I rubbed my fingers across his runes softly, then with more friction.

Fuck, I cried out in my mind, and fresh tears formed, threatening to overflow from my eyes. His hands grabbed mine in his, and he rubbed with his thumb in pleasant circles, but it wasn't the same. The tingling and warmth I felt from our bond... it was gone.

What have I done?

Before I could question him about how he was feeling, because he certainly wasn't admitting to any changes, the intercoms in our room chimed, and without any other warning Genbi's voice spoke, "A warship is headed through the planet debri-field, it's possible they will pass by and consider us part of the debri on their scanners, but you should head to the command bridge and prepare for contact."

Vareo took a moment to smile at me with softness in his brown eyes, before he kissed the stray tear that had fallen down my cheek. First he addressed Genbi, "We're close to AsunGor. Prepare a shuttle and hide yourself within the debri, making your way to the planet. If they pass us then we'll come to pick you up. If they don't, you have orders to stay on planet and convince the AsunGor to join the fight."

"They will honor a battle in their own orbit, but it is not the way of our clans to fight so impersonally," Genbi replied, but I already knew he wasn't waiting for any response from Vareo. The communication was already disconnected, and he'd already be heading to the shuttle bay and preparing to follow the command. They were like brothers, and there was a respect there despite their difference in species.

"You should meet him at the shuttle bay, the planet AsunGor has a hot spring that is infused with the planet's core radiation. It's possible it will help until the Krelis' ships are able to bring tarnpul from Estreldez."

"What are you talking about?" We hadn't been in contact with anyone, we were keeping a low profile, not allowing our communications to be traced, weren't we? I shook my head, realizing what he was saying. He didn't. He couldn't.

He eased himself from my core, and I ached with the absence of him. Gripping my hands in his, he sighed. "I was hoping we had more time."

"Vareo," I gritted, demanding he confirm my suspicions.

"The warship is the Viper-Raul. I knew they would trace the communication to Krelis and to Estreldez, but we can't keep you from your planet much longer. We both knew this was coming, but I agree with you on your plan. Go with Genbi, and lure the trill into a trap that they don't have time to fully understand. We need a trill ship on our side, and you're the one to make it happen. I know it."

My lip was trembling. He was asking me to leave him to deal with King Sylve on his own. "No," I said with a sob.

A sad smile showed me his beautiful fangs, and he pressed his forehead to mine. "I need you," he admitted, and it made my heart ache all the more. He'd never once said that so bluntly. I knew we needed each other, but for him to say it meant he didn't know if we'd see each other again.

"No," I repeated, and he captured my refusal with his lips, tasting the salt of my tears.

"I have a promise to keep."

"You promised, together," I reminded him, and wrapped my arms around his neck, pulling him close.

"Always." He placed his hand over my heart, where his mark showed on my skin. "No matter where we are, we are together."

I knew what he was doing. He was sacrificing himself and I wouldn't have it any of it. I closed my eyes as I accepted what I had to do.

"Always," I repeated his words with a sad smile, kissing his neck. I'd taken all of our mating glow into myself, and I let my loh extend from my back as much as they could. The jewel shards layered on themselves like deathly wings, and I surrounded our heads with them until I focused all of my energy towards my mate, warming his skin.

"Luan?" he questioned too late, before I saw the blue glow of my radiation dissipate through the room and I slumped in his arms. "What have you done?"

My hand slipped from his cheek, and I smiled. "There's a med pod on Viper Raul, use me as leverage to lure King Sylve back to Estreldez. Have Genbi use his connections on AsunGor to tell the trill they are complaining about a faulty nanobot they purchased from Necias Delta Fal. It's too minor of an issue to send a fleet, but I know the AsunGor are politically powerful with the alliance. They will send a ship. King Sylve can capture it."

Vareo rubbed my cheeks as I felt the warmth leave my body. He couldn't refuse my plan, not when Viper Raul had the med bay I needed, and I knew the mate bond between us wouldn't sustain me any longer. He could choose to go to AsunGor and bet on the hot springs, but I knew he wouldn't leave my life to chance.

He held my head to his chest and rocked back and forth, holding me close.

"I'll do it," he said finally, and I could hear the soft whine of the ship as I trusted our lives with the trust that King Sylve wouldn't turn away an opportunity to have control over a trill ship. He could betray us then, but it would be enough time to have the tarnpul infused with the moon's rays to reach us, and we'd have the support of the Krelis warships.

It had to work. For everyone's sake. This plan had to succeed.

Not injured like I was before, I knew the sleep claiming me was my body's way of preventing my radiation from being expended, but if this was the last thing I saw then I was glad it was within Vareo's arms as his jaw hardened into determination. Relaxing in his hold, I allowed the plan I forced on him to tumble into reality. I wasn't proud of my decision to take his choice away, but he already did the same thing to me when he contacted Krelis and Estreldez, leading the Viper Raul straight to us.

What a pair we made, I thought with a mischievous smile and closed my eyes.

Thank you for Reading Her Alien Bandit! Previously Titled Jewel of the Alien Bandit, but now with bonus content of a 15-page epilogue and a fresh new sexy cover!

Loved Reading Her Alien Bandit? Smash that star button or leave a review at all the places reviews can be found to help fuel more steamy goodness and encourage Sky Robert's next release to cum faster! (Wink.) You're welcome.

Review HerAlien Bandit on Goodreads

Review Her Alien Bandit on Amazon

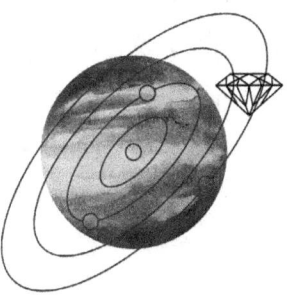

Author Note

T hank you for reading Her Alien Bandit! This was my first attempt into the alien romance genre, though I admit I endeavored into this genre because of my addiction to reading them, and then finding I was a mood reader that was missing a certain kind of alien romance to break up between the ones I was currently reading. I found I was reading a lot of the books I was reading had the couples accepting their love too soon, and thus the romance part of the story was resolved while the universe plot continued on with the added steamy scene here and there. I lost interest in caring about what happened to the universe because the romance plot line felt finished. So, I wanted to create my own universe with an interwoven plot line between all the books, which allowed me to have the tug and pull of the relationships and the standalone stories end when the romance is accepted, while the plot of the universe unfolds over the course of reading standalone romances. I get the alien romance hit I was craving, to have the tension back in the romance, and still unraveling the universe at the same time, what's better is that each book can be started at any time, in any order. They all layer without spoiling the romance of the others.

Your reviews, your ratings, your comments, and excitement for books helps fuel more books! So, thank you, and keep sending the love by leaving your own review/rating, sharing your love of the Trillume Universe to other alien lovers and let me know what you think of Her Alien Bandit! Are you excited to read Mabel's fated mate in Her Alien Prince next? Are there other characters you want to see more of? Your excitement and suggestions help fuel ideas and nudge me towards writing the next book as fast as my fingers can rub some words onto a page, so keep cheering!

Her Alien Prince is the next book in the universe, with Mabel and Trent. And yes, every book is a standalone and can be read in any order, but I HIGHLY recommend reading Her Alien Prince and Her Alien Savior to prepare for Her Alien Insurgent (as you meet GAVEN in Her Alien Prince and you meet ASHLEY in Her Alien Savior.) I also have plans to write a prequel romance before the alien exchange was established on Earth, that will probably come out in December.

To follow along on what's coming, see teasers, progress, what I'm reading, exclusive goodies, or just say, "hi", join my newsletter and grab Her Alien Exchange for freesies, or join the Sky's Smut Between the Pages on Facebook! I hang out on Instagram more often than Twitter these days, so give me a follow: @authorsteviemarie

Thank you so much for being a fan of my alien romances, it means the world to my squishy heart.

Sky

Her Alien Prince

T reasures of Trillume Book Two (Standalone-read in any order)– Available Now in Kindle Unlimited: Click here to borrow: https://books.steviemarie.com/heralienprince

MABEL

Three loh jewels: one tiny jewel on my forehead and two larger ones on my shoulder blades. That's it. That's all I had to absorb the moon's radiation. Because of that I'd grown small and weak in the eyes of my peers. No male had looked at me with more than pleasant acknowledgement, since coming of age to participate in the mating ceremony.

They weren't mean, not overtly.

I was simply ignored, and it wasn't difficult to be distracted by more accomplished estrelds that glowed in the moon's light.

The mating ceremony had been open to off-worlders for twenty cycles now. I didn't even know who my father was. Nor did I really care to. I'm different from most multi-species because female offspring usually take more after estreld genetics, having just as many loh to absorb the moon's rays as their mothers. Me, well, I only have three.

Three loh... and a freckle on my temple that glowed sometimes.

It was a sign of health to have many loh and, since most female offspring took after their mothers... Well, it wouldn't be wise to choose someone like me with so few loh to help an offspring grow and be strong. With the only mother I knew gone, the craving to have a family of my own burned inside like a cyclone of sand that my skin could hardly contain. I was one of many to my mother. She ran the offspring training center, raising hundreds, thousands even, of young. My only chance to raise even one would be to lure an off-worlder during the mating ceremony this cycle.

This year was my chance. According to all of my research as part of the M.R., Mating Research, team there has been a great correlation between offspring and an estreld's twentieth renewal cycle. I'll be twenty cycles this mating season, one of the first offspring spawn from an off-worlder. There was bad data collection that first cycle. My estreld foster mother didn't even know what species my father was, and my birth mother... well, it was easy enough to disappear into the fabric of duties and never return to the training center again. She could be anyone.

Sometimes, I'd look into the faces of females as they passed, searching for similarities between them and myself. Paying close attention to whether they were taking pity on the girl that had few loh, or if there was something more. Guilt, perhaps? It was foolish, and over the years I cared less about finding either parent. There were many to get to know, and there were many who faded the same way my blood parents did. Estreld males took turns caring after me in hopes of becoming my foster mom's sired mate. She never chose any of them. And I learned not to get too attached to any of them.

"Mabel, I'm glad you're here," Elder Ezra said without looking up from her microscope scanner. "I have your results back from your egg samples. Every estreld is required to be examined before participating in the ceremony, as you know."

She was always very clinical in the way she spoke about the mating ceremony. The future of our species depended on her, and she relied on my data collection from other estrelds by interviewing them before, during, and after mating. That was my job. The more we knew about the intangibles, the more it could guide Ezra's research on the offspring decline.

I correlated the data, and provided statistical probabilities of the likelihood of factors contributing to successful offspring.

"Did you do the tests yourself?" I asked.

Pressing her lips together flat, never a good sign, she clicked off her tablet. Again, not a good sign, prying her away from her work was never easy. Ezra took a deep breath preparing herself, she had never been great with the communication bit of her job. That's why she relied on me to do the social interaction necessary for the job.

"I reran the tests several times myself after hoping there was a mistake with the synthesizer. I wanted to inform you personally before Almder summoned you, as all results are automatically uploaded for her this close to the ceremony. She likes to review them personally and verify electronic data with verbal acknowledgements to confirm their accuracy." She was rambling and relying on facts to help her get through what she needed to say. My heart pounded in my chest, waiting for her to reveal what needed her direct attention. This build up didn't do me any favors, but I couldn't blame Ezra for that. "Mabel, you know as well as I do that we've yet to see any estreld establish offspring with no endometrium to attach to. There is simply no place for the eggs to secure themselves should they fall."

"What are you saying?" My voice quivered with fear for what I knew she would say but didn't want her to confirm. This would mean I failed my examination and would be disqualified from joining the mating ceremony.

"Mabel, if you meet a compatible mate... you would be risking your life. Dropping your eggs without a lining is dangerous. They could try to attach anywhere to seek purchase, and that anywhere could kill you and the unborn offspring. The safest thing for us to do would be to remove your sack from beneath your shoulder glands. You could still have some fun without risking your life," she explained.

I stared at her, stunned. I was twenty cycles... Perfect estreld age for offspring, for starting a family, and she wanted to remove my eggs. Gulping back my fear, I asked, "There's no way to wait until they drop and then safely transfer them to someone else? Or perhaps keep the eggs and test to find a compatible donor to incubate?"

Her eyes lowered and distracted themselves with a spot on the wall, not wishing to look at me directly. "So much technology," she said wistfully. "So much advancement, but I can't risk it. I can't risk you. Of course, there are tools out there," she motioned to the stars outside of Estreldez, "but we don't have an alliance with Trillume directly. We are on the outskirts of the galaxy. Everything we get outside of our planet is from Krelis, and we can't risk trade with Necias Delta Fal. They are outlaws from even their own kind. There's no telling when trill enforcers will return to bring order to this sector, or if we even want them to."

"What do you mean, 'if we even want them to'?" My eyes were stinging as I held back my emotions about being told I was broken. That I wouldn't have a family of my own.

Ezra quieted when she leaned in to say, "Sometimes being left alone is better than the cost of being 'helped'."

But the trill could help me, I thought rebelliously. "Allow me some time to process this," I said, trying to sound stronger than I felt. I knew she would want to perform the surgery to remove my egg sack sooner, rather than risk meeting a compatible mate when all the off-worlders joined shortly. Their ships were already orbiting our largest moon, and they'd be landing once their examinations were verified. It was my job to interview the mating candidates, and Ezra wouldn't want me around any mates if I might be compatible.

"Please return before the ceremony begins," she directed, her usual monotone, business-as-usual voice back in place.

I left the labs and went to meet with the leader of Estreldez, Almder, to see if I could get her approval to continue being her advisor despite my new status as infertile. There was more at risk besides not being able to have my own offspring; my whole career was on the line. Not only was I half estreld and half unknown, I only had three loh and had now failed my mating exam. I would be cast to a new position outside the palace, because it would be seen as a bad omen to have a mating advisor to be infertile. Perhaps I could convince Almder that I could at least train my replacement for a time being.

When I arrived at the central alcove carved from black tarnpul deposits to focus the moon's rays, Almder was busy speaking with a tall male with blonde hair... and horns. A krelin... in such close proximity to our leader, and her guards so far away? Whatever concerns I had for myself vanished as I watched with curiosity and a bit of fear. Luan would be appalled to see such trust shown to the krelins after what they pulled with our last import trade. I'd worked so hard to become an advisor to be of use to Luan when she took over as Almder one day. We were going to change Estreldez together. She'd risk going to the trill to help our planet, if need be. I knew she would.

"And the queen has agreed to this already?" Almder asked the krelin representative.

"Queen Kai seeks resolution to the tension between our trade agreements. It is reasonable to believe sharing biological ties between our species will bridge the gap we've found ourselves falling into of late. Krelin warriors are growing restless with our increased male population and are in need of females to calm their minds.

"As you well know, the hive shares a connection that all of Krelis feeds from. Many do not have the patience nor the desire to cull that connection when it overwhelms their sense of self. This has caused avarice to spread through the hive, infecting many warriors with a need to claim more than what is owed to them. Our export ships have taken advantage of their supply, and, without something for them to latch onto, they will continue to increase their efforts."

"Are you threatening Estreldez?" Almder thundered back, and I took a step back, feeling the increased tension in the room.

"Of course not. I am merely stating facts. I aim to prove the krelins are compatible mates with your females and promise you peace should you grant me the opportunity to prove the same to my species. To all of Krelis. Give me time with a strong leader of your clan. Should she reject me, I will respect her decision to do so." He bent down on a knee and bowed his head to Almder. It was very unlike a krelin to posture themselves in such a manner. To bow to someone other than their own queen was unheard of. It was almost like begging for them; their pride would never allow it, but there he was, kneeling at my Almder's feet.

"Very well," Almder conceded. "You've proven yourself to be reasonable for your species, and I agree with your queen that a union between our clans would solidify peace for many generations. I will allow you to join the ceremony, since you've passed all of our examinations. However, as you said, the final decision is not yours. It belongs to any female that is compatible with you. I will even grant you a single offering to spend some time with our strongest female this mating cycle, on the condition that you discuss other ways our clans may seek peace together once a union is formed."

"Agreed." The krelin male stood, and his back muscles flexed and bulged before straightening. He clicked his tongue, making noises that bounced within the stone carved dome. "You have company," he said without turning to see me there.

"One of my advisors," Almder explained my presence, and I flushed with embarrassment at not removing myself as soon as I saw she was already with someone. Something about the krelin made my feet plant where they were, and all I could do was stare.

All I saw was the back of his head, but he was very handsome. I shouldn't have thought like that at all, considering what he was, but my skin heated as I watched his shoulder blades move, and I gasped as I noticed something reflective that shifted along the leather strap across his back. He wore armor coverings all over—except for keeping his back exposed—but as the moon's light moved across him, it was almost like there were iridescent bones twitching as he moved. How could no one else see this?

He had wings!

Only the most powerful of the krelin warriors had wings, the ones that led the armies of their fleets. Not a single delegate had ever come to Estreldez with wings before. He was escorted out of the alcove by one of Loric's best trained guards, Gaven. Whenever Loric went off-world, he always took Gaven with him. It was a relief to see they wouldn't give the krelin free range around the palace.

Golden eyes captured me as the krelin passed, and like one of the glilor reptiles near the waterholes they blinked with a second lid that watched me with curiosity. I sidestepped and plowed towards the Almder with purpose, not wanting to embarrass the Almder further, should the krelin think I didn't belong amongst dignitaries. Of course, he'd have been right. I shouldn't have been here while she was discussing diplomacy with Krelis, but I was an advisor, and I wouldn't shame the Almder by letting the krelin know I wasn't summoned.

It wouldn't be the first time I'd gone somewhere I wasn't supposed to. The trading post on the farthest moon, a favorite of my excursions, was where I acquired nectar from a krelin called the Chief. The thought was almost enough to distract me from what I was doing here to begin with.

"Almder," I addressed, bowing my head. Her crystal, silver eyes dulled as she shook her head at me. As soon as the doors closed behind Gaven and the krelin with a thud, I cringed.

"I understand why you are here." She sounded sad. "You've always been like a seventh daughter to me," she explained, and my heart sank even farther into my gut. Luan was her only living daughter. Five others did not survive gestation. To be her seventh daughter was a great honor, and the sadness in her tone broke me. All I've ever wanted was family. Luan and my Almder were all I had left.

"I didn't mean to interrupt—"

She stopped me from continuing with a lift of her hand, I bowed my head once more to accept whatever punishment she saw fit for my intrusion. I took liberties with my role as advisor because of her affections. Being around her daughter since we were offspring, made me feel like I was family. A point that was often dismissed by others, but it was times like this one where the Almder looked at me with those caring silver eyes that I believed it to be true.

"Mabel, I received your exam report this morning." I flinched at the quick shift in the conversation. "This was going to be your first official ceremony as a participant, and not merely as a researcher for the M.R. team, and I recall how excited I once was as a fledgling into mating age. This must be extremely tough news to take, but I've already discussed things with Elder Ezra. Your life is priority, not that of life yet to form." Almder stood from her black, polished throne of tarnpul, carved with intricate murals of our history at her back.

Wearing flowing, black robes of the sheerest threads so as not to hinder her absorption of the moon's rays, Almder's every jewel shone and gave her an ethereal glow no other estreld but Luan, her own daughter, could match. She was mesmerizing to watch. So much so, I could forget why I was there, and why so much sadness tainted the brilliance of her eyes for me.

She bent her knees to be eye level with me, her delicate, long fingers leaned on her thighs. I was shorter than most females—a runt. It was unusual for the Almder to stoop for anyone, let alone someone like me, yet she still did it so gracefully and maintained a regality about her.

Almder continued, "It is the strongest of us that must bear the heartiest of burdens. It was not long after Luan that I was told the very same thing. I did not listen to my elders, and I suffered such great loss of sons and daughters I will not meet again until the end of my days. Their lives cut short before they even began.

"The souls of your offspring are out there in the stars. You need not suffer their loss, but embrace their new futures in their next life, as we all return to the moon's dust, and are born anew.

Mabel, I will not make you relive this feeling with every mate you interview. Hearing of the futures you will now not be able to obtain yourself; it is a burden I will not add to one I care for so deeply. I will devise a suitable position after you've had time to process this new phase of your life."

Her arms wrapped around my shoulders, and she kissed the top of my head as she would her own daughter. A warmth from her radiation flooded from her loh and through my body, giving me all of her love and a great sense of comfort, though I knew it was temporary relief from the weight building in the carved out cavity that once held my heart.

My Almder, my second mother, was removing me from my position as advisor of the mating research team. I feared this would be a possibility, but I didn't think it would happen so soon. After the ceremony perhaps, as all of our resources were stretched to the limit with the largest off-worlder invite to date.

I was not only told I could not participate in the mating ceremony I had been eagerly anticipating this cycle, but I lost the very position I had worked so hard for, despite not having many loh and being deemed weak and small.

Where would I go? What would I do?

Would I be sent outside of the palace?

Would the only family I had left send me outside of the city in some misguided attempt to keep me from harm? I was stronger than that. I was good at my job.

No, I thought with anger brewing deep in my gut, I was more than good. I was her best research advisor when it came to finding correlations in the efficacy of successful matings. Since I joined the team, our spawn rates have been steadily increasing. Marginally, but my research was bringing more offspring into the world. I knew it was.

But what proof did I have? Many could simply dismiss the small increases to other changes in the program. What proof was there that it was because of my efforts directly?

"My Almder... I can still do my job," I insisted, and she pulled away.

"I wouldn't hear of it," she dismissed as if she were doing me a favor, and perhaps she thought she was doing me a kindness.

"Please..." I choked, feeling the pressure build up behind my eyes. Fresh tears threatened to shed themselves at her feet.

She smiled warmly, pity in her silver eyes. "Take some time to consider your options. We can discuss after the ceremony."

That was the best I was going to get for now. I bowed and backed away. A sob struggled free from my throat, and I didn't want her to hear me cry. She would only use it as more evidence she was doing what was right. I was processing more than one kind of loss, and I'd already pressed more than any other estreld would dare with the Almder once she'd made a decision. My short legs walked briskly back the way I'd come. By the time I reached the doors, I felt close to running. The guards slid the doors aside for me, and water sloshed from my unruly eyes. I wiped away at them vigorously before colliding with Luan.

I cleared my throat to calm myself. Luan's hands grabbed my shoulders, but I kept my head lowered to hide my flushed cheeks with the strands of black hair that had escaped from my tie.

"Mabel?" she asked, gaining my attention with her silver eyes wide. They were so much like her mother's that it broke me further before Almder summoned her inside.

Forcing a smile to my lips, I shook my head at Luan dismissing my behavior, and rushed down the hall to be alone. I could hear Almder's voice carry through the halls before the doors closed, "Mabel has been informed by the M.R. that she is no longer eligible..."

My throat choked up as I steadied myself against the wall. If only it were as simple as Almder's words. Joining the ceremony was my chance to build something all my own. But my heart broke into painful shards that split and cut their way down my icy veins from the knowledge that it wasn't just a family lost, but my very purpose on this planet. I'd been dismissed from my duties to help the clan in the only way I knew how. Would I even be an advisor after this ceremony? Was Almder telling Luan at this very moment that I would no longer be acting as mating research advisor? How would the optics look, having an advisor being infertile? Broken?

"Those tests." Loric's voice startled me, and I wiped at my eyes once more, hardening myself for a conversation I didn't want to deal with. He was the Pride of Estreldez, Almder's favorite advisor on security and off-worlder politics. Loric had a lot of sway with Almder, and I had no choice but to listen to what he had to say. Running away from Luan was one thing; she was distracted, and, even though she'd be the next Almder one day, she was my friend, and she'd understand my need for some time to process before talking with her.

"I can still do my job, Loric. It isn't a debilitating diagnosis," I interrupted with a determination driving me to defend myself from being removed from the M.R. team.

His face softened. With a kindness he was known for throughout Estreldez he nodded before replying, "I know how much you wanted a family. Luan spoke many times solving the food shortage with Krelis being our main trade, so your offspring need only worry how to sneak out of the palace when she was watching them for you. You and Luan will always be family."

I sniffled, once more feeling my emotions overflow. It touched my heart to know Luan spoke of our futures together. I knew she relied on me to divert some of the attention away from her mating by spawning enough young for the both of us. She feared she'd be just like the Almder, like many of our clan, and have trouble conceiving. Stillbirths, miscarriages, and... infertility.

Almder would be even more insistent on Luan mating this cycle with my exam results on her mind.

"Perhaps, she'll have enough for the both of us," I replied lightly, forcing a smile that didn't quite reach my eyes.

"What I was going to say," he glanced over his shoulder to the window that looked over the palace gardens, "those tests aren't conclusive. The scientists can only work with the data they are given. Much is still incalculable. Elder Nen has spoken of how our loh are capable of healing great wounds when their essence is complete."

Covering my mouth, I chuckled through a hiccup. "Loric, I never knew you were such a romantic. It isn't often these days I hear an estreld speak of the fated mate bond, even in all the interviews I've had over the last few years."

He cleared his throat. "Yes, well, you scientist types tend to overlook the undefinable. Even Elder Ezra explains the fated mate bond in technical terms of pheromones and chemistry compatibility ratios, describing it as a reaction between two compositions."

"Well, isn't it?" I lifted a brow, already smirking at the welcomed distraction from my own issues.

Loric folded his firm arms over his exposed chest. His blue skin was covered in loh jewels, more than even our toughest warriors, a sign of his strength with the moon. Any female would be drooling to have his attention, but I'd grown up with him. His eyes were always on Luan. Whatever attraction I had for him when I was young was long since buried as I resolved that one day Luan would realize he'd always been there for her.

The Pride and the Jewel of Estreldez were the perfect match. Both of them worked so hard to help the planet in their own ways.

"Our loh are more than simply biological compositions," he said impassioned. "They are our connection with the moon, with our own souls. You can explain away the warmth as radiation energy conversion, but you can't explain the fact that it feels different for every estreld. When the Almder shares her radiation with us, it isn't merely her energy, it is her essence, her soul, speaking to us. Wishing us well. Giving of her love for her clan. You cannot tell me it feels the same when the scientists share loh energy with you versus when Almder shares it, or even when Luan shares it?"

The way he said Luan's name towards the end, I could sense the way his mood shifted to a different kind of passion. Ever since Luan had led the ceremony the last two cycles, Loric has been even more eager to have her participate. His loh glowed even brighter, and he was certain to be fertile this cycle if she joined.

Being curious, I'd already snuck a peek in the M.R. lab to compare their files. They were a very close match. Nearly perfect.

I never told either of them; regardless, it was their decision to mate or not.

"You're right," I placated him, but it didn't change my results, "it does feel different. Any scientist will tell you that we can't prove anything. All we can say is our data has yet to be disproven."

"Mabel," he chided, knowing I was deflecting. He was just trying to give me hope, but even that would be gone the moment Elder Ezra removed my egg sack for my safety.

"Fine. Until new data disproves historical results, there is a lack of evidence that some fated mate out there could heal a lack of lining to help support viable spawning of offspring." There was more bite to my statement than I intended, but it was a bitter hope to cultivate, knowing Estreldez didn't have the technology to do anything but perform preventative measures for my health. Estreldez didn't...

"I can already see the glorbins swirling in your mind. You are not like Elder Ezra, simply taking data for fact. Perhaps you need only find that new data yourself," he encouraged, then left me with my thoughts to go join Luan in the Almder's alcove.

My eyes were puffy, but who was I trying to impress? I rushed to the transport control to meet with Hazel, the lead advisor of the shuttle and space traffic control. She knew everyone and could help me find some potential off-worlders to interview. Until Almder officially removed me from my position as an advisor on the M.R. team, I still had complete access to all mate candidates.

TRENT

My wings bristled behind me. They refracted light camouflaged, until necessary. I didn't know the exact science of how each wing had its own frequency that created some kind of temporal hole in the way our eyes perceived wavelengths, but I didn't need to. Many couldn't see them when they were folded back. It was uncomfortable to restrain the leathery weapons, but that's exactly what they were, and it didn't help political matters to display them unless my intention was to intimidate. Estreldez was running out of time with my queen. She was set on conquering this land for the quarry deposits of the rare Ordin Crystal, which the estrelds called Glorbin Flower. I had very little time to sway the hive of Krelis away from forceful takeover. My queen has been busy stirring up the warriors' interests in the many females of this planet as our own females dwindle in number.

A cunning maneuver, but I'd use it against my queen's interests. If my plans succeeded in swaying the leader of Estreldez, I could convince the hive that the females would be available for their mating needs without invading. I would claim a strong mate for myself and prove to all, bonds can be formed without taking things by force. In time, even what my queen seeks will be hers by other means. The Ordin deposits can be negotiated, and our own warriors will aid in the extraction.

Finding a strong mate on Estreldez was my last resort to preventing the hive from following my queen's plans to invade.

Even now, I could feel the buzz in my head of royal influence trying to dig around in my mind seeking out my motivations. Like the nits that eat the molt before we add it to the hewve lard to preserve it for transport. Swat at them, and they scatter. My queen never did like my preference for disconnection, independence. Most warriors welcomed the intrusion and the several pleasure glands that activated when the queen, in particular, gave attention.

I was anything but a sycophant, stroking the glands as the queen's tendrils of influence wormed through their minds. There were plenty of other ways to relieve myself; listening to her 'check in on me' wasn't it. Since the last potential queen of our hive died of the Molt Fever without gifting the hive with spawn, my queen has become increasingly desperate to appease the hive's needs. No matter the cost.

The one I needed was Luan, the Jewel of Estreldez and future Almder of the clan. With her at my side, I could sway the hive, and she could lead both of our planets to victory against the coming war. There wasn't much time; Necias Delta Fal had already sensed the impending change in this sector of the universe, and many of their warships were approaching Estreldez, even as I knelt at the Almder's feet.

King Sylve had the same idea as our Queen Kai. Conquer Estreldez, gain control of the exports, and leverage against the trill. My queen had no intention of me finding a mate while here. Participation in the mating ritual was all a guise for me to acquire intel on how best to invade, but I had different plans.

My back bristled and I clucked my tongue to confirm the occupants of the room. I was a commander of the Krelis war fleet, first and foremost, and that feeling had never failed me in any battle I'd fought. The vibrations made it back to my horns' receptors, as I suspected, another had joined my meeting with the Almder.

I informed the leader of Estreldez, "You have company." It was preferable to distract her from our conversation as I had already received her permission to court her daughter, though not in so many words.

Whoever this newcomer was, they were not unwelcome. A softness filled the graying eyes of the Almder. My wings flexed as I rose to my feet from prostrating before the Almder in hopes she would trust that I wasn't as prideful as my queen. It was merely good politics to show my respect. Kneeling before her did not diminish my strength, nor my reputation among my warriors.

My second in command, Gho-ran, would agree, though he may not find it as easy to bear with a smile on his face. At no point in our time together had Gho-ran ever knelt at my feet, nor would I ever ask it of him. He was prideful, and popular with my warriors. Often, he was more dismissive of circum-stances than I would like of a second, but he had never let me down either.

A hum lingered in my horns that I couldn't shake since I'd scanned the room. It wasn't all that unpleasant like a warmth that spread from my horns to my toes. It reminded me of when my mother was less concerned with the hive's wellbeing and still proud of her first born. It had been a while since I'd had the touch of a female and being in a room full of them had me susceptible to a kind of nostalgia I'd rather forget. It was as good a timing as any to be in need of that touch when courting Luan to be my mate. Perhaps, finding an estreld attractive would be easier than I had once thought.

I'd made the decision to seek Luan as my mate the moment I'd caught my Chief of Trade smuggling home-brewed nectar at the trading station on Estreldez's farthest moon, Bina. They had chatted like old friends, and I felt like I knew her. Having never seen her directly, it was an odd feeling to have. I was worried over the disruptions of trade and I didn't need to be. Smiling at that thought, of course the future Almder of Estreldez would already be crafty in her efforts to keep peace between our planets. Then and there, I knew she'd make a wonderful queen.

Turning to take my leave, I spotted the guest. She too stirred an excitement within me I hadn't known was possible outside of the hive. Stunning. Her eyes were as green as the mountain tops of Krelis, and so bright. A roguish tie couldn't keep her black tresses secured, strands fell across her face obscuring those green gems as she commanded the space to stride past me without another glance my direction. Were all the females of Estreldez so fierce? I smiled to myself, looking forward to meeting Luan at the mating ceremony tomorrow.

I caught the movement of my escort, a warrior called Gaven, as he glanced over his shoulder back at the female who'd passed. It could simply be part of his training to assess all surroundings—estrelds didn't have horns to sense this themselves—but I felt myself tense at the extra attention he was giving to this advisor. Who was she?

The doors closed behind us, and whatever I saw on his features was expertly masked with a stoney expression.

"We will introduce all eligible mates during tomorrow's ceremony. Until then, you may rest in your assigned quarters, or be escorted around the palace gardens," he said, clearly indicating that he would be with me at all times during my stay, aside from when I was guarded within my quarters. At least the estrelds weren't completely ignorant to my potential betrayal. I'd have been disappointed if they weren't a bit cautious with my proposed peace agreement.

"Wonderful, and will you be joining the ceremony as well?" I knew he wouldn't be. He would always be within striking distance of me, or someone he trusted to do so. Seeing how he reacted to conversation was important to help me know who I was dealing with. I needed to know whether there were things I could take advantage of, or if he would be a hindrance to my successful mating with their future leader. My mission wouldn't be well received by all of Estreldez, just as it wouldn't be easy to sway the mind of the hive without a powerful mate.

He said nothing. We kept walking as he guided me to what I assumed would be my living quarters for the time being.

So, he was that type. That could be a good thing, if he was more focused on his job and less on intervention. It also meant it was unlikely he would leave any openings in his duty to keep me observed during my stay.

Passing the gardens, I noticed that the windows throughout the hall gave an ample view of the collection of foliage and rock. The palace was a fascinating structure that appeared carved from tarnpul and a strange dusky white stone that must have been one of the few tough minerals they didn't eat on this planet. A moon stone of some kind the estrelds held in high regard, called pan. Such a strange term; there wasn't really a translation in Krelis.

The whole palace was a large, open air dome with the center garden connecting it all. Weather on this planet was humid, making my wings feel sticky and creating the urge to unfurl them to feel even the slightest wind. It would provide relief from the heat that reminded me of the hatcheries for our spawn... suffocating. Though that was to be expected by keeping on my armor while all the estreld, even the warrior at my side, wore a sheer fabric barely covering much at all.

Estrelds were like walking radiation packs. The windows were everywhere to not only let in the moon's rays but amplify them.

Their bodies were capable of storing the radiation and utilizing it in blasts that could char the skin or even morph those pretty jewels into vicious weapons. I grinned. Yes, they were beautifully deceptive in their lack of clothing. It meant nothing of their defenselessness. Krelins were merely lucky that their radiation was harmless unless harnessed with a focused precision. Even their moons were armed with nanonets that could refocus the radiation at will and, with great accuracy, melt an invading warship. It wasn't flawless, though.

"While I'm here, I thought it prudent to take care of other matters before the ceremony. Would you care to escort me to the import station? There is supposed to be a final exchange planned before the rest of the off-worlders are granted access tomorrow. I'd like to overlook the process and make sure there are no incidents."

"We'll have to have it cleared with the head of transportation. The meet is on our farthest moon, Bina, as you already knew."

"Yes, it should keep us busy for the evening."

Gaven quirked a brow in curiosity. "You have no desire to snoop around the palace or sneak off to the quarries?" There was disbelief in his tone. He had expected some kind of subterfuge, which was what my queen wanted of me, but I fully intended to make sure the final trade exchange between our planets didn't screw up my plans to secure the future leader of Estreldez as my mate. I had suspicions of my own that my queen would have backup plans in place that didn't involve waiting to see what kind of intel would come her way.

"Should make your job easier," I said with humor.

He grunted, unconvinced. The warrior was right to be skeptical; I had no idea what we might be getting ourselves into by checking on this shipment. It could be nothing, or it could be an ambush that would take advantage of the stretched resources due to the mating ceremony and the influx of off-worlder ships surrounding the largest moon.

It was possible my future mate would be checking on the exchange, since my Chief of Trade had informed me of her increased visits to secure more nectar, and the last time she was absent... Ong decided that everything was solved with his crew and didn't oversee the trade directly. Mistakes were made that could jeopardize the peace we were both working towards.

I could say that my desire to make sure this exchange went smoothly was solely for peace, but a part of me knew that I hoped the future Queen of Krelis, my mate, would be there, and I could finally see her in person, instead of through Ong.

Continue Reading Her Alien Prince: https://books.stevie marie.com/heralienprince

Her Alien Exchange

R ead this book for free and join my author newsletter:
https://dl.bookfunnel.com/f2fwrjww4p

She thought joining the alien exchange would only be for a year...

Violet

Human Exchange Trade, H.E.T., was my ticket off Earth. Leaving the planet to get away was probably an over correction and impulsive, but I needed a change. And what bigger change was there than to hop on a shuttle to a large spaceship that would take me to an alien host on the planet ASunGor for a year. I get to learn a new culture, fool around with a few hot aliens, and come back to Earth with a better perspective on my life. At least, that's what I thought, before I rushed the whole thing, and my host wasn't there to pick me up. Another exchange girl named Evie was heading to the planet Necias Prime looking terrified, and I had time to kill, so what harm was there in taking a detour to make sure she was okay? I mean, my reasons had nothing to do with the sexy alien that had come to escort her.

Commader Roe-el

I was reluctant to leave Princess Klemon's protection when she told me to escort a human to my home planet for a mating experiment, but in my haste to return to her side, I left without asking the name of the human. When I got to the station... there were two of them waiting, and one of them was making me regret not having tasted a female in years. Her scent did things to me, and I found myself going into rut when it was my job as commander to protect the humans, not screw them. Humans were much too fragile for a necia warrior, but the fire in her eyes made me question my priorities, and I couldn't say no when she boarded my ship. Everything inside of me needed to claim her, but she needed to say, yes, first.

Dive into a fated mates, spicy monster love romance with instalust, exhibitionism, strong female empowerment, alpha male with consent, and alien extremities. Join the fated mates of the alien warriors of Necias Prime in the Treasures of Trillume Universe. All stand-alone romances, within a fun interwoven plot of the universe.

VIOLET

As soon as the Human Exchange Training was open to the public, I was first in line to join. That might seem reckless, to immediately seek to abandon Earth for a year-long, alien-job training program, but anything was better than what I had going for me now. My ex was psychotic, and he didn't take my whole let's-be-friends conversation as well as I'd hoped. You really don't see all the red flags until the end. Sure, I was feeling uncomfortable with him for a few months now, but all that crazy made for great sex and had my mind all addled over the idea of leaving him simply because he seemed a bit clingy when I wanted to hang out with the girls. I had a decent job as a marketing consultant for what used to be the biggest IT company. But ever since we—meaning humans—were introduced to how big the galaxy was by these aliens called the Trill, well, our IT was way behind the times.

Too many people were more obsessed with the technology the aliens had to offer instead of what mere human mortals were working on. IT took a huge dive, and so did my career. I was a bartender now; that's how I met Mick... and he needed some time to cool off and find a new obsession. Living for a year with aliens while also getting training in a new career sounded like a win-win.

I left the recruitment center more excited than ever after being accepted by an alien host from some planet called ASunGor. It wasn't too far from the planet Trillume, which was where the trill were from. ASunGor was beautiful, with its purples, yellows, and oranges, and red gaseous clouds that, if they didn't tell me otherwise, I might have thought were poisonous. Red was usually associated with warnings, like my ex with all of his red flags. But I was assured the red was merely a reaction to the iron particles in the air hitting the oxygen, and the concentration was mostly in the atmosphere, not on the surface where there was a reasonable amount of breathable air for humans to survive without any harm.

I got a data packet about the aliens that lived there sent to my brain implant, which was updated with an alien language translator, so all that was left was to wait for the transport shuttle to take me to the ship waiting in Earth's orbit. I'd be gone for a year.

Before I could think on it more, I was interrupted by a cringe-worthy voice that was all too sickeningly familiar. Damn it. I had been so careful about getting here without being followed.

"What do you think you're doing, Violet?" he said from behind me, leaning against the brick wall of the recruitment center.

Clearing my throat, I jutted a hip out in defiance while replying, "None of your business, Mick."

He rubbed his gorgeous face with his hands in exasperation. That's what got me the first time around. Mick was too damned pretty, and I let that cloud my judgement for too long. The kind of sweet, chiseled pretty that made you think he was both adoring and capable of sinful things. And he certainly was capable of all sorts of sinful things that I used to look forward to—with relish—but it wasn't worth it.

"I know the IT industry has seen a dive, and you weren't looking to be a bartender your whole life, but offworlding? Come on, Violet, that's low; even for you. There have been plenty of news stories about how most of those aliens want to experiment with us, and a pretty girl like you... Violet, if you need a good fuck, you don't need to jump on a shuttle to find it," Mick said with equal parts disgust and interest. It was amazing how he could twist his words to both insult me and imply that his dick was good enough for the job, all at the same time.

I smiled sweetly at him, but anyone with eyes could see my derision as I retorted, "Oh, honey. I don't have to go anywhere for a good fuck. I've got myself covered just fine." I showed him my two favorite fingers and then lowered one to leave only the middle, silently saying 'Go fuck yourself' and ending with a little wink. It wasn't right to tease him. He liked it when I played hard to get, but I wasn't playing at anything this time. I was more than happy with my own company. Anything was better than the constant, back-handed compliments I received from him regularly. At least my own fingers knew my clit was bigger than just the tip that was visible. It was a whole fucking organ, and he wasn't its musician anymore.

Mick pushed off from the wall, and my whole body froze like a deer caught in headlights. I talked a big game, but the dark look in his eyes was terrifying and crazed. That same determined gaze used to make me smile, knowing we were about to have some great hate sex. But when I wanted it to end, the feelings changed, and he wasn't willing to let me go. I gulped back my fear as he slowly approached, but my feet wouldn't budge. His knuckles brushed against my cheek, and I instinctively pulled my face away before he harshly pinched my chin in his grasp to force me to look at him.

"You know you like it when that foul mouth of yours wraps around my cock before you scream my name. Your fingers can still do whatever they want when I'm fucking the sin from your dirty thoughts," he purred, pushing his mouth on to mine. My hands scrambled to find purchase, to shove him off, but he held me firm, and I struggled to slide my mouth away from his, gasping for air.

"Get off of me," I growled, and he released me at the same time as I shoved, making me stumble backwards and I lost my balance. He let me trip, falling to my ass, and he shook his head at me like I was a piece of trash that he'd have to pick up for the betterment of the world. I wiped his saliva from my cheek and forced myself to spit at his feet, to rid the taste of him from my tongue. "You're disgusting."

It wasn't that I didn't particularly like dirty talk; I did. But the way he said things was anything but endearing. It was possessive in a way that made my skin crawl. Like I needed to burn the clothes I was wearing to get the feeling of his hands groping me seared from my memory.

"No one will touch you the way you want it like I do, Violet. Not even an alien dick, if they even have one, would touch you after they found out what makes you scream," he threatened while licking his lips, trying to get me to think about all the things he wanted to do with his tongue. "Don't make me wait too long; this game of yours is getting old." Mick left me there sitting in what I now realized was a puddle left by the rain from the night before. It certainly wasn't my own juices that had soaked through my pants this time.

"Fucker," I gritted out, getting back to my feet and stomping back to the recruitment center. I opened the door a little more aggressively than I'd intended, but I was amped and pissed. Waiting for the later shuttle to "gather" my shit wasn't an option anymore. I was leaving tonight, even if I had to sign some extra waivers or agree to an extended exchange program. I didn't give a crap. I was leaving now!

Mick was lucky I ever touched his dick, and he was right. The game was getting old, but not the one he thought we were playing. I was sick and tired of him harassing me, and the authorities said there wasn't enough to get a restraining order. Not that it would have stopped him, I thought with disdain.

"Miss Thorn... did you forget something?" my recruiter, Beth, asked with a quirked brow at my now soaked pants and probably reddened face.

"Yes, I need you to get me on the next shuttle."

Beth pursed her lips as if I were insane. "You have no personal items with you. And usually people wish to say goodbye to their friends, family, someone before they go. You should really wait for the next shuttle in a few weeks," she insisted.

"No," I snapped before calming myself to reiterate in a less intimidating tone. "I want to leave on the one I overheard you saying was leaving today." I paused, then added, "Please." I forced a smile to my face and waited for her to deny me because what I was asking for was ridiculous. It was the most insane thing I'd ever asked of someone.

She lowered her voice and wrapped her arm around my shoulder to lead me away from the prying eyes of the other recruits in the lobby, eying me with concern. "Are you in trouble?"

I sighed, not wanting to get into this with practically a stranger, but she seemed so sweet and trustworthy, unlike my usual friends I hung out with. They were more encouraging of my bad choices. This was not a bad choice though, I reassured myself. This was crazy, but it wasn't a bad choice. As far as decisions went, sure, I should probably wait for my scheduled shuttle in a few weeks. But what did I have to lose besides a creepy ex and girlfriends that didn't even know a single thing about me, other than I was fun to have a drink with? Come to think of it, they probably mostly liked the cheap drinks I got for working at the bar... I shook my head. I was over the whole thing.

"I've got an ex stalking me, and a year away will be good for both of us," I admitted, but I didn't let her know that a sick part of me knew that if I didn't get on this shuttle, two weeks was a long time, and I didn't think I had the strength to resist Mick when he reflected on his actions in a day or two. He'd come back, sweeter than ever, and we'd have mind-blowing hate sex, and I'd hate myself even more for letting him get under my skin. I deserved better than what he was offering. I knew that in theory. But in practice... he was right. I was fucked up, and I liked how he made me feel when he wasn't being a petty asshole. He knew how I liked to be touched.

This was for me. I needed to recalibrate my brain and my body.

I didn't need his kind of possessive veneration.

"Yes, but you won't have time to go home and grab personal items. No matter how strong a person is, everyone gets Earth sick and misses the smallest of things that remind them of Earth when they are away." Beth was trying to talk me out of it, and she was doing a shitty job. I didn't give a crap if I missed the dirt or way pizza tasted. Sometimes, cold turkey was the best way to change your bad habits. I'd just keep myself busy to distract myself.

"Beth, I see what you're doing here, and it's sweet, really. But if you don't let me on that shuttle, my life is more screwed than if you let me leave. Trust me." I could see her lips press into a fine line as she led me through the building, probably to a holding cell because I was likely to harm one of us if they didn't board me on the shuttle today. I was that kind of desperate, and pretty much too angry to see reason beyond what I'd set my mind to.

She sighed in what I hoped was resignation, but it easily could have been her annoyance at another crazy she had to deal with in a diplomatic way.

"Violet." She used my first name, which was weird. "You have to be sure about this. The shuttle is boarding now. Once you're on, there is no coming back until your exchange is completed. Do you understand?"

Well, that was unexpected.

"Like, now, now?" My nerves were getting the better of me, and I was just as likely to bolt as I was to follow through with my hare-brained idea of jumping on a shuttle to a different planet.

She laughed, which was refreshing to hear, before she nodded her agreement.

This was happening.

I was leaving.

She was going to let me on the shuttle.

ROE-EL

The Princess of Trillume rolled her eyes at me, and I grumbled. Princess or not, she was asking me to do something that was akin to fucking an animal.

"My Princess, I think I misheard you. I apologize." I tried to show my disinterest without actually outright denying her orders of me. I was a reputable warrior, and I'd never questioned my position to be in her service, but this was too much. She must understand that if any other had asked this of me, I would have considered it an insult that would have been remedied by a duel before I agreed to anything more. Only if I failed would I submit myself to this. My upper lip snarled.

"You didn't mishear," she confirmed with a sly smile. "I need you to train a human in the ways of the Necia and encourage this human to attempt spawning with a Necia warrior. It's important to my research. I'm not asking you to be the warrior that attempts procreation with the human, Commander Roe-el. I'm asking you to escort the human to Necias Prime and train them before they arrive, while encouraging the human to be open-minded about your species."

"You're asking me to have another warrior," I paused to wrinkle my nose at the prospect, "spawn with a human. Do you have any idea what you're asking of any Necia you have do that? Humans are fragile, and deserving of our protection, but they are like pets to us that we've used as entertainment and companionship on long missions across the galaxies. They are NOT mates," I insisted with disgust.

Princess Klemon nodded. "I'm aware. They are not so barbaric to be considered animals, Commander Roe-el. They are just... different, and, according to my research, potentially compatible mates as well. You are assigned to go pick them up right about... well, now. You should head out if you are to get there on time. I know how you like to be punctual."

"Princess, my assignment is to you. Not your project. I would be derelict in my duties to leave—"

"Commander," she stopped me before I could finish. "The project is the reason why you are needed to protect me at all. If it makes you feel any better, I'll be sure to stay hidden in the lab until your return. You're the only one I trust to escort our exchange human to their new host. You won't be gone longer than a few weeks. There and back."

I narrowed my eyes, uncertain if I could trust her to stay within the lab walls while I was away and still grossed out by the idea of mating with a human.

With a huff, she added, "I'll stay put."

"I will not mate with a human," I clarified.

She shook her head in a manner that made me think she thought I was humorous, which made my shoulder epaulets twitch in agitation.

"I'm not asking you to be the one to mate with the human. I already have a willing warrior who is trustworthy and understands my research and what it means to the whole galaxy, not just Necias Prime," Princess Klemon explained, then did that hand motion she used to shoo me away from her research.

"Fine, but if I find that you have left this lab for whatever reason, you will be hard-pressed to have me leave your side in the future. Keep that in mind, should you get the desire to go exploring without protection." It was my job to make sure her family didn't find her and that anyone who knew what she was working on didn't find her. She was right; her research was too important to risk. If she thought I was needed to protect the human, then that is what I would do for her.

Arriving at the waystation, I grumbled, realizing Klemon had tricked me into thinking I was going to be late when I was actually early. Wasting my time waiting grated on my nerves like no other feeling. She was being cheeky when she said I preferred to be punctual, I knew that. I always arrived on time... never early. If I'm to be somewhere at a time, that is the time I arrive. No earlier, no later. On time.

And here I was, waiting like a fool for some human to disembark from their transport to Trillume and then reboard my shuttle to head out to Necias Prime. All the human exchanges came to Trillume first, then to their destinations. Never a direct route, as the humans were strictly monitored and accounted for. Couldn't have secret humans being stowed away and sold off in the markets. We'd never hear the end of it. There would be an open war between species about who had more rights to the humans and to Earth. The only good thing about that was I wouldn't be bored on my glorified babysitter duties of a princess. I might get a few duels in here and there.

The humans left the shuttle and appeared as I expected them to be: like scared animals, shifting uncomfortably around until a new owner came to take them to their temporary homes. One by one, they were being plucked away by ambassadors from various planets claiming their right to have their own human for a while. I realized I hadn't asked which one I should be acquiring for her highness' research. I mean, there wasn't much difference between them all, was there? Did it matter which one I brought with me?

I liked the look of the larger human that appeared to be less likely to be harmed by our Necia females. He would stand a chance of surviving Necias Prime with his muscles, though he still wasn't quite as bulky as I would have preferred to ensure his safety. I cursed under my breath, remembering that Klemon had said there was a warrior who'd agreed to mate with a human, and I hadn't asked if they were female or male. I waited a bit longer to see if another planet was claiming the human male. Shortly, I found out that someone had indeed chosen this male for their own exchange.

There were only two females left after the rush, and I found myself unable to remove my eyes from the one with bright red hair, the color of Necias's oceans. Unlike the other female, who appeared as frightened as I would expect of most who ventured so far from their habitats, this one folded her arms over her chest, highlighting small mounds that had my mouth quirking up in interest. I closed my eyes to rid myself of the thought.

Did humans possess some kind of lure not recorded in their data assessments? Not one warrior had ever spoke of this kind of attraction at the mere sight of the curves of a human's frame. Possibly it was my subconscious playing tricks on me after the discussion I'd had with Klemon. She had planted this idea of fucking with humans, and I had been without a female for some time because of my current assignment. It was difficult to acquire interest, or even spur on a rut, with a protective detail and not many options for duels. There had been no need to prove my strength and encourage my use of bed play.

But there that human was, and, when I opened my eyes, I was still enthralled by her curves and the strong stance of what I could only imagine was her annoyance at waiting there for her host. I blinked, regaining my composure. Waiting for me, I thought, and a sudden surge rippled through my body, sending a jolt to my cock. What on Horv's great vine was happening to me? This couldn't possibly be a rut, could it? Was I so far gone that merely the idea of mating and the mission back to Necias Prime had sent my body into rut? Had I waited so long in a boring assignment that my body found any excuse to claim and conquer even an animal such as this human?

I grimaced, but that didn't stop my eyes from watching as the female adjusted her hips to favor her other leg. Those silvery eyes of hers looked out in search of her alien host, and it was only her and the other female left. What kind of ambassador arrived late to pick up their human? Sure, I was making mine wait, but I was here. Surely the other host would know who they were supposed to pick up.

Wasting time was making my mind wander, and thinking of that human's small, fleshy mounds pressed against me instead of those small arms wasn't doing me any favors in improving my mood. I refused to rut with a human, it was an abuse of my strength to claim such a weak being in such a manner. Humans were helpless creatures that needed protecting, not warriors—or even broodmares—capable of taming a Necia warrior's epulknot in rut. I'm not a monster, I repeated to myself in an attempt to calm the hardening length down my thigh. I had to pick up Klemon's human before I decided to call this whole thing off. I'd just grab the human that didn't make me doubt my sanity and be done with it.

Approaching the females, I tried to move slowly as to not frighten them further, and the dark-haired female flinched and tugged at the other's arm in warning. It was wise for humans to fear a Necia warrior. This female had good instincts for self-preservation. We were predators in this ecosystem. And yet, years of evolution did not stop the other from lifting a brow and smirking at me in challenge.

"It's about time. I was wondering if I had to walk over and get you. Didn't anyone ever teach you that it's rude to keep a lady waiting?" she snapped off in succession. Her words stunned me momentarily as my translator had to catch up with the harsh, yet intriguing, sound of her voice. I towered over her stature and yet there she was, chin held firm as she stared me down. Those silvery eyes had flecks of gold, now that I was close enough to see it, and I could see her beneath me as I tried to count every star in her mesmerizing portals and plunged into her depths. My mouth salivated, and my cock pulsed, seeking a reprieve I could not grant it. This was too far, even for a rut-inflicted mind. I had to control myself.

She was a human.

Not some seductive warrior seeking sport on my epulknot.

Continue reading for freesies: Grab Her Alien Exchange
here: https://dl.bookfunnel.com/f2fwrjww4p

SKY ROBERT

S.M. McCoy Writing as Sky Robert for Spicier Smuttier Romances

Sky Robert is a mom of two tiny humans in training, narrates audiobooks for fantasy/sci-fi indie authors, and when she isn't writing (which is MOST of the time) you can find her consuming copious amounts of coffee, promoting indie authors, reading alien smut, fantasy, sci-fi and romance books, chowing down on Indian butter chicken, and when she actually hangs out with people in person, in real life, outside of the internet (gasps), she's playing board or card games. All around nerd, lover of the strange, and all things fantastical.

More from the Treasures of Trillume Universe:
- ෧ Jewel of the Alien Bandit
  https://book.steviemarie.com/jotab
- ෧ Her Alien Prince
  https://book.steviemarie.com/heralienprince
- ෧ Her Alien Insurgent: Coming soon!

Necia Alien Warriors: (Part of the Trillume Universe)
- ෧ Her Alien Savior
  https://book.steviemarie.com/heraliensavior
- ෧ Her Alien Exchange (Free)
  https://book.steviemarie.com/heralienexchange
- ෧ Her Alien Warrior
- ෧ Her Alien Captor

Also by S.M. McCoy

The slow-burn fantasy romances
https://linktr.ee/authorsteviemarie
www.steviemarie.com

Divine Series:
- ☙ Blood Crescent Book One: Published 2018
- ☙ Blood Rebirth Book Two: Published 2019
- ☙ Blood Queen Book Three: Published 2021
- ☙ Available on Audible and Kindle Unlimited

Acatalec Series:
- ☙ Keys of Acatalec Prequel: TBA
- ☙ My Abett Book 0.5: Published 2022
- ☙ Kingdom of Acatalec Book One: Published 2022
- ☙ Available Wide on all Retailers including audiobook
- ☙ Acatalec Chosen Book Two
- ☙ Acatalec's Sword Book Three

Want More?

For more information about upcoming books in the Treasures of Trillume or Necia Warrior Series (or any other books by Sky Robert) like me on Facebook or subscribe to my newsletter.

Thanks for reading! You are a book hero!
All the squishies,
Sky